Praise for Mark Henry and
Happy Hour of the Damned!

"Dark, twisted and completely hilarious. I loved this book!"
—Michelle Rowen, author of *Lady & The Vamp*

"Call them the splatterati—werewolves who always know what to wear, zombies with bodies to die for, and vampires who know their fang shui—just don't call them late when it comes to happy hour, or the drinks might be on you."
—David Sosnowski, author of *Vamped*

"*Happy Hour of the Damned*—is it a comedy? An urban fantasy? A whodunit? Who cares! Mark Henry's written such a clever and engaging story that fans of any genre will totally adore it. Amanda Feral is the freshest, funniest character to come out of fiction since Bridget Jones and my only regret is she's not real and we can't go out for drinks. (Because, really? Zombies are the new black.) In short? I loved this book!"
—Jen Lancaster, author of *Bitter is the New Black*

"*Happy Hour of the Damned* blends the hilarious narcissism of *Seinfeld* with *Night of the Living Dead*. Who knew skincare-obsessed zombies were so much fun? I couldn't read this book fast enough."
—Jeaniene Frost, *New York Times* bestselling author of *Halfway to the Grave*

"More brisk, batty, raunchy, and catty than a room full of cougars with a margarita machine. *Happy Hour of the Damned* is funny as hell."
—Cherie Priest, author of *Not Flesh Nor Feathers*

"Gruesome, ghoulish and utterly groundbreaking. Mark Henry is daring and scathingly funny."
—Jackie Kessler, author of *Hotter Than Hell*

And advance praise for *Road Trip of the Living Dead*!

"What can I say about *Road Trip of the Living Dead?* It's irreverent, gross and disgusting. All in a good way. I LOVED it!!"
—Jeanne C. Stein, author of *Legacy*

"In turns hilarious and twisted, *Road Trip of the Living Dead* is a book I'll never forget. Who knew fashion-obsessed flesh eaters could be so engaging? Fans of any genre won't be able to put this book down as they fall into the darkly comedic world of Amanda Feral and her undead companions. Edgy and evocative, *Road Trip* is a must read! I'm looking forward to reading future works from this talented author."
—Anya Bast, author of *Witch Heart*

"Hilariously wicked and twisted, *Road Trip of the Living Dead*'s Amanda Feral's antics had me rolling on the floor with laughter. Between the snarky footnotes and the quirky, sassy voice, this book rocked my world."
—Tate Hallaway, *New York Times* bestselling author of *Romancing the Dead*

"A spew-licious snark fest straight from Winnebago hell—Mark Henry drives this adventure with masterful wit!"
—Dakota Cassidy, author of *The Accidental Human*

"I didn't see how Mark Henry would be able to top Amanda Feral's first adventure, but *Road Trip of the Living Dead* is even more raucous, lewd, and hilarious. How could I have doubted his genius? His *savoir faire*? His ability to create scenarios so horrifying *and* guilt-inducing funny? Amanda Feral rules the urban fantasy landscape. To miss out on this novel would be *très gauche!*"
—Michele Bardsley, nationally bestselling author of *Wait Till Your Vampire Gets Home*

ROAD TRIP OF THE LIVING DEAD

MARK HENRY

KENSINGTON BOOKS
http://www.kensingtonbooks.com

KENSINGTON BOOKS are published by

Kensington Publishing Corp.
850 Third Avenue
New York, NY 10022

ISBN-13: 978-0-7582-2524-5
ISBN-10: 0-7582-2524-5

First Kensington Trade Paperback Printing: March 2009
10 9 8 7 6 54 3 2 1

Printed in the United States of America

To the two most ravenous readers in my life:
my mother, Edna,
and my goddaughter, Delaney
(who better not read this until she's old enough!)

Acknowledgments

A second novel in a surprise series (I had no clue that I was getting into more than one book here—still can't believe my luck) shouldn't have been anywhere near as easy as *Road Trip of the Living Dead*. My fantastic editor, John Scognamiglio, forced me out of my seat-o'-the pants style, heralding the age of the outline. Thanks, John. Seriously. The book turned out better than I could've imagined.

I'm forever indebted to Jim McCarthy, agent, editor, comedian, and pop culture reference guide. Your advice and suggestions are invaluable. On the downside, you've encouraged a dependence on apple pie milk shakes.

I seem to have picked up a slew of first readers. First up, Stacia Kane (whom I'm sure I'll mention again): Her encouragement and critique helped to make this book so much better than it started. The South Sound Algonquians, for the second year in a row, have put up with my filthy public readings, offered support, and even added a bit of their own brand of nasty. A hundred thank-yous to Monica Britt, Dolly Ceehar, Ned Hayes, Manek Mistry, Megan Pottorff, Sherylle Stapleton, and Tom Wright.

So often writing is a solitary activity, and for most, so is the promotional aspect. I was lucky to find like-minded friends to help stave off the loneliness. Team Seattle, for one, Caitlin Kittredge, Richelle Mead, Cherie Priest, and Kat Richardson—thank you, guys, for putting up with all the crude jokes and laughing, anyway. To the League of Reluctant Adults (because blogging doesn't have to be lonely), thanks Stace (there she is again), Caitlin, Jackie Kessler, Jaye Wells (Blue Drank!), Anton Strout, and Jeremy Lewis. And even our fallen comrades, Ilona Andrews and Jill Myles (who've never really left).

One of the most surprising things to come out of this whole published-author thing is the great readers who have found me. The Glamazombies*, as I've dubbed them, are such a fun group, and I'm totally enamored of my plague carriers, Missy Sawmiller and Todd Thomas. You guys Rock!

I promised myself I wouldn't write another two-page acknowledgments, but clearly I can't keep my word, so I'll continue. . . .

Two author peeps kept the Montana events in this book on track, Patricia Briggs and Diana Pharoah Francis. Thanks to you both, and Patty, I still have that Butte map on my wall.

My friends continue to put up with my crazy schedule, God bless 'em. Thanks, Kevin Macias and Jo Rash for all the support and free dialogue! Three more friends: Synde Korman, Duane Wilkes, and Barbara Vey—your enthusiasm for books and the genre is inspirational. You guys are awesome, and I'm glad to know you.

Finally, Caroline, my lovely wife, she's my magic. She is everything to me and contributes so much to this series.

Thank you.

For your time.

For your love.

*Join us online at http://groups.yahoo.com/group/markhenry

Chapter 1

Raising the Dead
for Fun and Profit

Nowadays, anyone with a wallet full of cash and a little insider knowledge is getting into the Supernatural life. And, I do mean anyone. Criminals, politicians, even—brace yourself—entertainers are plopping down tons of cash for immortality.

—*Supernatural Seattle* (June 2008)

Gil brought lawn chairs to the cemetery—not stylish Adirondacks, not even semi-comfortable camp chairs (the ones with those handy little cup holders). No. He dug up some cheap plastic folding chairs, the kind that burrow into your leg flesh like leeches.[1] He arranged them in a perfect semicircle around a freshly sodded grave, planted an iBoom stereo in the soft earth, pulled out a bottle of '07 Rose McGowan,[2] and drained half of it before his ass hit plastic. Granted, he managed these mundane tasks in a pricey Gucci tuxedo, the tie loose and dangling. On any other day, this would have been his sexy vamp look, but tonight . . . not so much. His eyelids sagged. His shoulders drooped. He looked exhausted.

I, on the other hand, looked stunning.

---

[1] It's like he had a time machine and a white trash childhood.
[2] Celebrity blood donation is quite lucrative. You'd be surprised who's giving it up for the vamps.

One of those movie moons, fat and bloated as a late-night salt binge, striped the graveyard with tree branch shadows, and spotlit your favorite zombie heroine reclining starlet-like on the polished marble of the new tombstone—there was no way I was subjecting vintage Galliano to the inquisition of plastic lawn chairs; the creases would be unmanageable.

Wendy didn't take issue with the cheap and potentially damaging seating. She wore a tight pink cashmere cardigan over a high-waisted chestnut skirt that hit her well above the knee. She crossed her legs and popped her ankle like a 1950s housewife, each swivel bringing attention to her gorgeous peek-toe stilettos—certainly not the most practical shoe for late-night graveyard roaming, but who am I to judge?[3]

The dearly departed were our only other company; about twenty or so ghosts circled the grave—in a rainbow of moody colors and sizes. A little boy spirit, dressed in his Sunday best and an aqua green aura, raced by, leaving a trail of crackling green sparks; the other, older specters muttered to each other, snickered and pointed. Popular opinion aside, zombies do not typically hang out in graveyards—ask the ghosts. We don't crawl out of the ground all rotty and tongue-tied, either. We're created through bite or breath, Wendy and I from the latter. So you won't see us shambling around like a couple of morons, unless there's a shoe sale at Barney's.

"You're killin' me with The Carpenters, can't you skip this one?" I stretched for the iPod with my heel trying to manipulate its doughnut dial. Karen was bleating on about lost love from beyond the grave—and just a little to the left. "She's forcing me to search my bag for a suicide implement. I swear I'll do it."

"No shit. Her warble is drawing the less-than-present out of the woodwork." Wendy looked over the top of huge Chanel sunglasses—she seemed to wear them as a joke, so I refused to

---

[3] I'm a total shoe slut. Jimmy Choo, Manolo Blahnik, Christian Louboutin: this is an open invitation. Feel free to run a train on me. The cost? Stilettos, duh.

comment. She'd be more irritated with every second that passed. Such a simple pleasure, but those are often the best, don't you find?

"Bitches." Gil opened an eye. "This is a classic. Besides, Markham put this playlist together."

"Who's that?" I'd decided against self-harm and opted for a smart cocktail. I pulled a mini shaker from my bag and followed that up with miniature bottles of vodka, gin, and rum. Who says Suicides are just for kids? I mixed while Gil chattered.

"Him." He jabbed a thumb toward the grave. "That's Richard Markham; they call him the Beaver King. He's a millionaire, entrepreneur, and genuinely bad guy. He owns a chain of strip clubs, you might have heard of them. Bottoms."

When neither of us registered a hint of recollection, he became animated.

"You know. He's been in the news re-

> ### *The Beaver King's Maudlin Resurrection Jams*
>
> The Carpenters • *"Superstar"*
> Harry Chapin • *"The Cat's in the Cradle"*
> Barry Manilow • *"Mandy"*
> Captain & Tennille • *"Muskrat Love"*
> Gordon Lightfoot • *"If You Could Read My Mind"*
> John Denver • *"Leaving on a Jet Plane"*
> Carole King • *"So Far Away"*
> Melissa Manchester • *"Don't Cry Out Loud"*
> Judy Collins • *"Send In the Clowns"*

cently because of some shady business deals. He also coined the phrase 'All Bottomless Entertainment'."

"Don't you mean 'all nude'?" Wendy asked.

"No. 'All *Bottomless*.' He's decidedly anti-boobs. His clubs feature blouses *and* beaver. It's a very specialized niche."

"Well then, this should be fun." I stuck a straw into the shaker and sucked.

It was nice to see Gil's enthusiasm; he had been a complete ass-pipe since he'd opened Luxury Resurrections Ltd., stressing about every little detail. I had to hand it to the guy. After the money dried up—his sire left him a hefty sum in their bank account and then left (said Gil was too needy)—he launched his plan to charge humans for vamping. He was one of the first in Seattle, but the copycats were close on his heels. A few months later he bought into my condominium—not a penthouse like mine, but a pretty swank pad, nonetheless.

"Explain to me again why we're out here?" Wendy struggled to separate her legs from the sweaty straps—I cringed, afraid that she'd leave some meat on the plastic; we were fresh out of skin patch—they finally released with a slow sucking sound. She massaged the pattern of dents on the backs of her legs. "It's not like vampires need to rise from the *actual* grave. It's a little melodramatic. Don't ya think?"

"Yeah." I drained the final droplets from the shaker with loud staccato slurps. The alcohol seeped into my veins, flooding them with welcome warmth.

"I told you, I have to provide an experience with the Platinum package," Gil huffed, then snatched up his man bag and dug through it. He pulled out some Chapstick, spread it on in a wide "O," retrieved a crumpled brochure, and tossed it at me. "Here. Service is the only thing that's going to set my business apart from the chain vampire manufacturers. I provide individualized boutique-like vamping, at reasonable prices."

"Mmm hmm." I slid from the headstone, carefully hopscotched across the grave—I'd hate to misstep and harpoon Gil's client, or worse, break off a heel in the dirt—and stood next to Wendy. I smoothed the crinkled paper and turned to catch the moonlight.

"The Platinum Package," I read aloud. "Includes pre-death luxury accommodations at the Hyatt Regency, voted by readers of *Supernatural Seattle* as the best undead-friendly hotel in the city, a thorough consultation with a vamping specialist, a fully realized death scenario, including funeral and interment, bereavement counseling for immediate family, and an exclusive orientation to the afterlife from the moment of rising. Hmm."

"I spent a lot of time on that." Gil beamed.

"Yeah, at least fifteen minutes." My eyes found a series of numbers after the description, that if it weren't for the dollar sign, I'd have mistaken for binary code. "Can I ask you a question?"

"Sure."

"Is this the price down here?" I pointed out the figure.

"Yep."

Wendy took a slug from a crystal-studded flask—she couldn't find her usual Hello Kitty one.[4] Immediately, her skin took on the rosy glow of most living alcoholics. I love the look: almost human.

"One million dollars, Gil? You call that reasonable pricing?" Wendy did a spit take that flecked the brochure and my hands. "Jesus! So, if that's the platinum, what's the bronze package, then?" Wendy asked, wiping at the Grey Goose trickling from her nose. "A drive-by vamping?"

"Cute." Gil tongued and sucked at his fangs in irritation.

He shrugged off our outrage and plopped down in his own lawn chair. "Five hundred grand is the going rate nowadays, the markup is for my fabulous luxury features. It's not cheap, but look what you get . . ." He swept his hands from his head to toes like a game show hostess. ". . . a super hot greeting party. And . . . a couple of hot go-go dancers."

"Where?" I looked around. "Are they late?"

"Why, you two pork chops, of course. You remembered to leave the panties at home, right?"

"Oh yeah. Of course." I plucked a miniature Goldschläger from my purse and drained it. "When am I not airing out the chamber of horrors?"

"Me, too," Wendy said. "Totally commando."

---

[4] The folks at Sanrio are really kicking their adult line up a notch.

"Gross." Gil covered his mouth, heaving. "Let's not talk about the vage, anymore. I think I'm traumatized."

"You started it." I tossed the empty bottle aside and dug for another.

From there, the conversation dwindled to nothing, an uncharacteristic silence settling over us like a late summer fog. The ghosts had even settled down. Except for a particularly downtrodden specter pacing under a nearby tree, the rest seemed content settling into their various routines (friendly visits to neighboring graves, a spirited game of cards over by the mausoleum, a display of ghost lights in the woods). Relaxing, even.

And that's when I opened my big fat mouth.

"I got a weird call today."

"Oh yeah?" Wendy asked. She must have been bored because this normally mundane news had her wide-eyed.

"My mother's hospice worker."

"What?" Gil twisted in his chair to face me. "Hospice? She's dying? You never even talk about her. I thought she'd already kicked it."

"Yeah, right?" Wendy muttered.

The dead are so sympathetic. If you're looking for an honest opinion, and don't want any handholding or softeners, this is the crowd for you. Not that we're auditioning for friends, just now.

"Nope. She's still alive. The doctors say she's in the end stages of stomach cancer; it's pretty much spread everywhere. Been at the hospice for a few weeks now. Apparently, it's not pretty, nor is she." Inside *or* out, I thought.

"Wow."

"That's bad."

"Yeah." The truth was, I wasn't feeling any pain about it. Ethel Ellen Frazier had been a rotten mother, wife, and human being. You name it. Now, she was rotting inside. Ironic? Harsh? Sure, but she'd earned it. Every wince of pain, bout of vomiting, and bloody toilet bowl—the caller had gone into some unnecessary specifics.

Let me give you a little "for instance."

When I was young, Ethel convinced me—through months of badgering and ridicule—that I could benefit from a gym membership. Dad tried to talk her out of it, but like always, he had no say. So, off we went to Happy's Gym and Pool. Happy was just that; he had the kind of smile I could never seem to muster, broad and beaming. I think it was even real. The gym and pool were in the same room, a massive barn-like structure with the pool in the center, the equipment to the right, and the men's and women's locker rooms on the left, separated by a dry sauna. With about ten minutes left on the treadmill, I noticed a growing number of horrified expressions. I took off my headphones. Screams were coming from the sauna. Long screams. Then, choppy short bursts. And in between low gurgling moans reminiscent of the ape house at the zoo.

I scanned the room for my mother; I didn't expect to see her. She was behind closed doors. And I was out in the open, 15 years old and humiliated. Happy's smiling face was nowhere to be found, either. I suspected it was crammed firmly between my mother's thighs. But I was wrong. The security guard cleared up the mystery by opening the sauna door. There was Mom. On all fours and facing a captive audience, Happy behind her caught up inside like a shamed dog; his perpetual smile replaced by an embarrassed "O". I could see the words play across Ethel's lips, as I ran for the exit. "Shut the door, dimwit!"

Now, tell me she didn't buy herself some cancer on that day.

Did I mention how lucky I am to have friends like Wendy and Gil? I can always count on them to turn the conversation back around to . . . them, and I was glad to have the heat off this time.

"Oh my God!" Wendy grabbed my arm and shook it like an impatient kid in the candy aisle. "I totally knew about this. I was talking to Madame Gloria just the other day and—"

"Here we go." Gil snatched up the bottle of McGowan and finished it off.

Madame Gloria was Wendy's telephone psychic. According to our girl, she was "moderately accurate," whatever that meant.

"Shut up, Gil. Madame Gloria said that someone was going to die and that we . . ." she pointed at Gil, herself, and me, "we would be going on a trip. A road trip."

"Jesus." I swatted her hand away. "You think she's talking about Ethel? I'll be damned if I haul my dead ass across three states for that bag of bones."

"It might be good to get some closure." Gil's face was attempting sincerity. It missed. He did succeed in pulling off a smoosh-faced version of constipated.

"Alright. So, before the two of you go all psychotherapist on me, let me tell you a few things. The reason I never talk about my mother is that she's a bitch. In fact, the last time I saw her was my high school graduation, where she blew me off to go to my ex-best friend's party. I can't say as I miss her."

Wendy waved me off. "None of that matters, anyway. Madame Gloria says we're going. It's fate."

"Yeah. It's fate." A sly smile played on Gil's lips.

"Like Hell it is." I punched his arm. "What was all that shit about breaking free from your family?"

He sneered, rubbing the spot. "What are you talking about?"

"When I first met you and you took me to see Ricardo?"

"Not ringing any bells."

"Ricardo told me that I needed to make a clean break from any living family and friends."

Ricardo Amandine had filled me in on a lot more than mere survival tactics. The club owner had become a mentor of sorts, doling out words of wisdom over drinks, shopping, and the odd kill. He was hot as hell, but as is the rule with male zombies, totally asexual.[5] Shame.

"True," Gil said. "But this is different. Your mother's gonna die, anyway. And look at poor Wendy. Don't her feelings count?" He gestured to the other chair.

---

[5] Something about the lack of blood flow.

Wendy's lips pursed into a pathetic pout. She was even batting her eyes.

Christ.

He continued. "She's totally bored. Would a road trip be so bad?"

I imagined dirty rest-stop bathrooms, rows of trailers substituting for motels, a general lack of shopping opportunities. A zombie has certain needs. The upside? Cute country folk have cute country flavors.[6]

Wendy nodded. "What were *you* planning to do about the situation?"

"I thought I'd pretend I'd never gotten the call. Denial's my friend, and all."

"Yeah, okay. Just say you'll think about it. Please?"

"Fine. I'll think about it."

I lit up a cigarette; the smoke caught on the thinnest of breezes and spun off like cursive. The trail stretched off toward the single ghost who was still interested in our presence. He stomped through the haze, passed us and then stopped about ten feet away, leaning against a rather confusing headstone of a gargoyle eating a hoagie—or was that a salmon?

"I've been meaning to talk to Hans about making me some of those," Wendy said. She was pointing at the black-papered cigarette dangling from my lips.

"I'll ask him to make you some. Any particular colors, or outfits you're trying to match?"

The ghost started coughing. Expansive rattling coughs. He must have wanted attention, as he never looked away. So dramatic. "It's not gonna kill ya, buddy!" I yelled. He scowled.

Wendy disregarded the exchange and continued. "An assortment would be great. Only no orange. I look horrible in orange."

"Tell me about it. Remember that track jacket you kept trying to wear out in public. You looked like a road worker. I was fully prepared to club you."

---

[6] Without all the nasty additives you find in city meat.

"Oh yeah," she said, as though I'd brought up some long-lost treasure. "Where'd I put that?"

I shrugged. The truth was, Wendy hadn't put the track jacket anywhere. I'd snuck it out of her hall closet while mama was putting her face on and promptly dumped it in the trash chute. I was doing her a favor, really. She looked like a big pumpkin in that puffy satin piece of shit.

Gil adjusted his butt in the chair. He'd taken note of our visitor. "Is that ghost eavesdropping?"

"Probably."

"I can't have anyone, or thing, fucking up my shit. Not tonight. Markham's not a flexible guy."

"Maybe he thinks you need a third judge of your vampire making—"

"Vampires?" The ghost choked the words out from over my shoulder. I staggered to the side to avoid any spectral germs or whatever. "I can't stand me no friggin' vampires. Piss on 'em. They should all rot in iron boxes."

"That's a little harsh," Wendy commented.

"Harsh?" The ghost spit a glob of violet-hued mush at Wendy's feet. "I don't know 'bout that. Seein's they're the one's suckin' people dry. I'll say it again. Piss on 'em."

Up close, the ghost looked like a vagrant. His face was all scruff surrounding a nose the size of a kosher dill, his eyes obscured by thick tufts of brow hair. Dirt clung to his ethereal form in spots, as though even death couldn't hide the residue of boxcar or alley dumpster. There was even a scent in the air, pungent and sour like milk gone to clot.

"You one of them fuckin' vampires, boy?" He kicked at the back of Gil's chair, foot moving right through and ending up somewhere inside Gil's stomach.

"What if I am?" Gil stood and faced the bigot. I almost interceded but thought it might be important to witness some honest-to-God vamp bashing. If only just to say I had been there, and act disturbed and offended. I could give my report to the late evening edition of *Supernatural Seattle Tonight*. They love me.

"Then I got somethin' fur ya. You stinkin' mosquito." The ghost started to reach down inside his pants.

We all gasped in horror. Well not all, Wendy seemed genuinely interested—craning her neck to get a good look—but she doesn't count, being a slut and all.

A low scraping rose from beneath us, a lonely hollow scrabbling, as though rats were burrowing through wood or Gil's client had shredded the tufted silk of the coffin lid and was clawing through mahogany. Yeah. It was that last one for sure.

The noise drew the ghost's attention, as well. He hiked up his pants and re-secured them with what looked like an electrical cord.

The scrabbling gave way to several deep thuds.

"Couldn't we just dig him up and save his manicure?" I asked.

Gil shrugged. "It builds character. Besides do I look like I'm dressed for grave digging?"

Gil was up out of his chair, folding it and gesturing for me to do the same. I looked around for Wendy and to my immediate dismay caught sight of the homeless ghost. He stood atop the soon-to-be vampire's headstone, pants unzipped, and dick in hand.

"*Ew*. What do you think you're doing?" I asked.

"What does it look like, girly?" He bounced on the balls of his feet in preparation.

It hit me then. "Oh . . . shit. Gil, he's gonna piss on your guy's—"

"Piss on 'em. Piss on 'em," the ghost chanted.

Gil looked up from packing away the chairs just in time to catch Boxcar Willie pissing a steaming stream of ectoplasm onto the grave. It glugged from the guy like Mrs. Butterworth's, glowing an enthusiastic obscene purple.

"Gross!" Wendy yelled from behind me.

"Jesus!" Gil dropped the folded chairs and made for the

ghost just as the Beaver King broke ground. Markham breached the surface and was birthing straight through the manhole-sized puddle of ghost piss. Globs of the stuff dribbled down his arms and mingled with the mud on his face. The ghost shook a few errant drops loose. They plopped on Markham's face like thick blobs of mayonnaise.[7]

"What the fuck!" The new vampire spat, scooping the ectoplasm off his face. It oozed from his hair and plopped onto the shoulders of an expensive pinstriped suit that really seemed like overdressing for either digging oneself from a grave, or pee play, for that matter.

Gil started backing away, and gesturing for Wendy and me to do the same.

Markham had extricated himself from his burial place; he stood there like Carrie on prom night: humiliated, covered in that obscene fluid. He swung at the ghost, pummeling the air with impotent fists. The hobo's laughter echoed across the cemetery. The spirits playing poker by the mausoleum looked up.

One said, "Earl must have found him a vampire."

Their laughter joined a growing cacophony, as news spread amongst the dead.

"Where's that piece of vampire shit? I'll kill him!" Markham yelled.

Those were the secret words, apparently. We took off through the graveyard like someone had announced happy hour, bounding over headstones, and skirting spectral presences. Wendy broke off a heel in a concrete vase holder. I nearly tripped on a wreath Gil knocked over in his mad dash for the car.

In the distance, Markham was still screaming. "Luxury my ass! I want my money back, vampire! Every fucking cent!" Despite being the evil villain type, the Beaver King couldn't chase for shit.

I turned to Wendy. "Did Madame Gloria see that one coming?"

---

[7] I don't have to tell you, this kind of treatment would not be considered luxury service, by any means.

Chapter 2

Hood Ornaments of the Damned (and Bitchy)

Might I suggest a zombie plan—no, nothing as absurd as a defensive arrangement—a plan to have any plastic surgery or body art installed prior to your transformation.
—Horchata Romero from her appearance on Channel Dead's *GHOULAG* (episode 21)

We barreled through tight residential side streets, skidded on mounds of soggy leaves at nearly every corner and churned through puddles at breakneck speeds, coating one unfortunate woman with a shower of mud so slimy it clung to her head like a veil. Wendy and I busted up screeching like school girls while the woman spat obscenities foul enough to make a two-bit crack whore blush.[8]

"God, that was close." The back of Gil's head filled the rear-view mirror. He was noticeably shaking from the scene, but his hair looked great, thick and shiny. I let him be for the moment, rather than pointing out the understatement of the year. Wendy, unfortunately, had none of my restraint.

"You think?" She twisted around and jabbed him in the back.

[8] On that note, I hope women aren't spreading their legs for under a hundred. It seems a shame to exploit yourself (and your poon) for less than the price of a Toki Doki Messenger Bag. Which are totally cute, right?

"Ow!"

"What the fuck was all that, Gil?"

"What do you mean? *That* was us escaping from a psychopath drenched in ghost piss."

"Don't you mean *paying client?*" I shook my head. "You're gonna have to straighten that shit out, Gil. He'll badmouth your business into the ground, if you don't."

"Or worse!" Wendy crossed her arms.

Gil sunk back into the seat and covered his face. "Jesus."

"Let's just swing by the Well and talk to Ricardo, he'll have some ideas."[9]

"Fine," Gil said.

I suspected he acquiesced to shut me up, rather than from any real sense that Ricardo could help. I'd ever seen him so downtrodden, and frankly, I didn't care for it.[10] There was something defeated in his posture that had me wondering exactly how dangerous the stripper pimp was. Markham certainly wanted his money back, but would he really try to kill Gil? It seemed a tad petty considering the man's business. I mean, honestly, what were a few golden showers to the king of kink? It probably wasn't even the first time someone had pissed on him.

Still. Gil was scared.

He's a vampire, sure, but that doesn't mean what it does in books, on TV or at the movies. Down here, in the real world, if Tom Cruise gets burnt to a crisp, he's not going to show up shiny and new in the back seat of Christian Slater's car.[11] They're a lot more vulnerable than you'd imagine and rapid healing only helps if there is something left to heal. I'd seen vampires pummeled to death that didn't make it back.

It wasn't helping any that my driving was a tad erratic.

At the next intersection, I nearly clipped a faux-wood panel

---

[9] Ricardo Amandine, mentor, cocktail-shaker and go-go boy—I mean go-to guy, of course (he'd kill me if I left that little joke in there).

[10] As a rule, downtrodden is not my favorite look.

[11] Not without a great beard by his side.

van filled to capacity with bouncing welfare children, fully un-leashed from their seatbelts, their mother smoking away with the windows rolled up. It was embellished with those creepy stick fig-ure families on the back window. Normally, I thought of those as menus, but this time, I was just happy to avoid another accident.[12]

"Jesus Christ!" Wendy screamed. "Bruises equal money, Amanda!"

I pointed the Volvo into a 7-Eleven and parked. Wendy snatched her purse from the center console and darted into the store. Gil and I sat for a moment, silent.

"Do you think he'll really try to kill you?" I asked.

"It's a distinct possibility. He's not one of the good guys, you know?"

"We're not, either."

"We're the good bad guys. He's a bad bad guy."

"Oh . . . got it. I'm glad we straightened that out." I rolled my eyes.

It was then that a transparent head slipped through the wind-shield. "What's with rong faces?" The ghost pointed his finger from Gil to me; the glow smudged the air a weak teal.

"Hi, Mr. Kim."

The first thing you'd notice about my Volvo is its unusual hood ornament.[13] Most people have metal emblems festooning their cars; I have to have a ghost. 'Cause if anyone would be stuck with one, it'd be me, right? Mr. Kim is a permanent fix-ture in my life, since he died for the second time in the front seat of my car. It was about six months ago. I jumped in next to the zombie, who grinned at me through a trickle of liquefied brains draining from a hole in his forehead. He was gone. *Gone* gone. Or so I thought. A couple of weeks passed and there he was lying on his stomach on the hood, ankles crossed in the air and beaming, like a cheerleader photo.

---

[12] That's right, I have a little problem keeping my cars dent-free. What of it?
[13] Well, if you were dead yourself you'd notice. Are you? Dead, I mean?

"What got you upset?" he asked.

"Gil's gonna get murdered." I couldn't resist a jab. He's lucky I held off for as long as I did.[14]

"Oh God, it's true." Gil reverted to his standby head in hand pose. "I'm dead."

"No you're not. I was kidding. Why would he kill you, Gil? What for? A little piss play? He's probably cleaned up and draining hookers all over town, enjoying the dead-life."

Gil's brow arched and he allowed the slightest of smiles to creep across his lips. "You've gotta admit, a hetero guy with an aversion to breasts is probably not the picture of mental health."

"True. Let's just see what Ricardo comes up with. I'm sure it won't go any further than this. You'll see."

Inside the convenience store, Wendy browsed the aisles like a lazy Sunday antique shopper. I honked. She startled and scurried for the counter. I hadn't really intended for any of us to go in, I just thought I'd stop to avoid another car accident. She plopped a hand basket in front of the cashier and eyed the car nervously.

Wendy was probably back on the Twix. I kept telling her that those candy bars would be the death of her, again. Doesn't matter what I say, of course. Food addictions are strong among the undead, even though it is impossible for our bodies to process anything we eat. Wendy would just have to live with the residual splatterfest. Oddly enough, she seemed fine with that. Didn't mean I couldn't fuck with her a bit. She opened the door and fell into the passenger seat.

"That's a big bag you got there."

"Yeah. Yeah, I guess so." Wendy shrugged, looked out her window.

"Did you get any Altoids?" I winked back at Gil, whose gaze said, "I'm on it." He leaned in between the seats.

"How about some gum?" he asked, knowing full well that

---

[14] Empathy is not my strong suit.

gum and mints were all zombies could feasibly get away with without an adult diaper. "Did you get some gum?"

"Nope." The reflection of her face in the window moved into sour territory, so I was pleased.

"Hmm."

"What's that supposed to mean?"

"Nothing. Nothing at all."

"She think you got Twix in there, Wendy. You got Twix?" Kimmy swept an ethereal hand through the plastic shopping bag. "I think I feel something."

"Shut up." Wendy snatched the bag from his reach and gave us cat anus face.[15]

Ricardo lounged at our regular booth, his arm slung around my assistant, Marithé, in a loose comfort that I still wasn't used to. She was laughing, gregarious. One of the few times I'd seen her break from true bitch form. And . . . if I can just say, the silly grin didn't suit her. Not at all.

About a year after I was turned into what I am,[16] I cleaned house at my advertising firm. I bought out my partners—with the financial and mystical help of a silent partner—canned the entire staff, and groomed Marithé for undeath. She warmed to the idea almost immediately.

Almost.

In true Marithé style, she made me detail every element of the experience and provide written references. She planned for future body ornamentation, understanding that clit piercing wouldn't heal unless she went through with it before I turned her.[17] Do you see my logic? I couldn't afford to lose someone that upfront and organized. In fact, after her rebirth, she had

---

[15] There's no finer victory evidence.
[16] Fabulous zombie socialite. Gorgeous vision of death. Envy of all. Take your pick.
[17] That's hood ornament #2 for those of you counting.

Feral Advertising staffed with qualified supernaturals within a month. The turnaround was amazing.

Don't let my admiration for the woman mislead you. Marithé is a real cooze, a class A bitch, and I'm not talking out of turn here; she's won awards. Normally, I'd love that—look at Wendy. But I work with her and don't care to see her socially. So you can understand my irritation when her interest in Ricardo panned out. The two were disgustingly inseparable. Touching each other, slobbering on each other like dogs.

Gag with me, won't you?

The Well of Souls was crowded, despite the grand opening of Goblin Bar, two streets over. It was a real testament to the club's appeal, and in no small degree to the great DJ Despair— currently spinning his own remix to *Fuck the Pain Away* by Peaches, in case you're interested.

We scooted into the semi-circular booth, one after the other, forcing Ricardo and Marithé around until her ass hung off the seat. The handsome Latin snapped for a waitress who brought a pitcher of mojitos without all the pesky soda, sugar syrup and muddled mint.[18] Being a polite kind of gal, I poured.

"So what's the problem, sweetheart?" Ricardo's deep vibrating bass swam in the air and skid across my skin like a skipping stone on a placid lake.

"And make it quick please," Marithé added. "We have tickets for *Spinabifida the Musical*,[19] and we don't want to miss curtain."

"I hear there's an awesome duet between a lobster-clawed boy and a pinhead," I said, swizzling my drink.

"Absolutely. It's supposed to be awesome." Wendy nudged a sour-faced Gil. "Huh, Gil?"

"Sold out for months," he said.

"Ricardo has connections." Marithé winked at her beau.

---

[18] Got your wheels turning? Straight rum on the rocks. 151, actually.
[19] A celebration of deformities . . . and song.

Of course, Ricardo had connections. He was the biggest super-natural club-owner in the Seattle area. In fact, until recently, he held a near monopoly on the nightclub world. There were a few independents like Les Toilettes (gross), Garters (not nearly as sexy as you'd think) and Convent (a great willing victim market), but for the most part, Ricardo had the city by its dancing, cock-tail-swigging balls.

Now, that said, and no matter how loyal I am—and I am—I was totally going to hit the Goblin Bar opening after all the Gil drama settled. I couldn't very well miss a red-carpet paparazzi showdown, and my outfit was way too hot not to be fawned over and envied in the next issue of *Belle Morte.*

"So what do we need to talk about?" Ricardo asked.

"Gil got himself in some trouble. We wanted to get your take on the situation." I shoved an elbow at Gil. "Tell him."

Gil recounted the evening from the funeral service through our flight from the scene of the pee. Ricardo rubbed his jaw.

"Well, you've messed with the wrong sicko, that's for sure. Markham has been known to hold a grudge, too. You may have given him eternal life, and all, but if he sees it like your service did not meet his expectations, then . . . God. Piss? Jesus."

"How was I supposed to know that derelict would do something like that?"

"It really was just bad timing," I suggested. Gil stared straight ahead, his eyes drifting away.

"Doesn't matter. I've heard some really nasty stuff." Ricardo tapped a cigarette on the table.

"Like what?" Wendy lingered on that last word like a secret.

"Well, a few years back, one of Markham's 'girls' showed up to work fresh from a weekend meth-a-thon, tweaking like crazy. The boss man stripped her nude, shook a whole box of itching powder on her and pushed her onstage. By the end of her dance, she'd picked herself bloody and half the audience had ei-ther run out, puking and blood spattered, or . . . shot their wads, to put it crudely."

Marithé added, "Well, I heard—"

"How do you know about Markham?" I asked.

"I get around," she said.

I looked from her to Ricardo and back. "Yes . . . you do."

She gave me her patented "fuck you" look and continued, "Like I was saying, I heard that he keeps a bag of ball bearings in his office and if a girl slips up and accidentally gives the crowd a peek at the girls," she shook her chest to accentuate the point, "He hammers their tits like a mafia thug silencing a snitch."

"Oh that's lovely." I glanced at Gil; his eyes were wide and dry. "Is that all, or does someone else want to toss a rock at Gil's house of cards? Wendy?"

"I got nothin'," Wendy slurred, between greedy swallows of rum.

"Well . . ." Ricardo ran his fingers across his lips.

"Yeah?" I eyed him.

". . . there's the . . ." He looked over each shoulder and then spat the words across the table. "The Oatmeal Scotchie."

Gil gasped. "Oh my God, how do you know about that?"

"Uh—" Ricardo grimaced.

I glanced at Wendy. Her eyes caught fire—I imagined mine had as well (this was too juicy)—as though a terrible family secret had been revealed. "So . . . you're not referring to a delectable butterscotch cookie, I take it?"

Ricardo shrugged and let loose a sly smile. Marithé concealed a giggle behind a stiff hand.

"Just shut up, all of you!" Specks of blood clung to the air around the sound, curling and undulating between us like a living thing. "I don't want to talk about it."

"Ooo." I pointed to his face and drew an invisible circle. "What's all this about?"

Pinpoints of crimson appeared on Gil's pale cheeks like freckles—Rose McGowan's blood was fresh in his system . . . and mobile—the effect was more Pippi Longstocking than all-

American boy. The closest thing to human I've seen from him in a while. Cute, kind of.

Wendy broke in, "I know, right? So testy."

"There might be something that could play in your favor." He leaned in and motioned for the rest of us to do the same. "Markham has a memory problem, ever since a car accident from his youth. Becoming a vampire doesn't heal brain damage. He might forget the whole thing in a matter of days, so if you just lay low, got out of town maybe." Ricardo held up a finger, his face turned deadly serious. "Do you think you can do that?"

"Sure. Of course."

"I mean it, now. You'll have to offer some sort of refund and an apology. But, I wouldn't do it anytime soon. Let the man cool down and maybe he won't kill you." He said it like the situation actually *had* a bright side.

"Oh God." Gil's head lolled back on his shoulders.

Wendy jumped on the suggestion and slapped my arm. "We could totally go see your mom! It's like another sign."

"Looks like you may get your way, girl," I said.

Wendy bounced in the seat, clapped her hands and prodded Gil, like he wasn't going through a crisis. He cringed.

"What's this about?" Ricardo asked. "You were all planning a trip anyway?"

"Oh, my mother. She has cancer or something. Wendy's telephone psychic predicted that we'd take a trip to see her."

"Telephone psy—" he began.

"Madame Gloria has a 92 percent accuracy, people. I won't have y'all maligning her."

She had us there. The medium, or whatever, certainly predicted that we'd all be going on a trip, and as soon as we made an appearance at Goblin Bar, we'd be free of obligations. After all, Marithé would be perfectly capable of running the business in my absence. I guessed there was no avoiding my own issues.

Ethel Ellen Frazier.

I drained the pitcher and drank. The alcohol warmed my frame and I imagined the scene at my mother's deathbed. She lying there, dried out like a mummy on display, crispy fingers beckoning me closer.

Amanda, she'd say. *You've come to beg for my forgiveness, haven't you?*

Uh . . . nope. I've come to watch you croak.

Mother would completely ignore this crack and respond with something like: *Ah. Sweet girl, go ahead and make your apologies. I'm open to them.*

Apologies my ass, bitch. It's you that should be begging my forgiveness.

Rest your mind, child. I forgive you.

Can you hear me, old woman? I'd yell.

I forgive your neglectful ways, your whoring, your—

I hate you.

I know, baby. I love you, too. Doesn't it feel good to tell each other, after all these years?

Aaaaah! I'd scream, right before I bashed her head in with her bedpan.

I returned to the present. Ricardo and Marithé were vacating the booth, saying their goodbyes and wandering off through the crowded masses on the dance floor.

"Yep," I said.

"What was that?" Wendy asked.

The image of Ethel's still corpse fresh in my mind, her normally smug face stretched into a grimace, I found myself beaming.[20] "Let's go see Mom."

---

[20] Not that I was lost or anything. Oh . . . wait. I kind of was.

Chapter 3

Bitches: Trannies, Werewolves, Otherwise

The Goblin Bar marks a new era for supernatural clubbing. Ricardo Amandine has some real competition this time . . .

—*Zombie-A-Go-Go*

First off.

There was no valet at Goblin Bar. Do you have any idea how much I hate that?[21] We ended up parking across the street at a pay lot. Say it with me, "pay lot." I had to park myself at a club opening, like regular people, and shell out funds to do it; that's all kinds of wrong, no matter how you slice it. So you'll forgive me for being irritable.

The other thing.

The Emerald City drizzle was plotting to ruin my new outfit, a tighter-than-tight, scoop-necked cashmere sweater in a pale blue that made my eyes glow like dying stars, over a tan wool pencil skirt that tapered at the knee with such severity that with every step my hips swiveled with burlesque-like abandon. The heels were suicide high, and almost embarrassingly expensive.

---

[21] A butt-load, which is far worse than an actual shit-load, in that a butt-load is perpetually hangin' on. You know what I mean.

Almost.

Wendy had a bit more room in whatever it was she was wearing, some loose fitting smock that may have been the talk of New York and Paris, but looked like a cinched-up nightgown, and was thin enough, had she been alive and susceptible to cold nipple syndrome, that it would have been split open at the tits. She twisted around and collected the umbrellas from the back-seat.

And Gil—well, he was meeting us, said he wanted a second escape vehicle on the scene in case Markham showed up. His need for attention was going to get him killed one day, but he did look hot in formal wear and if anything's worth the risk of death and dismemberment, it was a photo-op.

We were just about to cross the street when Wendy stopped me. She was gawping at the entrance of Goblin Bar, eyes wide in horror.

"Oh my God. Is it ugly day?"

There was a frightening scene unfolding in the club's queue. Fashion victims, at least fifty of them. I'm talking bad weaves, atop poorly conceived cosmetic palettes, propped on cheap clothes, and in some cases flats, a parade of the grotesque, each one more hideous than the next.[22] Dare I say, an average evening in Seattle? The fashion quotient had taken a real nosedive since the '90s. Grunge may have been *très important* as a musical statement, but it really did a number on the whole aesthetic around these parts.

"Something," I agreed, as we crossed the damp road arm in arm our umbrellas battling above.

"I mean, honestly, have you ever seen this many—" she stalled on the word.

"Skanks?"

"Yeah. It's like a convention."

A particularly scary and hirsute woman with the pointy face

[22] I may be exaggerating, but only slightly.

of a rodent curled her nose at us, whispering something to her friend, who sneered.

"Yeah, you." Wendy pointed back at the woman, chuckling under her breath.

"Wendy, stop. Let's just go in."

"Oh shit. Look at that one!"

I followed her startled gaze to a woman picking at her hair with what looked like a chopstick. She was really digging in there, too. Chasing something. She had the pale-as-death skin of a vampire and arms striped in so many different colored pastes that it was obvious she was a cloudhead—a real frequent flyer from the look of it. She looked familiar, though.

"Hold up, that's Giallo."

"Who's that?"

I pulled Wendy in close. "Giallo was that model. You know. The one that was famous for killing her photographer during a *Vogue* cover shoot. I though she was dead, but didn't realize she was . . . actively so."

"From the looks of her she's a little cloudy, just now."

Giallo withdrew the chopstick from her ratted hair. She'd caught whatever it was she was hunting. The bug was still wiggling. She plopped it in her mouth.

"No kidding," I said, pointing her toward the gauntlet of photographers at the front of the line. Her expression brightened at the sight of flashbulbs. It shouldn't have considering the outfit. I could see the headline in ZWD[23] now . . .

Undead Socialite Spotted in Mu-Mu, Moo. Moo.

She'd be devastated. But I can't save my friends from everything, least of all negative media attention.

We stood for a few carefully posed shots and then approached

---

[23] *Zombie Wear Daily:* The source for the fashion-conscious zombie.

the gigantic trannie with the clipboard. She was seven foot if she was an inch, and the curly blonde weave added at least half a foot. She was a werewolf for sure and had her claws out to prove it. They would have been much more threatening, though, had they not been airbrushed pink and polka-dotted.

Wendy marched straight up to the beast. "Wendy Miller and Amanda Feral."

A single pastel claw scraped through the names, up one column, down the next, slowing near the bottom of the third page. Her face scrunched at something she saw there. She snickered. "Sorry. Not on the list." She craned her neck to look behind us. Her lupine face brightened. "Oh hey, girl. Long time no see. You go right on in."

Two zombies in cheerleader outfits and pigtails bounded past, asses hanging out from under the too-short skirts.

"Are you serious with this shit?" Wendy tried to grab the list, but the werewolf snatched it away.

"Oh yeah. I'm serious, bitch. You better back off and head to the back of the line."

Wendy's face was contorted in a glower, the bones in her jaw clicked and popped, moving, reshaping her jawline. Her arms clung to her side like logs ending in two tight fists. They resembled a pair of sledgehammers.

I slid in between the two. "What's your name, gorgeous?"

The blonde wolf grinned. "Tanesha Jones." When she voiced the last "s" she accentuated it with a finger snap. "I don't need to ask your name, girl. I see you all the time on TV."

"Oh stop." I winked. She could continue for several more minutes, at least, and it wouldn't bother me a bit.

"No. Serious. You're my party girl. Way better than Paris."

"But twice as deadly." I winked and gave her a practiced snarl.

"I know that's right." Tanesha giggled and flipped her hair over her shoulder.

I mimicked the activity on my end. If I'd learned anything

from my mother it was how to manipulate, and this one was nearly on the hook.

"Are you sure we're not on that list, Tanesha?"

"Um." She wrinkled her muzzle, looked away. "Well—"

"Yes?"

"It was on here, both of you were, but—"

"What do you mean 'were'?" Wendy had flanked me, her hands on her hips. Had she learned nothing from watching me work? You'd think that some of my skill would rub off, but no. Pesky emotions.

Tanesha reverted to her seemingly natural bitch state, lips curling for maximum canine exposure. "And why would I tell *you* anything, bitch?"

I reached for Wendy's arm and drew her close. "Not another word. You're fucking up my shtick. Now, just stand over there and be quiet."

"That's right, you better get ahold of your girl."

Wendy stomped a few feet away, and straightened her gown, as much as the puffy frock could be fixed. We were going to have a talk about that dress; I was having a hard time looking at it. I returned my attention to the job at hand.

"You're going to have to excuse my friend. She's had a bad night." I leaned in close, conspiratorially. "She's experiencing a little flaking, downstairs, if you know what I mean," I whispered, winked at Wendy in the distance, and gave her the thumbs up. She eyed me suspiciously.

"Ooo girl, I'm glad I've still got a heartbeat. The worst I deal with down there is a little yeast." She eyed me, watching for a response.

"Don't you mean head cheese?"

Tanesha erupted into a deep raucous laughter, shoulders jumping. "You nasty," she managed to choke out. "And I love it. Now come close. I'm not supposed to tell you this but the owner had us cross your name off the list just an hour ago."

"What?"

"Yep. Mr. Markham called the manager and nixed you from the opening night festivities. Cold, I thought."

"Damn. Markham, you say?"

Tanesha tilted her head like a threat. "Not a word, girl. I can't afford to lose this job."

I looked back at Wendy, the crowd that was going to watch us shuffle away, and the cameras that would be documenting it all. Markham or not, this wasn't just a dangerous situation, it was quickly becoming a PR nightmare. "Shit, that's embarrassing."

"Mmm hmm. Do you want me to make a scene so you can get out of here without people noticing?"

"No thanks, Tanesha. I'm a big girl, I can deal."

"You're good people, Amanda. No matter what they say."

"Sometimes the news gets it right, girl." I smirked.

"You're bad." She chuckled in a deeper tone than she'd liked and cut it off instantly. I turned to Wendy and shook my head no.

As long as I'd been dead—I was going on two years now—I hadn't missed a single social event. And now, I was blackballed. What the fuck? I can see Markham banning Gil from his club, but me? That's insane. Could my popularity be waning? I know it seems unlikely.

"Come on, Wendy. Let's go."

We turned from the velvet rope into a tidal wave of flashbulbs, and enough questions to clog our ears for days.

"Miss Feral?" Cheshire grin.

"Wendy?" Wrinkled nose.

"What's happening?" Smirky judgment.

"Not going in?" Giggles.

"What's the story?" Sarcastic tone.

I gave them a publicity grin. "No news here, boys, just forgot something in the car." The stalkerazzi were unconvinced. We posed for a couple of mercy shots and then took measured steps past the line of photographers. Too much speed would seem urgent and call for a chase, and I didn't intend to end up like Princess Diana, no matter how much publicity it'd get me.

"Jesus, those pictures are going to be everywhere, tomorrow," Wendy said, as we moved out of earshot. She'd sucked her lips inside and nibbled, a nervous tick that made the pretty blonde look toothless.

"Stop sucking your lips and don't worry, I'll figure out some kind of spin and have Marithé leak it. It'll be fine." I had to be strong, Wendy could freak out at any second and draw more attention. It's not like my heart wouldn't have been beating out of my chest.[24] So humiliating, right? But, like I said, I had to be strong. "Let's go eat a wino. You know how that always cheers you up."

"Okay." She stretched the word out, as though unconvinced.

"C'mon, girl. We'll go down to Pioneer Square and make it a smorgasbord!"

She giggled. I linked on at her elbow and we Blahniked toward the car, hips bumping.

"What the hell do you think happened back there?" she asked. We stopped at the car. Since, at some point during the horror show, Seattle had decided to stop the rain, we tossed our umbrellas in the back.

"Oh . . . I think it has a little something to do with our buddy, Gil. Where is he?" I looked at my watch. He was twenty minutes late, not that that wasn't just like him—or any of us. I usually followed strict "fashionably late" guidelines, myself. But, to keep us waiting twenty minutes when something as catastrophic as a velvet rope denial had happened? Unacceptable.

I didn't have to wonder for long.

A blood-curdling scream split the night into before and after,[25] a scream that blended the feminine quality of a horror movie starlet with all the masculine panic of a proctology patient.

---

[24] Had it not been a blackened husk, of course.
[25] As far as screams go, blood curdling is the way to go. Don't settle, victims.

Gil burst from around the corner of the next street, feet pounding the wet pavement and arms waving. He wore his trim Gucci suit in monochrome, making his hysteria all the more comic in its formality. "Car!" he yelled. "Car! Car! Car!"

Two massive dogs emerged behind him, snapping, snarling, and scrabbling at the cement. They were held back from a full charge by leashes that ended in a familiar, yet horrifying presence.

Markham howled more than his dogs, deep, guttural and menacing. Blood from his cheeks vaporized with each yell, filling the air between him and Gil in curling tentacles of vampiric spray. Between screams, his face was wild and his lips curled back from a pair of particularly nasty looking fangs dripping red condensation down his face and onto a white dress shirt, already striped with gore.

Sloppy fucker.

Wendy and I split off, leaving the SUV's hatch open, and darting around opposite sides of the car.[26] We were in and cranked before Gil hit our side of the sidewalk. Wendy screamed from a barely cracked window, "Hurry! He's almost on you!"

"No shit!" Gil dove between two Japanese imports, forcing the dogs to scrabble up and over the hood of one, crushing and dimpling it, and slowing them down only slightly. From this proximity, it was clear they weren't dogs at all, but fully shifted werewolves. Slobber flung from snapping maws in large enough globs to splat on the sidewalk like water balloons.

I put the car in drive and as Gil dove into the trunk space, floored the accelerator, careening between two cars in the rear of the lot. Markham's blood screams spattered the windows in flecks of crimson. I hit the wipers and cranked the wheel right, pointing us at a nearby alley. Gil swatted at the swinging pull of the rear lid, and closed it just as the werewolves reached the car. Their claws scraped across the window, etching it with their

---

[26] No small feat in stilettos.

fury. They were on us until the curb at the next street, where a sliding pivot flung them from their purchase on the bumper.

Markham planted himself in the middle of the street and bellowed. The blast of expectorated blood should have emptied him. The eruption was conical and expanded, catching on the buildings, and sending rivulets down the grey glass. He was still there when I turned onto Denny Avenue.

Blood rained from the sky.

Chapter 4

Winos, Witches and Winnebagos

Willing to relocate? Enthusiastic about the recent strides in clairvoyant technology? Leading medium accepting applications for Psychic Technicians 1 and 2, must have excellent communication skills and triple-digit Intelligence Quotient.
—Employment Section, *Seattle Supernatural Daily*

We didn't really talk about our next step, it just sort of . . . happened. No one even spoke until the car was barreling up Interstate 90 toward the pass, Mr. Kim snoring quietly in the back. We all looked like zombies, even the two that weren't.

I turned on the radio.

"A mysterious red rain fell on the downtown core, around 1:00 this morning," a man's voice reported. *"Centered just north of Belltown, the odd substance, that some described as diluted blood, fell for only a few minutes, but the evidence of the event can be found on every car, building, and bystander unfortunate enough to be caught in the downpour. We talked to Mara, a waitress and witness to the bizarre rain."*

"The reapers are gonna have to work a miracle to sort this out," Wendy said.[27]

[27] Reapers: the supernatural world's cleaning crew. They fix all the little messes that could expose our presence (but only in larger metropolitan areas where they can extort the most money from a side-business of zombie healing). Nasty little bitches.

"No doubt, they'll be working those little asses all night cleaning the streets and washing memories."

Gil squeezed his torso between the front seats, elbows up on the seatbacks. "I almost feel sorry for them."

"Sh! I'm listening." I cranked the volume up.

"It happened all quick. Like super sudden. I'd just stepped out the door when the first drops fell. I'd be pissed if it weren't a uniform."

"Mara's shirt is covered with red spots and streaks, much like everything else in the area. The police are treating it like a crime scene at this point . . ."

There was a pause in the news report, a subtle crackling static that seemed to take over for only a few seconds, but was likely much longer. I looked at Wendy, who nodded. Gil slid back into his seat, relief spreading across his face. The interruption subsided.

"We have with us Seattle Police Department spokeswoman, Gail Charles. Officer Charles, have you found the source of this unusual—"

"Absolutely—nothing of any import, simply a busted water main and a little rust. City water is on its way."

That was quick.

The reapers wielded their magic with the impatience of only children. I imagined the scowls of contempt on their faces as they moved through the crowds, snapping fingers and clearing minds, all with the springy-stepped footing of child stars. The massive mouth portal would be open, chomping at the blood debris, and licking windows clean.

"I wish I could have seen them show up," Wendy said.

"Ew. I don't." I glowered. "I owe those brats twenty grand

for last time I cut myself. If I'm not more careful, I'm gonna be broke and broken. Plus, they're just fucking creepy."

"I think they're adorable."

"So you've worked through that porcelain doll phobia, then."

"Shut up." Wendy's eyes squinted.

"No. *You* shut up."

"You're the one that made us go to Markham's club."

"How was I supposed to know? It's all Gil's fault anyway."

"Um. If I could break into girl-talk for a minute." Gil's face was slack. He stared off in the distance.

I followed his gaze. Didn't see anything. "What's up?"

He looked down at the dash clock. 4:30 A.M.

"That's dawn up there." He pointed toward the break in the mountains. A dim light clung to the trees like the faintest dew. Only a vampire would notice. I didn't pick up on the importance of the statement, right away . . . and then it hit like a wave.

"Oh crap." If we didn't find shelter, Gil was going to either burn or be forced to claw into the earth

"Is there a motel nearby? When was the last exit? How far are we from the next exit?" Gil broke free from the stupor that claimed him. He spat his words, and clung to the seat backs with white-knuckled intensity.

"Calm down. This is America, there's got to be some sort of commerce blighting the landscape just over the hill there." I pointed to the cresting roadway.

But there wasn't. Just more of the same, trees, more hills, and the higher we climbed the more obvious dawn became.

I'd never seen a vampire fry before and you can bet your ass, Gil wasn't about to be my first. He told me, once, about seeing it happen on an underground video that made its way through the suck circles.[28] The female vampire was tied to a table in a

---

[28] Suck circles: A group of vampires (sucks, colloquially) that get together for conversation about books, film, and music, and not, as you presume, some dirty blowjob party. Why must my readers have the filthiest minds?

forest clearing, face up and nude. The light simply tanned her, at first, and then seemed to ignite in her veins, searing her flesh in a web pattern, before bursting from inside and engulfing her. Finishing her.

A shudder rolled through me.

That wasn't going to happen to Gil. I wouldn't let it. "The way I see it, we've got another two hours before direct sunlight, maybe more in the forested areas. We can't be more than an hour away from a town with a motel, or something."

Gil warmed to this idea. "I agree. Okay. Anything sounds like a plan right now."

Always the breath of fresh air, Wendy said, "I knew we shouldn't have wasted all that time driving around the city. What if you guys are wrong about the timing?"

The sound of Gil's teeth grinding sent shivers rolling through me. "Do you have a better idea?"

"Maybe." Wendy snatched her purse from the floorboard and dug inside.

"What are you doing?" I asked.

She pulled out her cell phone and spoke two words, "Madame Gloria."

"Jesus."

"It couldn't hurt, Amanda," Gil said.

A minute later and we had another voice in the car. Wendy's telephone psychic had joined us on speaker. Her voice was rich and buttery like a jazz singer's, hypnotic. Ear crack. There was no wonder Wendy called on her so often. "Here's what you're going to do, children. Take the next exit."

She had no sooner gotten the words out than the next exit was on us. Hearing no dissent, I pulled the car off the freeway. At the top of the off-ramp a sign pointed toward a campground.

"Follow the signs to the campground, when you arrive at the gate, turn off your lights."

This was beginning to sound dangerous, but no more so than a flaming vampire in the backseat of my Volvo, so I kept going. The road to our destination was worn and potholed, and entirely unlit. This was the kind of dark that scared the living, and it was beginning to scare me. My headlights seemed swallowed in the dense forest on either side, and the paved road gave way to dirt before too long.

Then we came up to a sign. It hung from a chain that blocked our way.

> **Green Gulch Camp**
> *Closed for Season*
> **STAY OUT!**

"Shit!" Gil screamed, defeated.

Madame Gloria's voice attempted to soothe, "Now, now, ease yourself, vampire. Shelter is at hand. Drive into the campground and at the curve, you'll find what you seek." Then, "That was twelve minutes, Wendy, shall I add it to your bill?"

Wendy looked from me to Gil, sheepishly. She clicked off the speakerphone and whispered, "Yeah, that's fine . . . I know." She glanced in my direction, not quite meeting my gaze. "I know," she said, again, and hung up.

"Hmm."

"What?" Wendy snapped.

"Are you sure about her?"

"She guarantees her visions to be *moderately accurate*."

"Well, in that case—"

"What?"

"You realize that means she's only right part of the time."

"Well I have faith that she's right about this."

"Okay." I shrugged.

Wendy turned to her window, her scowl reflected in green dash light.

Gil left the car to unhook the chain, and hook it closed behind us. The further into the campground we drove, the wetter it became. Not from any noticeable rain; the dampness just seemed to be its natural state, permeating everything, condensing on the windows. Muddy puddles splashed dry as we churned through.

"Turn off the ligh—" Gil yelled, then cut himself off, then whispered, as though someone could hear us inside the car. "She told us to turn off the lights!"

I clicked them off and we bounced over the rough road in darkness for a moment, before a dim glow appeared in the distance, flickering on and off as though with candlelight. I stopped and turned off the engine. "That must be it."

"Yep." Wendy clutched at the dash; she was chewing her lips again.

"Why are you scared?" I asked. "Did that witch tell you something?"

"No. It's just kind of scary, that's all."

"We're the monsters, ladies." Gil opened his door and hopped out. "Remember?" He pushed the door shut with a quiet click, and then a soft bump to secure it.

I pulled off my heels and followed suit. Dirty feet were far preferable to ruined designer shoes, even if I had to drive barefoot.

Wendy didn't move. "I'll stay here and guard the car."

"That's what Mr. Kim's for, wake his ass up." The gentle snores continued from somewhere other than the backseat, probably somewhere in the heater vents.

"He can't defend it if someone strikes. He's clear for Christ's sake." Wendy crossed her arms, and sneered.

"Who's going to 'strike' our car Wendy?"

"I don't know."

It was certain Madame Gloria had told her something. I acquiesced and trod off in the direction of the light. Gil was already moving, low and catlike. The light emanated from a smallish RV, obscured behind an overgrowth of wild rhododendrons. Gil pressed his ear to its side and held a finger to his lips. He was in hunting mode, which would have been arousing had we played for the same team. Well, actually, it was still arousing. Gil was sorta hot, ask anyone.

"Someone's in there. Definitely."

I sniffed at the air—my only useful hunting skill, truth be told. At first the only scent was pine, and bark, the wet rot of needles. Then something else snagged on the moist air. What I caught was familiar: coffee grounds, tobacco, sweat, piss, shit. Body odors, of a specific variety. "Homeless guy," I said. "Probably mentally ill."

Gil nodded. He'd learned to trust my nose. His could tell you the vintage of any celebrity blood donation in production, while mine was only capable of detecting disgusting body fluids and psychiatric problems.[29]

"Just knock." I elbowed him in the side, causing him to flinch like a girl, forcing me to mouth that simile. *Like a girl.*

He made a fist at me, dropped it and then shrugged an okay.

After the third rap against the metal door, a quiet raspy sound came; it could have been, "Who there?"

"Amanda and Gil," I said. It didn't really matter if the poor guy knew our names, he wasn't going to make it out of this alive anyway. It's a sad fact about our kind that you're hopefully used to by now.[30]

The door swung open, "Who?"

First impressions are terribly important, don't you find? I know I do. The trailer's occupant didn't. Clearly.

The man was a tiny scrap of a guy and filthy—not unlike my feet—the dirt seemed ground into him, staining his skin in a way that was totally unsavory and obscuring any ethnicity.

He blinked tired eyes. They adjusted and widened, fear welled up—though I can't imagine what was frightening, other than the total mess that was my outfit. He made a quick attempt to slam the door closed. Gil intervened, his fingers getting crunched

[29] Useful skills? Some would say yes. Crime scene investigators, dogs, certain therapists.
[30] And if you're not, please try to keep up with the rest of the class. You're dragging down our scores. Thanks.

between the door and the frame. The air whistled as he cringed, sucked up the pain and jerked the door back open.

Inside, the man fell back onto a ratty banquette, shook his head, as though shaking a flea loose from the rat's nest on his head and busied himself arranging various objects on the faux-wood table before him, as though the exchange had never occurred.

We climbed inside.

The trailer was surprisingly cozy, albeit decorated in dingy shades of yellow and cream, the effect reminiscent of an oozy yeast infection. Somehow, I was certain Todd Oldham would have been either mortified or intrigued.[31] What no one could stomach were the piles of dirty dishes on the lone countertop, which had become a battleground for a roach/fly war.

I scanned the man's collection. Weird stuff. Thimbles, fish-hooks and safety pins, were lumped with doll heads, fingernail clippings, and Ziploc baggies of pop can tabs (the kind you're supposed to collect to buy precious time for loved ones on dialysis machines, but never end up anywhere but the trashcan). He arranged them on cocktail napkins, lined up in a row of eight, and each imprinted with the words: Can Can Saloon with a tiny silhouetted dancer lifting her skirt—for the boys, presumably.

His work was meticulous. Each item took up a prime location on the scraps of paper, thimbles to the left of doll heads, tabs under fish hooks, and so on. Not that there was any reasonable pattern at work.

I slid into the booth opposite; Gil followed me in.

"Whatcha doin'?" I pointed at the napkins.

The man continued his business, sorting, shoving a thimble inside an empty doll head, and placing it back on the napkin. Repeating these movements with measured determination.

---

[31] Todd Oldham: Fashion/Interior Designer. In love with kitschy retro in a totally unwholesome way.

"I . . . uh. I . . . uh. Sorting," he whispered.

"What was that?" Gil's face was crinkled and registered more than a little concern.

Clearly, the man was crazier than a shit-house rat, probably didn't even realize we were there.

"Do you live here?" I asked.

"Seat under my bottom, ain't it?"

"Yes, you're sitting down, that's true. Does that mean you live here?" I put on my most charming smile, but the man didn't look away from his task.

Gil put his arm around me and pulled me so close I felt his lips against my ear. "I'm going to look for the keys to this rig. You take care of him." He pulled back and winked. He slid back out and shuffled through the paper bags and other garbage that littered the aisle, heading toward the driver's seat.

I turned my attention back to the man. Who was looking directly into my eyes, a sly smile on his dirty lips.

"They're comin', girl," he said.

"What did you say?"

The man returned to his task, as though no exchange had occurred. Twirling a three-pronged hook between his dirty fingers.

Gil jingled something from the front, and yelled, "Found them!" My eyes darted to the keys dangling from his fingers and then back to the vagrant, just in time to hear a gulp. His fingers were empty and fast, apparently.

"Did you just eat that fish hook?"

"I . . . uh. I . . . uh. Yes."

I couldn't quite wrap my head around what had just happened. "Why would you do that? Why would you eat that?"

The man just smiled, cracked lips opening to reveal teeth blackened with decay. There was a twinkle in his eyes though, a spark of knowledge that implied he knew a little bit more about what was going on than I gave him credit for.

"You're insane." I snapped my fingers for Gil. "Get over

here! This crazy fuck just ate a fish hook!" I turned back to the table. The man's hands were creeping toward the napkins. I noticed that fishhooks sat atop five of them, instead of the seven that were left. "Did you just eat two more?"

He smiled again, this time licking a thin trickle of blood from his chapped lips. Brown bubbles of saliva cluttered the corners of his mouth.

"Did you hear me, Gil? We've got a problem here."

Gil stood next to the table staring down at the man, who in full, unobstructed view reached out, picked up three more fishhooks and popped them into his gaping maw. His head bobbed like a chicken as he swallowed the sharps down

"Well that's that," I said, holding up my hands as though turning myself over to the cops. I imagined the effects of chowing down on the human fishing line would not be pleasant. I'd be lucky to survive it and with no reapers around to play doctor, I certainly wasn't going to risk it. "He's all yours. I'm not going to chip a tooth on that shit, or snag my lips, or anything else, for that matter."

Gil frowned, but lunged toward the man's throat, anyway, pulling back the filthy winter coat and exposing the grayed flesh underneath and scars—so many scars—all of them circular and dashed. Obvious.

Gil gagged and let go.

"Jesus! He's barely alive. He's been used so many times." He pivoted and threw open the camper door. "I think I'm going to be sick."

I reached over and pulled the jacket back, again. He wore no shirt underneath and the scars covered his neck and torso, as though he'd made the error of swimming in a moray eel's nest. The man had been around vampires; that was certain. He'd probably been driven insane by their feeding, escaped, and retired from service out here where no one would look, let alone bother to camp. He looked away as my eyes took in the abuse of his body.

"Well, buddy." I shut his jacket, patted his shoulder and slid out of the booth. "Today's your lucky day." Although, it wouldn't be if any of those hooks shredded his insides, or maybe that would constitute a lucky day for someone who'd lived through such a trauma. Then, to Gil, "Did you try to crank this piece of crap?"

"Unh uh. Here." He tossed me the keys. His face was even paler than normal.[32]

I left the old guy to sort the remaining objects and took a seat behind the wheel. The camper cranked right up on the first turn. I could see the Volvo through the windshield. Beams of sunlight were filtering through the trees.

"You better find a place to sleep, back there. It's about that time." I watched as Gil wandered through the RV opening cabinets and two doors in the rear. One led to a bedroom that would be bright and sunny due to the large window at the back, the other led to a toilet/shower combo that after giving it a shocked look and a glower, he wedged himself into and locked the door behind him. I think he even cried himself to sleep, or at least that's what I'd tell Wendy, later.

---

[32] Pretty pale considering he got no sun, and had developed a sensitivity to bronzer.

Chapter 5

The Inexplicable Allure of Cowtown Couture

Several very fashionable boutiques have begun to cater exclusively to our otherworldly population, in fact, just this week former supermodel Giallo opened EMA-CIATED in the new veiled area by Pioneer Square. Her goal, to provide budget-breaking couture to the skin and bones set, is a smashing success . . .

—"Fashion victim" column, *Otherworld Weekly*

Fifty miles east of Green Gulch, Fishhook—as I'd christened him—snored himself awake, staggered up the aisle and plopped down in the passenger seat. I hadn't really thought about him since we pulled out of that moldy excuse for a campground. As it was, I had the Winnebago sailing down the other side of the pass—careening might be the more accurate verb—so he really was taking his life in his own hands just by moving around—of course, no more so than sharing your veins with a herd of thirsty vampires.

At that thought, I glanced his way, in what I hoped was an expression of empathy.[33] He responded by ripping the wettest fart I'd ever heard, a massive gelatinous ass moan, that woke a gag reflex in me that I thought I'd lost with my death. He gave me an exaggerated wink in response. The bastard.

---

[33] I'd seen that look on TV before, but mimicry isn't my strong suit, so it's hard to say whether I nailed it or not.

"Jesus Christ! Did you burn a hole through the seat? Open a window! Gawd!"

His laughter was a stutter of grunts, and I soon realized why. With every inch the window cranked down, the air molecules seemed to have bonded with shit. We'd rolled into a cloud of methane gas that could easily power a small island nation. The fucker knew it was coming, too.

His laughter became deep and rolling and I, in turn, began gagging and shouting, "Shut that fucking thing before I puke."

"I . . . uh—"

"I . . . uh nothing, asshole. I know a lame joke when I see one . . . or smell one."

The man nodded, grinning wildly and showing off those pearly blacks. The smell dissipated slower than I'd like but anything was an improvement to full exposure.

Crazy ass got back up and shuffled back to the table where I'd first seen him.

What are we going to do with him?

At the very least, he was going to need as much of a hosing down as this camper, to be at all presentable.

We rolled into a small college town called Ellensburg, where cows seemed to outnumber the human population by a mile. The stockyards were the first evidence of the place and they stretched from the freeway to the distant hills, a sea of shit, sectioned off by gridlines of fence post and barbed wire.

The town itself was straight out of a Norman Rockwell painting, if good old Norm had been caked in shit and three beers shy of a nasty cirrhosis. A mid-sized college kept the population stocked in taverns and cheap restaurants, poverty chipped in on the thrift stores. Lucky for me, visiting parents require moderately habitable hotel rooms or I'd have nowhere to freshen.[34]

I pulled into a newish motel called the Round Up—which,

[34] You didn't think I'd be freshening up or lounging about in that rat trap on wheels, did you? If so, you've got some serious catching up to do.

if I'm not mistaken is also the name of a weed killer. Wendy parked the Volvo next to the camper and waited for me in front of the office.

"You stay right here. You understand?" I leveled a glare and my index finger at the freak, and then reached down into his fishhooks and thimbles and mussed it up. He gasped and waved his hands over the rolling debris, and then busied himself re-assembling his collage of crazy.

"That ought to keep you busy," I said.

I opened the door and let in a burst of air thick with bovine butt funk. I gave the man one last threatening sneer and slammed it behind me. At the far end of the parking lot, a scruffy-haired youth traded balancing on his skateboard for falling on his ass. The stink didn't seem to bother him.

"Why, might I ask, would anyone choose to live in this hell-hole?"

Wendy shrugged nonchalantly. Too nonchalant for my taste. The day Wendy doesn't have a snide comment, is the day she's hiding something. This, I suspected, was that day. When she finally looked me in the eye, I saw a thin streak of brown below her lip that couldn't be anything but the gooey, sweet and creamy afterbirth of . . . wait for it . . . chocolate.

"Oh, honey," I said.

"Hmm?" Her brows rose in genuine interest, or so it would seem.

"What's that on your lower lip? Are you trying out a new liner?" I prodded.

"Huh?" Wendy scraped the chocolate with the point of her nail and examined the roll of brown that clung there. The evidence. "Aw shit. Alright, already. You know it's chocolate. Of course, it's chocolate. What else would it be? Why do you have to do that?"

"Do what?" I raised my palms to her, horrified. Had I committed a social faux-pas?[35]

---

[35] A rhetorical question, obviously. I don't need to hear it from you, too.

"Be so goddamned critical all the time. It's called an addiction, okay?"

"I . . . uh . . ." I didn't know what to say. One of the few times I'd been at a loss for words. Wendy stomped off down the sidewalk knocking on each of the motel doors along the way. She did so love to disturb the humans. "Sorry!" I called after her.

She raised a fist in the air, then flicked up her middle finger. She knocked on the last two doors and then turned the corner toward the back of the building. As she did, the frazzled guest in the second room down, stuck his head out, a question mark where his face should have been. "What the fuck!" he yelled.

I pointed out the skateboarder, watched him launch off toward the poor kid in his loose-fitting boxers and bare feet, and ducked into the manager's office, just as the man unleashed a torrent of expletives on the unsuspecting youth.[36]

With Wendy off sulking somewhere, I had no choice but to rouse Gil from his eternal slumber. I banged on the door to the dirty camper john, and yelled, "Gil! Wake up! I need to talk!"

"Wha-wha?" His voice slurred like a dementia patient's.

"Wendy and I had a fight."

"So?"

"So? Help me get over it?" I leaned against the door and kicked the bottom with the toe of my shoe.

"Stop that racket. You know I've got to sleep."

"C'mon. What should I do?"

"Jesus. Apologize?"

"Why do you assume it's my fault?"

Silence.

"Well?" I asked.

"Isn't it?" he sighed.

---

[36] What? I'm sure the kid did something to deserve it. They're not all angels.

"Shut up and go back to sleep already." I turned and examined Fishhook.

With the vagrant and nothing but four "budget beige" walls to occupy my mind, I was left with no other choice than to give him a makeover. I stood in the camper doorway eyeing the biohazard. His hair was shoulder length and ratty, starting on the top and working his way around his mouth like a dirty mohair scarf. What skin left exposed was ruddy and dry to the point of flaking. And the clothes—Christ—too tattered to salvage. Thank God for American Express Black; re-imagining Fishhook's persona was going to cost a fortune.

"I . . . uh . . ." he whispered. Because that's all he ever seemed to say, except for those comments.

They're comin', girl.

My first thought rushed to the vampires, those gluttons that fed from the poor guy so liberally. But it was daylight, and there was no way they were following, right now. Then I wondered if he could be referring to Markham and his werewolves. But how could he possibly know about that? We didn't even know that, for sure. I suspected Markham was on our trail, but I hadn't seen any proof. Madame Gloria hadn't mentioned it, and, honestly, wouldn't she have? I thought back to the moment she spoke to Wendy privately and a strange theory batted its way into my brain.

Maybe she was in on it. But, she'd led us to a safe place for Gil. Didn't make sense.

I was getting completely fucking paranoid.

I shook off the fog of thoughts and eyed my quarry. This time he was responding to my visual assessment and seemed to know he was looking down the throat of a bored zombie with a keen fashion sense. For a crazy guy, he seemed to put together the puzzle pretty well. He reached up and brushed his beard into a point, loosing food debris and at least one cockroach that dropped to the table and scuttled through the grid of doll heads and buttons, taking refuge in a toppled thimble.

"Oh yeah." I nodded. "It's project time."

Fishhook flinched.

He was surprisingly easy to herd into the motel room; a rolled-up newspaper prod didn't work but flashing a tit got the hobo shuffling right along. His eyes crinkled as he stepped into the sun.

Getting him into the tub was another story.

Bubbles exploded from the rush of steaming bathwater. I'd swiped six miniature shampoo bottles and a can of Ajax off the maid's cart just to be sure we'd have enough cleansers for his soaking.

The first step was my obstacle, not his. You see I wasn't really prepared to see the guy naked. Not after seeing all the dimpled scar tissue circling his neck. I'd seen a show on scarification as the next big body art movement. Looking at Fishhook, I wasn't buying it. Not for a second.

The scars tracked down his arms, chest and stomach, a trail of pain marking every bit of flesh loose enough to get a mouth around. Some were fresh specked with the yellowed ooze of infection. Fishhook needed antibiotics and a good plastic surgeon. What he had was me. He watched with those sad eyes, assessing me this time. I imagined him wondering if I was disgusted.

I was. Probably wasn't hiding it well, either.

He undid his belt and dropped his pants, catching me off guard, ruffling me—and not just because he wasn't wearing underwear. The scars continued down past his waist, a mass of swollen indents blossomed across his buttocks, traveled the length of both thighs and calves, set off against a canvas of mottled bruised flesh. There were even a few bites on the sides of his feet.

Savages.

Fishhook did have one thing going for him. He was hung like someone had left the sausage machine unsupervised. I found myself staring, mouth unhinged. The sight was moderately frightening, I must say, like someone had traded a normal dick for a fresh kielbasa. I'm not even going to talk about the foreskin.

Understand this: I don't do cheese tray.[37]

I must have sneered. Fishhook cleared his throat and formed a coherent sentence.

"You may not like it, but I'll bet that friend of yours enjoys a little hood."

"Oh . . . I see. You're talkative, *now*."

"Everyone knows Gummi bears taste like dick cheese." He rocked his hips, spanking his thighs with the monstrosity.

"Gross. Just get in the tub, you perv." I reached to snatch his putrid clothing off the floor but he beat me to it, rummaging through linty pockets, until he retrieved a small green Tupperware container. He gave it a shake, rustling up a muted scraping sound and then hugged it between his palms. He slid into the tub, eyes never leaving the container.

I sat on the toilet. "Do you remember what you said to me back in the camper?"

He shrugged.

"You said, 'They're coming.' Who'd you mean?"

He closed a fist around the lidded cup. "I didn't say nothin' to you." His words clipped off at the ends like a bad haircut, choppy; defensive or embarrassed, but hard to say as he didn't have any other social skills that could be construed as normal.

"Yes you did," I chided.

"No I didn't."

"Did, too."

"Uh-unh."

"What's in the box?"

"None of your business."

I crammed his rags into the trashcan, through with his bullshit. "I'm going to get you some new clothes, but since you can't be trusted to clean your own dick, I'm certainly not leaving these filthy rags for you to pull back on after you've bathed."

---

[37] . . . or dickies . . . or turtlenecks . . . or mushroom caps . . . or squash blossoms . . . call me picky.

He snickered and I backed out of the room, slamming the door behind me. A moment later, I heard sloshing. "And shave off that goddamn beard. It looks like a badger's taking a shit on your face. I think there's a razor on the counter. I'll be back in a bit and take you to get some coffee and food."

"I . . . uh. I . . . uh—"

"Great." I stepped out of the motel room, nearly falling over a clearly eavesdropping and knee-level Wendy. She dropped over on her side.

"Dammit!" she squealed.

"Oh, sweetie. I'm sorry."

She snatched her purse from the cement and brushed at her already-ruined sack dress. "I'm fine."

"No. No. Not about running into you, about before."

She brightened. "You were right. I'm a freak."

"Still. I shouldn't have." I lifted my hands in surrender.

Wendy's clutched her hips with mock indignance, and pouted. "You're supposed to tell me it's perfectly normal to have cravings for human food. That's a friend's job."

"Hello? There's nothing *normal* about us. I'm just worried that you feel like you have to hide it." I pulled out my best psychotherapy voice for the next bit, a manner I had a great deal of experience with, being a habitually inappropriate patient. "Secrets erode families."

"Can we just talk about something else?" She looked at the wastebasket in my hands. "Like what's in there?"

"Oh, just Fishhook's clothes. I need to toss them in the dumpster. I've got him bathing right now and there's a topic that'll trump a pesky eating disorder. The guy's wiener is scary big."

"What?"

"Oh yeah. He needs a chamois for that hose."

"You're kidding. I thought you said he was gross."

"Oh, he is. Totally covered with scars from his neck down, the poor guy."

"Then what were you doing checking out his dick?"

"Um . . . hello? I'm a perv. Now, let's go shopping."

The rest of the afternoon was spent searching for suitable travel attire in the Town That Fashion Forgot. The population must have had to drive elsewhere for their clothing needs—or, God forbid, duct tape some burlap together and call it a dress (like this one bitch I saw[38])—all we could find were a thrift store and a western wear shop, both of which caused me to itch like crazy just looking at the signs. Despite my own personal anti-cowpoke sentiment, Wendy dragged me into Mandy Jo's Tack and Tatters; she didn't seem to have a problem wrangling into low fashion.

I did.

Mandy Jo, as I insisted on calling the shop girl, wore a flared skirt and boots with a leather vest festooned—and there's no other way to put this—with spare change, a centerfold from *Penthouse*'s "Girls of Panhandling" issue, or at the very least a runner-up.

"Hey ladies. Can I help find you some cute western wear outfits?" Mandy Jo snapped her gum with a jaw cracking like a TMJ poster child. She rested her hands on her hips

"Ew." I shook my head as I looked her up and down. If I'd thought about eating this one, it was only for a second, chewing through that outfit would surely cause a rash in even the most hardy of skin types.

Wendy stepped in front of me. "Absolutely, hon. I'm gonna need some jeans, boots and one of those darling hats."

"And for you?" the girl addressed me directly.

"Thanks, but no. I'll just watch my friend make a fool of herself."

Wendy sneered and waved me off.

---

[38] Swear to God!

"Suit yourself, but I have to tell ya, bolo ties are half off and we got some real cute ones in the last shipment."

"I'll bet you did."

Mandy Jo loaded Wendy's arms with indigo jeans, a couple of muted plaid shirts, the requisite shit-kickers, and led her to a curtained closet. I grabbed a seat by the mirror. Within a couple of seconds, the sound of Wendy's jaw ratcheting open echoed from the changing room, followed by the clear shredding of fabric and a shower of threads and plaid scraps launched over the curtain rod.

"Are you alright in there?" The shop girl kneaded her hands, her jaw clenched under a forced smile.

"Purrrrrvection!" Wendy tossed back the curtain to reveal her creation.

Mandy Jo gasped, her hand quivering over her mouth as though some welfare brat had just vomited on the floor.

While Wendy strutted back and forth along her makeshift catwalk of carpeting between the cash register and the front door, I applauded, and shouted, "Gorgeous!" I had to give it to her, she was workin' it like a ho in her re-purposed daisy dukes and plaid strapless halter made from shredded menswear shirts. Even the cowboy boots weren't entirely wrong, though the hat was a bit much. What brought the whole thing together were the layers of gold chains, big '70s hoop earrings and pink tinted porn star sunglasses, which had to have been hiding in Wendy's huge hobo bag. "Chic and tawdry at the same time. Genius!" I yelled.

"I hope you're going to pay for *that*." Mandy's Jo's face curled up into a shrew's snout.

"You act like it's *not* an improvement." Wendy busted into laughter, cut it short and belted with a snap, "Add it up, bitch. We're ready to go."[39]

---

[39] If you didn't love Wendy before, you do now. By the way, that's not a question.

★   ★   ★

The thrift store was where I was forced to work my magic.

Second Hand Rose was the name of the dive and was also suitable designation for the sales staff, a dusty girl in a beige sweater with a face to match. I waved her off before she could eke out a syllable. Menswear is the first stop in any used clothing store.[40] I snagged a white cotton Van Heusen dress shirt from a nearby rack, tore out the offensive label and let it parachute to the dusty floor, from the boys' section I snagged a pair of flat-front khaki pants and on my way to the dressing room I snatched a fading black tablecloth from housewares and held my head high as I breezed through shoes,[41] thought twice and snatched a pair of penny loafers from the rack.

When I emerged from my cocoon (read: dressing room), I was channeling early Ralph Lauren casual. The winter white shirt draped open almost too far across my cleavage, and khakis rolled up to show off my calves—lucky for me I'd done the full makeup treatment and my dead skin was covered and pristine. Lucky for everyone else I knew how to put together an ensemble.

I marched up to the only mirror I could find and took in the majesty.

"Oops." I pulled a long strand of pearls from my bag, threaded them around my neck twice and let the rest fall where they may.

"The hotness." Wendy returned the favor of a fashion show "lady clap."

I have a decent eye for men's clothing and how they should fit, so I picked up a few marginally embarrassing outfits for Gil and Fishhook and we were outtie.

★   ★   ★

---

[40] A Rule: Men hate to dress up. Go rural and this rule is amplified. Thus men's dress shirts are less likely to be polluted by yellow armpit piss. You're welcome.
[41] I wouldn't be caught dead in someone else's foot sweat. Oh . . . wait.

It was dusk when we got back to the motel, so I knocked on the Winnebago's side hard enough to wake the dead. And by dead I do mean Gil. A low muffled moan come from a tiny frosted window near the back I didn't realize was there. I gave it a tap.

"Jesus! What!" Gil yelled.

"Good morning, Sunshine," Wendy said.

His response was more mumbles and moans.

"How'd he sleep with that window, anyway?" she asked.

"I dunno. I here him whining in there so he must be okay." I skipped over the curb and yelled a warning through the room door, "Hey Fishhook? You're not jerking off in there, are you? 'Cause we're comin' in."

"Nope, but I *am* indecent!"

"Just like I left you, then." I turned the key in the lock and opened the door onto a bulimic's dream.

The man lay propped up in a drift of pillows, naked to the waist where he was covered by bedspread. Around him in a pile were five Domino's boxes, two open and stained with grease, but empty otherwise, one open on his lap and coagulating. The other stacked and ready for the mood to strike him. He grabbed one and pushed it in our direction. "Hungry?"

Wendy grinned and nodded.

Fishhook's face registered the threat and his smug expression melted into a simpering grin. He attempted a diversion and pointed at the television. "Look! Maury's revealing the results of the paternity test. Bitch is such a ho, it could be one of these three guys, a felon, a 14-year old, or her cousin."

The diversion worked.

Who could resist trash TV? Certainly not zombies—daytime talk shows are like an inside look at our food industry. Maury, Springer, that new show with Jerry's bodyguard, if some supernatural wanted to make a fortune, they could deal with those producers for leftovers—except for Oprah's crowd, which probably has people who would miss them.

Hold on.

"How'd you pay for these pizzas, Fishhook?" I asked.

"Put 'em on the room bill. The front desk guy seems a little scared of you." He winked. "Might be he suspects somethin'."

"Bullshit, motels don't have room service contracts. Nice try."

He shut the box on his lap and rubbed his scarred stomach. Wendy made like she was throwing up. "Alright, but I promised not to say. A guy came looking for the owner of that Volvo out there."

I rushed to the curtain and peeked outside. "Holy shit! What'd you tell 'em?"

Wendy turned the deadbolt.

"I told him I'd tell him what I knew for some food. That's when he called the pizza place."

"So?"

"So what?"

"What do you think, what did you tell him?"

"I told him you two traded your car for some guy's Camaro and then took off toward Spokane leaving me stranded and hungry."

"Serious?" Wendy asked.

"Yeah. And that you guys were a couple of lesbians." He glared past her toward the TV and hollered, "Argh . . . I knew it was her cousin."

I shut the curtain and collapsed on the corner of the bed. "Did he believe you, do you think?"

"He totally bought it, had you both figured for muff divers, now get out of the way, I can't see the fight."

"I meant about us leaving."

"Totally."

I wanted to believe the guy, but he didn't seem all that reliable, considering his mental health when we first found him. But now, he was alert and articulate. Or as articulate as a guy can be who watches Maury.

Still.

We had five pizza boxes of proof in front of us.

Chapter 6

Dust Devils and Dirty Mothers

*Don't be mislead by the recent vampire research tout-
ing 'beef as the new human'; the statistics don't add up.
Live pig is, and will always be, the closest meat, both in
texture and flavor. Still, there are side effects . . .*
　　　　　　—Undead Science Monitor (Winter 2007)

There's nothing that says celebration more than an impromptu
hunting party. This one was to commemorate the official start of
our road trip, rather than the clarification that we were definitely being hunted and probably would end up shredded balls
of dead meat at the hands of a snarling talon-clawed wolf thing.
That said, a party is never an inappropriate reaction.

First we had to lure Gil out of the RV.

"Yeah we're sure. He's gone," I said.

"You're basing this on something a schizophrenic tap told
you?" Gil crossed his arms over his chest and slunk back against
the musty camper cupboards.

"Listen." Wendy put her hand on his arm, gave it a reassuring
squeeze. "He knew enough to send the guy off in another direction, we totally have time to pull together some food."

"If you're sure." His eyes were full of concern.

"We're sure. Now come on."

Wendy and I rustled up a pair of migrant cow-town drunks
outside a cinderblock gym that advertised "Mexercising" and

"Personal Traners" without the "i"—which, despite the not-so-subtle racism and misspelling, was far more appealing than the "Shame-based Spinning" class that Wendy forced me to every other Thursday. She worried that we'd "atrophy" just sitting around in bars all the time. I contended—and continue to believe—that a well-made cocktail keeps the joints oiled slicker than a steroid shot or a tab of glucosamine, and certainly more than an emaciated exercise bulimic named Gretchen.

I'm reminded of this fact by the particularly pickled nature of our evening snack. The two brown-skinned gents were totally soused and remarkably flexible in their staggering. Twisting and leaning and righting themselves with hands that darted out to walls, lampposts and garbage cans.

"Look at that." I pointed out one of the cowpokes bending down in an odd angle to retrieve a lit cigarette from the gravel. "Don't tell me liquor doesn't grease the hinges."

Wendy nodded and waved them over. "Hey boys! Want a ride?"

They did.

Before they could wrap their pickled brains around what we were, the telltale clicking of spreading jawbones had begun. Wendy dove in first, her mouth stretched over her drunk's head and shoulders like an anaconda, lifting him from the ground and shaking as she bit down. Not at all dainty. But at least she dabs the corners of her mouth when she's finished.

Hold on . . .

I know what you're thinking. Do zombies normally have such elasticity, strength and impeccable table manners? Absolutely not. We are the exceptions. Most of those shambling idiots we call mistakes are the sort with which you might be familiar. Sadly, with my luck our story will probably involve more than a few of those atrocities.

Let's get back to it.

Mine had the dazed look of a chronic late stage alcoholic

and the busted-out nasal capillaries to back up the assessment.[42] I took him in three bites and balanced against the building kneading my swollen gut until it returned to normal size.

How is that possible you ask?[43]

We cleaned up behind the place, where bushes blocked the line of sight from the road. But since we weren't in Seattle where our little indiscretion would likely go unnoticed, I had to say, "This isn't Seattle, you know?" while I picked at my teeth with my pinkie nail.

"Oh yeah-yeah-yeah . . . hold on." Wendy opened her hobo bag and dug around in the bottom, her face twisting and tongue thrusting from the corner with effort. Out came a coupon caddy, garish with neon daisies and a ragged scrunchie barely keeping the bulging thing from an impromptu game of 52-card pick-up. She shuffled through cards, matchbooks and empty condom wrappers with the efficiency of a Vegas dealer until she found the perfect thing for the occasion.

"Lookie here." She slipped her arm around me and held the business card up to the streetlight. It had lots of things written on it, but the only thing anyone would see was:

U.S. Department of Homeland Security
Citizenship and Immigration Services

"Nice maguffin."

"Huh?"

"I'm just sayin', people will assume they're illegal."

"But what's a—"

"Just toss the goddamn thing and let's get going."

Wendy flicked the card at the wall, where it banked into a puddle of piss still reeking of hops and barley.

Gil was just around the corner, in an alcove by the garbage

---

[42] Over time, one becomes a connoisseur.

[43] Will you shut up already and apply for a research grant. I don't know everything, Mother.

and recycling bins, pressed up against a burly homophobe named Gard. Occasionally, but not often, Gil liked to plug his victims before he drained them, if you catch my meaning. Being cursed with the worst man magnet I'd ever seen, Gil seemed to draw out every closeted homosexual within miles of his presence— none of whom were particularly pleasant, yet had no problem grabbing their ankles when their buddies weren't around.[44] Gil gives them the physical release of their dreams, for a price. You can't blame him—he gets thirsty—as with all tragic relation- ships, someone's bound to die. Right?

Gil tossed *it* in the dumpster when he finished. Wendy handed him a wet-nap.

"Did you two forget to say the blessing? Because I'm pretty sure I stepped in poo back there." He scraped the square-toed black shoe against the curb. The dog feces rolled up like a holi- day sponge cake and dropped from the toe.

Wendy held her palms together in prayer. "We'd like to thank the Lord, Jesus Christ, for minimal tread on Italian loafers."

"You're both going to Hell . . . and yet I'm amused." I giggled. We all laughed and tramped back to the Winnebago.[45]

By 3:00 A.M. we were rolling along the Interstate, heading east. Next stop, wherever, since we still hadn't bothered to pick up a road atlas. Gil had chosen to follow in the Volvo, opting for the comfort of the seats. During the previous night, he'd been forced to sleep holding a plank of cardboard over the bathroom window, and complained of a crick in his neck as a result. He insisted heated seats were the cure. And after we'd tin-foiled up the bedroom window in the back of the Winnie for his next hi- bernation.

---

[44] A note to closeted homosexuals: keeping secrets has a tendency to make one a tad bitter over time, or so Gil says. That bitterness affects the flavor and consistency of your blood. Think about the vampires for once and get some therapy; only you can save a palate.

[45] A sentence I never expected to write, I assure you.

Ingrate.

By dawn, eastern Washington proved to be nothing to look at. Hills rolled off into flat dusty farmland, already harvested and tilled, like the Evergreen State's dirty brown secret. There were no trees, very few structures, nothing really to look at; even the few cars, at that time, were stuffed with faces so drawn and exhausted as to be completely uninteresting. Gil locked himself up in the back, Wendy buried her nose in fashion magazines at the table, and Fishhook talked me into driving the Volvo for a while. I didn't expect that he had anywhere else to go and his social skills pretty much guaranteed he wouldn't be making many friends, so I went with it.

The low drone of the engine lulled me into memories.[46]

Of Chapstick and diarrhea.

This is how bad my mother was—probably still is. Oh, who am I kidding? Definitely still is—one year, my father (the real one, not one of Ethel's scaly substitutions) took us along on one of his trucking routes. It was a cause for celebration, as he'd never brought us before and, thankfully never brought us, again. I was eight at the time and even then into my mother's make-up, which she loathed.

"Don't touch my goddamned mascara, Amanda Shutter. You'll get germs on it. Do these eyes look like they want germs on 'em?"[47]

I didn't know whether eyes *wanted* anything, or noses, or ears. But lips—I can tell you—lips *want* Chapstick, if for no other reason than to mimic my mother's lipstick routine. She wasn't a smearer, nor did she line. Ethel Ellen Frazier was a patter. She'd pat that tube of blood red paste on in the tiniest overlapping circles until her lips were as rosy as a Chinese jewelry box.

[46] . . . and I hate that.
[47] A perfect example of why I hate memories. Secrets pop up. Yes. My real name is Amanda Shutter. I had it changed during college. One of my feeble attempts to escape my mother's reach. New name. New city. Not a chance.

"Dad!" I yelled from the backseat. "Can we pull over and get some Chapstick? My lips are dry."

"Sure thing, soon as I see me a 7-Eleven." Dad's face was well-lined and tanned, and the cigarette dangling from his lips bobbed with every word. It was a skill.

"Oh John. You're spoiling her, next thing you know, she'll be hounding us for mini-skirts and alcohol."

"She's eight, woman. She's not interested in boys or booze."

"You keep tellin' yourself that, hoss. I know girls. It starts early." Ethel shot a glance into the back cab, daring me to say something back. She hated backtalk.

"I'm not interested in—" I began.

"What? What? What?" She was in one of her moods and normally, I'd acquiesce or she'd come up with some ludicrous punishment like licking hot peppers, or going to the humane society on Monday morning, or as she liked to call it Ash Monday.

"I'm not *interested* in boys."

"What do you know? Nothin', that's what."

Dad pulled the big rig into a convenience store, and we hopped out. My mother clopped over to a phone booth, lit up a Virginia Slim and sucked at it like a blowgun. My father led me into the store and let me pick out a cherry Chapstick and a Coke-flavored Slush Puppy. He picked up a pack of Winston Kings and when Ethel strode in she flicked her hand in the air and as if she'd spoken, Dad nodded and asked the clerk for a pack of Virginia Slims.

She came out after us and handed me a chocolate bar. She said, "I'm sorry I've been so crabby, lately. Here's a little peace offering."

The bar was dark, chewy and rich, but there was a bitter flavor underneath. It wasn't Hershey's and I didn't like it, but I ate a few squares, anyway, because—well—it was chocolate. I rolled it around in my mouth. There was something medicinal about it. Something oily, maybe. Something wrong.

"How do you like that, back there? Good, huh?" Ethel asked.

"Mmm hmm." I spit out the last piece and dropped it into an old McDonald's bag shoved in the corner.

Twenty minutes later, the cramps started and then the diarrhea. We pulled over at a truck stop, where I sat on the toilet long enough for both my dangling legs to fall asleep—this made wiping a monumental task. Outside Ethel and Dad were yelling back and forth about something called Ex-Lax.

See?

Do you see what it was like?

No jury would convict me if I just walked into that hospice and put the bitch down. Maybe, we could have her cremated for half price on Ash Monday. I'm sure the Humane Society wouldn't mind.

No more quiet moments for me. I needed a distraction. "Wendy!" I yelled. "Get up here and talk to me, the lack of scenery is driving me crazy!"

"Can we talk about . . . anything?"

"Of course. Why do you—"

"Even the *Cosmo* sex quiz?" Wendy flopped down in the passenger seat and popped the cover up like a Union banner.

"Oh God. Except that."

"C'mon. It's been how long since you did it?"

"Not long, since last month's edition, anyway."

"I'm talking about *it*." She bit at the word. I could almost feel the jab of it in my side.

"Shane was the last time and you know it. I don't need a man to make me happy. I don't even think about it. I don't." God I sounded like an idiot. Who was I trying to convince? Not Wendy.

Shane was the last guy I'd slept with, euphemistically speaking.[48] He was a lousy lay and in the end turned out to be a

---

[48] If you haven't noticed, zombies aren't big on sleep. We're not wired for it.

lousy person, so I blew him. Okay, granted that sounded dirty, allow me to reiterate. I mean I blew "the breath" into him. I've got this gift. Remember when I said we weren't like other zombies? Well I'm even more rare.[49] I can turn people into zombies with a single exhalation. It's kind of cool. I only know one other that can do it, and that's Ricardo. The trick is they've got to be alive when it happens. Plus it can be a pretty effective weapon. Vampires like Shane, for instance, can't handle the pressure in their dead lungs; it kills 'em dead like Raid.

"Mmm hmm. Question one," Wendy said. "You meet a guy for a quote coffee date unquote. He's cute but shy, doesn't ask questions, or offer anything about himself. You've got to do all the work. Do you, "A," take control of the situation and give him an old-fashioned interrogation, "B," sit quietly, finish your coffee and thank him for meeting you, quickly quote losing unquote his phone number, or "C," take him home and fuck the shit out of him, right on your new egyptian cotton sheets from French Quarter?"

"It does not say that." I snatched at the magazine.

Wendy pulled it away. "I swear to God it does."

"Well, then." I pretended to consider the options, although there was really only one answer. "A then C and then lose the bastard's number."

Wendy tossed the magazine on the dash. Gwyneth Paltrow or Martin or whatever smiled out of the airbrushed cover. "You're full of shit. When? When have you ever not strung the guy along? Always confusing sex with a relationship. You totally did that with Shane, and he turned out to be a real monster."

"I can be slutty. Is that what you're asking? I can *be* slutty." No I couldn't. Wendy could be slutty. Totally. But I tended to latch on to people. Which was really new for me, I'd been a loner for so long. but I like to think I was adjusting. "What's this quiz called anyway?"

---

[49] Thank you.

Wendy flipped through the pages. "Are you a man-eater?" she read.

"Well . . . duh."

We nearly had aneurysms laughing about that one, until a flash of orange shattered our cacklefest. A Ford Mustang, the new kind, the kind that was trying to look old, sped into our lane, causing me to slam on my brakes. The worst of it? The color, of course, it was truly offensive. It's not the new black, no matter what anyone says. I caught only the slightest glimpse of the driver, a blonde guy. At least his hair coordinated with the car color. It was the nicest thing I could say about the piece of shit.

I laid on the horn, Wendy leaned forward and flipped a double-bird, and the car sped off. Weaving between a few travelers in the distance. Bastard.

Wendy's face was crumpled in concern.

"What's up?" I asked.

"Do you think that was one of the werewolves chasing Gil? I know we haven't talked about it much, but Markham really seemed to want Gil dead. What if that guy back at the motel was sent to kill him, or worse, all of us."

"Maybe you should call Gloria."

"I'm serious."

"I know. It's possible. Maybe Fishhook's lie threw them off the scent."

"Maybe." Wendy sucked at her lips.

An exit was coming up, the signs said Ritzville, though if anything were certain it was that a town in these parts would be anything but ritzy.

"Pull over. I want to get some Chapstick."

"What did you say?"

"That I need Altoids. I'm out. What's your damage?" Wendy dug through her purse, tossing out hollow tins and crumpling empty packs of gum.

"Alright." This driving was making me crazy. I needed a break, anyway. We pulled off and parked the RV on the road across from a 7-Eleven. Quite a few people were milling around the store. Outside a pretty Asian girl with honey-streaked hair chatted with a ghost-skinned blonde wearing, of all things, white.

Wendy trod off toward her quarry. Fishhook parked in front of the store and followed her in.

"Hey!" I cried after them. "Grab a pack of smokes, would ya? All that's left are these shitty menthols." I snagged one, crumpled the rest, and tossed the pack in the back of a rusty convertible. I found a spot near the back of the store and lit up, sucking on it like a blowgun.[50]

Since the lungs don't exactly function, smoking has become way more of an oral fixation than when I was living. You'd think I'd garner nothing from the act, since I wasn't getting any nicotine, and all. But, what can I say? I still enjoyed it. Maybe it was the act itself, the feel of the paper, the curly tendrils of smoke. Who knows? It's not like it's bad for me, nor am I recommending brands to children on the schoolyard. So before you start up with your judging, remember, I don't count your calories, do I?

Now . . .

Here's how you know you're in the middle of nowhere: the dust devils are the only movement on the horizon. Such was the case behind the 7-Eleven. It must have been farmland or something, only shit-brown and stretching across eastern Washington like miles of dirty carpet.

There were three of the swirling miniature tornados, tortured contortionists each. I watched the biggest coil and strike, swirling about and seemingly approaching. Was it actually coming closer? Unfortunately for me, it was. The twister cut a thin line onto the dusty soil, stopped about five feet from me, and slowed to reveal a pale sandy figure, humanish, male and tall, only see-through.

A ghost.

The memory of worn stubbly skin stretched across his

[50] Damn you, Ethel! Just when you think you'll do things differently.

rugged features. Crow's feet put him at about forty at the time of his death, or a well-tanned thirty. His eyes barely hung on to a pale blue. Handsome, I supposed, in that intangible, inaccessible, dead kind of way.

I looked down at my thrift store miracle outfit and noted several flecks of dust on my white shirt. I blew at them and responded appropriately. "What the hell do you think you're doing?"

"Why, I'm comin' over to say hello, sweetheart, is that a problem?"

I pointed out the grime on my top. "Uh . . . yeah. There's a problem. You're whipping up manure and chemicals and shit and flinging them at my outfit. I'd say that's a problem."

The ghost perused my shirt, grinning, settling on a long stare at my cleavage. "I am sorry ma'am, but you've got nothin' to worry about, seein's this here's organic soil."

"Oh! Well that's okay then."

The ghost moved closer, hands reaching for my chest. "Well maybe I'll just help you brush those right off."

I backed away but collided with the brick wall. I slapped at his hands, but went right through, only succeeding in coating myself with patches of beige grit. His hands found my breasts and passed through Mr. Van Heusen's hard work. My nipples hardened from the sudden chill.

"Fucker. You better step back."

He giggled. "Or what?"

"Or . . . or . . ." or what, I thought. It's not like I could hit him. Sure I could take some swings but that wouldn't do anything. And in the meantime, the spectral bumpkin was deep enough in to scrub out my lungs. "I'll leave and you'll have no one that can see or hear you."

He withdrew his hands with a jerk leaving two baseball-sized brown spots on the fabric. My outfits were being put through hell. If anyone deserved a shopping spree, it was me.

"Jesus." I brushed at the ruined fabric. "You've got a lot to learn about courting a woman."

"Well, you're not just any woman, now are you?"

"You'd know."

The ghost eyed his handy work, grinned.

I crossed my arms across my chest. "So how do you manage to free range? Shouldn't you be stuck hovering around your grave, or sitting on your tractor or something?"

He laughed. "I'm a traveler. We're a pretty rare sort, but you'll see us around. Spinning, painting these plains, and watching, of course. My name's Cort."

"I'm Amanda."

"Pleasure is all mine."

"So does all that spinning make you dizzy?"

The ghost shoved his fist through the side of his head. "Nope. Not a bit."

"Then you're just normally obnoxious?"

"Absolutely."

"And on that note . . ." I walked off toward the corner of the convenience store and a pair of loafing teens. A greasy-haired youth caged a pale blonde to the wall with his arms, making the kind of snarling open-mouthed gestures that adolescent boys think are sexy. The girl's skin was as pasty white as an Edward Gorey death.

Behind me the air began to whistle. The ghost was following. "Where you headed?" he asked after me.

"None of your business, motherfucker."

The boy glanced in my direction. I pretended to search through my purse.

"Well. If that's the end of our chat then, I should probably tell you I've heard whispers about you."

I stopped. "Whispers? What are you talking about?"

Even the little albino was staring now. But I didn't care.

"You travel as much country as I do, you're bound to hear things here and there. Well, the whispers say trouble's a-comin'. And from the looks of you, it's heading your way."

"Trouble?" I lowered my voice to a whisper and strolled back to the ashtray.

"Big trouble."

I lit another cigarette. Exhaled through his body. "Care to elaborate?"

"The word is that you and your friends are drawing a dangerous element to you. Bad energy. That you think you're running away from evil, but it's all around you and you're heading for more."

I thought instantly of my mother, thinning out like jerky in the hospice. "You got that right," I said.

"You best take care of yourselves. I'll keep an eye out."

"That's comforting."

The air whirred and the dust devil spun off into the field, pulling at the earth until he'd puffed into an impressive funnel. I stepped back from a puff of dust that rolled the ground like a wave. In the distance, the ghost met up with two other dust devils. They swirled around each other as if in some square dance box step, and then scurried off in opposite directions. Gossip, presumably.

Back inside the RV, Wendy was behind the steering wheel. "Jesus. What took you so long?

I slid into the passenger side. "I ran into a real dick."

"That seems to be happening a lot, lately. Did you take care of him?"

"More like he took care to finish off my shirt." I flashed her the dirty spots.

"All hands, huh?"

"No hands, actually."

"Ew. Not sexy."

"Tell me about it."

As Wendy pulled the Winnebago back onto the freeway, I caught a glimpse of orange. The Mustang from earlier was parked on the side of the convenience store, the same tall sandy-haired man leaning against it.

Watching.

Chapter 7

Snacking at America's Favorite Child Abuse Palace

Tired of the same old same old? Remember the Golden Rule: prey upon those that have few praying for them. Sure it's sad, poverty is a curse. But, you'll never run out of tasty options if you stick to cruising the low-end retailers. Happy Hunting.
— *Tips for the Modern Dead*

We found the thrift store equivalent of a KOA just south of Coeur d'Alene—The Shady Glen Campground and Swap Meet proved a perfect hideout, dark, decrepit and deeply set into a hillside sluice. Where better to hide a moldy Winnebago and a lethargic vampire, only an hour into a bad blood hangover? The place was so run down, it wasn't likely to gather many guests, unless the homeless were on holiday.[51]

Twelve grassy camper slots overlooked a tin-roofed cabana, its grayed clapboard walls so worn and knotty a deer had better not take a piss or it would sag and collapse. The sign on the front read: The Washout—which is exactly what would happen in the next big rain—I was fairly certain.

A ramshackle cottage, tin-roofed, with paint peeling off of it in ribbons, sat in the webbing between the two hills. I was de-

---

[51] If only we could be so lucky.

tecting a theme.[52] Cheap roofing and wood rot: downtrodden as the new cozy. Lovely. It's a good thing I didn't sleep anymore because there was no way I'd be closing my eyes in this shithole. Open them and find a toothless overalled hick named Hoss pumping away at your behind with a pud like a corncob. Not a pleasant image.

Near the front of the property was the swap meet. The sale was no more than a barn filled with tables of crap that over-flowed past the doors into piles of damp stuffed animals (bound for Sugar Loaf machines near you), racks of clothing (again, in-sipidly western-inspired), and metal-rimmed wagon wheels (destined for someone's exterior decorating mishap or—God help us—a coffee table.

Wendy ran into the cottage and registered for a place to park the monster, and after a particularly heinous scuffle with some tree branches—Mr. Kim shouting suggestions from the hood of the nearby Volvo the entire time—I backed the RV into the slot.

We rested on the back bumper.

"I'm starving," Wendy said.

"Me, too. I could eat a horse, or at least a large jockey."

"Where we go?" Mr. Kim yelled from the Volvo.

"Into town. I'm feeling peckish."

"Oo. Me, too."

The sound of two ghost hands clapping is silence. Regardless, Kimmy was happily clapping away.

"Well I'm not going," Fishhook said, walking past us to a hammock sagging between the trees. He flopped into it like a professional loafer.

We left Shady Glen in a swirl of dust.

When it comes to mid-day snacking, I really can't resist slum-ming it at one of America's finest child abuse palaces, Kmart. On

---

[52] By the B-52s, of course. Can't you hear Kate Pierson, just now?

any given Sunday, a quick scan of shoppers will undoubtedly produce the following:

- An overweight single mother cursing and swatting one or more of her dirty children in the snacks and chips aisle.
- Sad divorcées perusing the Jaclyn Smith collection for happy hour outfits.[53]
- Lumbering men pushing steel-toed boots onto holey-socked feet.
- Woefully unsupervised children running amok through the candy, toy and/or CD aisles.

Plus, there's usually a Kmart in even the smallest burg. When there's not, a Wal-Mart or Dollar Store will have to do, but Target is never an acceptable substitution; there's something about that particular meat that gets the police involved. Our Kmart was a mere six blocks away, which spoke poorly to our accommodations. Inside was exactly what we expected: those unlikely to be missed. We settled into a location by the books and magazines.

"What about that one?" Wendy raised a finger to point across the top of her *Country Living,* in the direction of the main aisle, where a filthy homeless guy was skittering amongst the intimacy planning—as if he had a chance—and the douches, which I had no doubt he was in desperate need of. His movements and frequent pinching at his cheeks simply screamed tweak show.

"Yeah . . . no. I like my downtrodden with a little less spring in their step."

"Good point."

A pretty, and totally out of her element, Asian girl passed through our aisle, her once-dark brown hair streaked with honey tones. In fact, she smelled of the thick syrupy stuff. It must have been her shampoo. My eyes fluttered, drifting to that place . . .

[53] Mmm, happy hour.

"Amanda!"Wendy socked me in the arm.The girl's eyes met mine as she turned the corner toward the Martha Stewart stronghold of linens and housewares, out of sight. "What do you think you're doing?" She reached in her purse, withdrew a napkin, and dabbed a thin stalactite of drool hanging from my chin.

"Ew, gross. Sorry."

"Did that girl look familiar, or something?" Wendy asked.

I thought back to Ritzville, to the Asian girl and her pasty friend. A distinct possibility. "Yeah. I guess so."

Unlucky in periodicals, we replenished our waning supply of Handiwipes and Altoids and made our way to the registers. An elderly woman and two hideous youths—one a greasy pimple of a boy, the other a stringy-haired wisp, who looked like she was shooting for an anorexic porn-star look—unpacked the cart ahead of us. As they did, a CD case fell from the mound of toilet paper, housedresses and canned goods, rattling on the floor.

Gold and diamond-toothed rappers represented from their discounted plastic prison.

"Grandma, now you know you gotta be careful. See. You done dropped your CD."The girl stooped to pick up the disc, pelvic bone popping loud.When she stood, she gave us a quick sneer before tossing it at the checker.

Grandma had no response. Her face was blank. Eyes blurry. Drunk, I thought. Who wouldn't need to knock a few back with kids like *those?*

Wendy leaned into me and whispered, "Because what granny don't like G-Unit?"

"I think we've found lunch."

The family—for lack of a better word—lived in a mossy doublewide trailer sinking into the mud about ten minutes from the next sign of life. We slowed to a crawl about a hundred yards back, where I pulled the car off the road into a nestle of bushes and silenced the engine.

We rolled down the windows, watched and listened.

"You better get them groceries in the house now, Grandma! If you expect any food tonight," the boy yelled, lighting up a cigarette and giving the old woman a stumbling shove.

"Yeah!" the girl agreed.

The elderly lady shuffled from the trunk to the house four or five times, hefting the Kmart haul while the surly youths supervised from the porch. The girl picked cigarette butts from a rusty coffee can and handed them to the boy who emptied the leftover tobacco into a pile and rolled it in a new paper. Wendy sucked at her teeth and grumbled under her breath. We'd chosen well, these kids would be a tasty snack and an heroic action all rolled into one. How often have you been able to say that about your last trip through the Burger King drive-through? It's like we're heroes.[54]

"Johnny, don't smoke all that, now. I need me some nicotine." The girl rubbed her hands up and down on her thighs as though chilled.

"Shut your pie-hole." The lanky kid stood and kicked through the mud puddles of the front yard, thumbs hooked in the back pockets of his jeans, and cigarette dipping from his lips with every stride. The girl bounded after him through a break in the fir trees and became shadow in the darkness there. The screen door on the trailer clapped shut behind the old woman and the final bag. The scene quieted.

Wendy was first to reach for the door handle.

We followed a gulley that ran parallel to the road, avoiding the collected water and crouching as we crossed the open space beyond the yard. The smell of moss and pine needles floated on the slightest of breezes while the birds sang along to a country twang burrowing from inside the trailer walls like rats. As we reached the path, I barred Wendy's progress and held a finger to my lips.

The teens were a fair distance, since their grating voices were no more than a whisper.

---

[54] Please refrain from applauding. Send checks instead.

"I'll lead." I stepped into the gap between the trees onto a welcome carpet of needles and forest waste that dulled any announcement of our approach. The brush tightened on the path a few yards in and the thick smell of wet wood smoke made its presence known gradually. The canopy thinned and the brother and sister's voices became audible.

"When I get older I'm going to get the hell out of this place and move to Cleveland or Detroit." The boy's voice cracked and crumbled, adolescence or the cigarette kicking in at his vocal chords.

"Detroit? What the hell are you going to do in Detroit?"

"Build cars." He coughed.

"Hand me that cigarette."

We crept up to a massive evergreen trunk that signaled the entrance to a clearing. The teenagers sat on a fallen tree in front of a small mound of branches and logs producing more wet smoke than heat and fire. It snapped and popped like a five-year old with bubble wrap.

"Well I'm moving to Hollywood and I'm going to be a huge star."

"Yeah, a regular Katie Morgan," he giggled.

"Who's that?" The girl's jaw jutted in his direction as she dragged the glowing cherry down the cigarette.

"Porn star." He snatched the cigarette from his sister's fingers and stuck it between his teeth.

"Don't!" she yelled, punching his arm. "You're gonna nigger lip it."

I'd heard enough. I stepped into the clearing. Wendy flanked me and cocked her hip out. Her outfit seemed much more appropriate than mine, considering the occasion.

"Hey." I called. "Either of you guys holdin'?" I hoped this was the correct terminology. It'd been at least ten years since I'd scored pot for a party. Not that we had any intention of buying any, it just seemed a good in with these particular kids who seemed to be so brain damaged that drug use was likely. I had my answer soon enough.

"I know where to get some, yeah." The boy smirked and puffed his chest. He browsed Wendy from tits to ass and back again. She flipped her blonde waves and blew him a kiss.

It seemed the icebreaker was successful. They wouldn't try to run until we were already on them, then it'd be too late. As you've seen we're not what you'd call dawdlers.

"Aren't you cute?" Wendy sat down next to the boy and ran her hand through that greasy mop on his head. It was a bit gross, even for Wendy, who has a history of, shall we say, lewd conduct.

I claimed a spot near his sister and stood there with my hand on my hip, waiting.

"Not as cute as you, baby." His lips curled back on a handful of dirty teeth that clung to his gums like grave markers in an old settler's cemetery. One bony hand crept from the log across Wendy's bare thigh. "Oh," he said, drawing back his hand. "You're cold."

"You have no idea, Johnny." Wendy scooted across the log toward him.

The boy flinched.

"What's the matter?" she asked.

"I didn't tell you my name." He looked over at his sister. "Raylene?"

She shrugged and continued to puff on the cigarette.

"Looks like you've found us out."

Don't worry fans. We made it quick. In the end—and if you have any knowledge of dysfunctional families—it was a public service. Had they been allowed to continue on their path, they would have simply bred more welfare recipients and third-strike offenders. I think we can all agree, we don't need more of those, now, do we?

All that was incidental anyway, because as we were leaving, scraps of clothes and odd bone matter sizzling on the fire and Wendy thumbing through her red herring caddy, the blonde Asian stepped into the clearing.

At least, I thought it was her.

I was kind of focused on the gun.

Chapter 8

A Taste of Honey

Shun human fads, embrace the new supernatural!
Bite me!
—Graffiti from the wall of McAlinden's Tavern

"How about you bitches sit your dead asses down on that log, before I put a couple of holes through your heads?" The girl had the bad-ass lingo and rigid stance of a killer combined with the fashion sense of a, well, of . . . me. Her fair skin was a striking canvas for a gorgeous pair of almond-shaped eyes and cherry lollipop lips. The clothes were the real thing. White banding clung to her lean torso like Saran Wrap and cut just below the snatch.

I had to admit, I hadn't been so afraid of a teenage girl since Laura Wilks shunned the no eyebrow-plucking edict in high school.[55] She hadn't seemed nearly as threatening in the sweater set and jeans she wore at Kmart. Even then, I thought she'd looked familiar. She'd been following us. I assumed she was one of Markham's. There's no reason a girl couldn't shape-shift into a bloodthirsty wolf. It's just, so well . . . butch.

"Well I guess that establishes that you know who you're dealin' with," Wendy said.

The girl shoved the gun forward, lining her sights up on

---

[55] I still get chills. Hold me.

Wendy, which, while far preferable to having a gun aimed at me, was still pants-stainingly terrifying.

Bullets leave holes.

Holes are neither pretty nor fashionable.

I didn't want any holes.

Wendy didn't either. She straddled the log and pouted. I joined her.

"I couldn't say for sure but your little fiesta here looked remarkably like a double homicide."

"Well, if you want to get technical," Wendy said.

"Dude. I'm about through with your sass." The girl turned the gun sideways, gangsta style.

Busted! Could it be as simple as just that? Markham's goon or concerned citizen, either way, I needed to take control of this situation, before Wendy's smart mouth got us both killed. "Listen. We don't want any trouble. Those kids were abusing that old woman in that trailer out there, they earned their punishment."

"So you bitches are like public servants?" We nodded our heads in agreement. "Social Workers with Shark Teeth? Is that what you're trying to tell me?" She kicked through the leaves sending a spray of gravel into the fire, which cracked and popped as though she'd thrown some bubble wrap into a day care center.

"Exactly, I knew you'd understand." I beamed and sighed, as though that were the end of the conversation. "See? She's totally reasona—"

"Shut up! You make me sick. Both of you. Fucking zombies." She began to pace, then slowed and cocked her head, toward me. "But, since you seem to be in the mood for chatting . . . let's hear about what you did to my brother."

Wha? Huh?[56]

I hoped she wasn't talking about food; it's so hard to remem-

---

[56] In case you're keeping score, that's 0 for 2 in the assumption category. Damn.

ber every meal. It's not like a chomp on the homeless is fine dining.

"I don't know what you're talking about."

"My brother, Dae-Jung. Ring any bells?"

"No. Not a one." And that was no lie, the only Korean guy I knew was Mr. Kim and I'd never done anything to harm him. Except for leaving him in a car, instead of inviting him into a succubus pit. But surely, I wasn't being blamed for that. He was already dead when that happened.

"Well, allow me to enlighten you." She continued to pace.

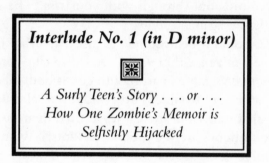

Interlude No. 1 (in D minor)

A Surly Teen's Story . . . or . . .
How One Zombie's Memoir is
Selfishly Hijacked

"When I left for Denver—" she began.

"Rehab?" I suggested.

"No," she snapped with two syllables, just like the ones in "duh." "College."

"Oops . . . sorry."

She took a deep cleansing breath—like they teach you in anger management class—and continued. "Like I was saying, when I went away to college in Denver—this was last year, by the way, so not long enough to get foggy on the details—Dae-Jung was having some difficulty coping with life as a zombie—God knows why, it runs in the family. My mother was the one who turned him. Purely by accident, of course.

"She's a breather, but I suspect you knew that, and, not dead yet. She was carrying the ability into her old age, savoring life and really living. She was careful. Except for this one time. Dae-Jung drove her to the herbalist for her tea. It was a late spring day and the sun was shining through a squall. Like they do.

"They were halfway through the intersection when the taxi barreled into them, punching into my brother's side of the car. Mother knew he would die. He was barely breathing. He'd never survive until the ambulance came. She didn't tell me exactly how she did it, but by the time the paramedics cut the doors open, Dae-Jung climbed out of the car without a scratch.

"He was fine for the first day and then he started sniffing around like a dog. I woke up and found him standing at my bedroom door . . . drooling. He needed to feed, you see? We were all ignoring it. Mother and I took him to the temple.

" 'You take him. Talk to him. Make him not be hungry,' she said to the priest.

"He was an older man with bright wise eyes and eyebrows that could use a good trimming, if you know what I mean. But he was kind and he took Dae-Jung into the temple, gave him sanctuary, and promised to offer guidance during these troubling times. Mother and I turned to leave. The wooden latch scraped on the door to the priest's rooms, shutting us out. That's when the screams began . . . and I don't mean my brother's. A heavy thud shook the door and blood washed out from underneath onto the stone tiles of the temple floor.

"It was all very quick. Afterward, we could hear my brother's sobs.

" 'Open the door, Dae-Jung,' I said, standing to the side of the puddle as I knocked. 'Let us help you.'

" 'You go away!' he cried. 'Now!'

"We heard a sound inside the rooms. A hollow tearing that echoed through the building followed by the scuffling scrape of little feet. Mother and I backed away from the door, into the shadows of the carved columns nearby. The sanctuary was barely lit, but we could see the door and the blood. It pulled itself back into the gap underneath, like it had a mind to do so, willing it-self to return. Whispers filled the air, silenced, a loud pop sounded and the door opened. Dae-Jung stepped out. Clean. Quiet.

"For the next few days, he wouldn't talk. Not a single word, and then he did.

" 'Reapers,' he said. And then packed his things and left.

"He stayed away for nearly six months and then came home to tell us he'd joined a group that would help him with his problem. He seemed genuinely hopeful, and started visiting Mother every day.

"That's how it was when I went away to college.

"Then Dae-Jung stopped coming to the house. He didn't answer his cell, and never returned any messages. We had to pick up his furniture from a small condo in Ballard. He'd stopped paying the rent. His car was gone.

"So, I came home and started looking for this group." She flicked the gun in my direction. "This is where you come in, so listen up. I talked to a Ms. Baumgartner. Very nice lady. Helpful, too."

Oh shit. I knew exactly where the girl was headed. I tried to stop my hands from shaking. Wendy scanned my face for some help in understanding. I didn't give her any.

"She remembered my brother, told me that the last time she'd seen him, he was getting into a car with a strange woman that had come to the group and really messed things up."

"Mr. Kim." I nodded. "Mr. Kim is your brother."

"Her brother is Kimmy?" Wendy yelled.

I nodded. "He is."

The girl lowered the gun for the first time since her diatribe began. "Is? Dude. Did you say *is?*" Her face was scrunched with confusion, like someone had taken all her conviction and re-placed it with a big fat question mark. There was hope there, too.

Unfortunately.

"Well . . . yeah. He's around, in fact, he's up in the car." Wendy pointed back up the path.

"What? What do you mean?"

"Now don't get excited," I cautioned. "He *is* dead and—"

"Duh!" The girl turned and darted from the clearing.

I socked Wendy in the arm. "Stupid bitch! Why'd you go and say that? She can't see him, or touch him or hear him. All that's going to happen is she'll be even more pissed off and come back gun blazing."

"Ew. I didn't think of that."

"No shit. Now let's hurry after her before this gets really fucked up."

When we reached the Volvo, the girl's ass was hanging out the passenger door. "Dae-Jung!" she yelled.

Mr. Kim was jumping up and down on the hood, clapping with the joy of a slot machine jackpot winner. "Hyon Hui! She here! She here!" Clearly her English was much better than Kimmy's. He pointed inside the car. His excitement shook some ectoplasm free and it floated about him like balsamic vinegar in salad oil.

"Honey!" I yelled from the end of the gulley.

She pulled herself from the car and glowered, slammed the door and trained the gun on me. "He's not here."

I raised my hands in the air. "Honey?"

"No, Hee-on Hui." Mr. Kim pronounced for me.

"Your brother says your name is Hyon Hui. Is that right or am I just butchering it?" I pulled my advertising smile out hoping for sincerity but settling for scared shitless.

"What did you say?" she came closer. Her arm sagged a bit.

"I said, 'Your brother told me your name, Hyon Hui.'" This time she smiled and looked around the car, even bending down to peer underneath it.

As she did, Wendy ran from the woods and tackled the girl. They rolled off the road into the muddy bowl of the gulley, wrestling for control of the gun. I ran to the opposite side of the car.

"Don't hurt her! Don't hurt her!" Mr. Kim screamed the entire time.[57]

From further up the road, another girl was running. Her friend, the unmistakably white, Whitey—we'll call her, just for the sake of a name. She wasn't far enough away that I didn't notice her polka-dotted Holly Hobby dress or the scary shotgun she wielded.

I threw open the car door, slid behind the wheel and cranked. The wheels spun as I floored the car toward the ghostly creature running toward us. The maneuver worked. When she saw the car coming she twisted in the opposite direction, dropped the gun and bolted.

I parked the Volvo at an angle and retrieved the dusty shotgun from the gravel road. From back where I'd left them, Wendy was prodding Hyon Hui forward with her pistol. The girl's face was stuck in an unflattering cringe, forcing her eyes into slits narrower than an overly thankful Renée Zellweger.[58]

"If it's any consolation, your friend back there was super helpful."

She flinched.

"Oh Honey. We're not going to hurt you. We all love a little violence now and again. Why when Naomi Campbell busted her assistant with that cell phone, I laughed just like everyone else. But you can't pull a gat on the ladies after dinner; that makes us cranky."

"I'm sorry," she said, and tried to crack a smile. God bless her. But, I could tell she was plotting and who could blame her? I know I hate to lose the upper hand.

---

[57] The whole scene was enough to give a girl a migraine, if my nerve endings still functioned, that is.

[58] Right? Right? I'm right. I know it. I'm not buying that act for a second.

"Good girl. Now let's go get your friend and have a talk. 'Kay?" I put my arm around her shoulder to guide her back to the car.

Mr. Kim was already in the back seat, waiting. Pink beads slipped down his poor little see-through cheeks. The sight was almost enough to make me go moony over family reunions.[59]

The whitest girl ever followed behind us in a hideous purple Geo Metro, while Hyon Hui must have experienced the most bizarre car ride of her life, silently staring at the empty seat next to her that was the entire focus of our conversation.

Mr. Kim started in immediately, "You must promise to protect sister. You owe me that much."

Wendy rolled her eyes at me. "He's talking to you, bitch."

"I hope you know, I'd never let anyone hurt your sister, Kimmy. Even this one up here." Our eyes met in the rear view mirror.

"Swear," he said.

"I swear."

"Make her swear." He cocked his head toward Wendy, who turned an offensive glare back at him.

"I've got no reason to hurt her."

"What about you run low on candy bar? Huh?"

Wendy twisted in her seat with the speed of a prizefighter, swinging a right hook though the gap in the seats that breezed through the ghost's head and into Hyon Hui's shoulder.

"Jesus!" she yelled, reaching for the door handle. "What was that for?"

"Aaaarggh!" Mr. Kim roared from the back seat, his spittle solidifying into dark blue jelly that crossed the distance in less than a second and settled into a dripping mess off the brim of Wendy's cowboy hat. She rolled down the window, snatched off the woven mess and tossed it out.

[59] Almost.

Pouting followed.

"Enough!" I shouted. Mr. Kim had never expressed such an open emotional reaction, at least not in front of me. It was oddly cathartic to know that family could have such a strong connection, that a sister would put her life in danger to find a brother, that a brother's love could actually reach beyond the grave. "We'll take care of Hyon Hui. You have my word."

He narrowed his eyes, but ultimately nodded his trust. He slid his arm around his sister's shoulders. "Tell her I'm right here."

She shook off what appeared to be a chill. The ghost withdrew his arm and sulked.

"Those goose bumps just then were from your brother. He was giving you a hug."

"Yeah. Whatever. You two are insane."

Chapter 9

Does Anyone Actually Own Shower Shoes?

. . . then there are those unpredictable werecreatures.
What are we to do with them? On the one hand, who
can resist their sheer animal magnetism, but on the other,
can a zombie really risk the cuts and bruises for even a
single night of passion?
                    —*Zombie-A-Go-Go* (April 2006)

The albino chick's name was Becky—get this—by choice. She
was born Granita Graham; Granita . . . like the delicious ice-
cold beverage and not Grenada like the island. Which, if she
preferred Becky, why'd she even bother explaining her previous
name. That's just weird, right? There's just no accounting for
taste. For example, I knew this girl in high school named
Elizabeta Von Regens.[60] She was this gorgeous exchange student and everyone thought she was royalty. Well, she wanted
people to call her Lotus, which, for my taste, is just way to similar to *lettuce*, which is what I *preferred* to call her. Lettuce could
you get out of my way, *et cetera, et cetera*, you get the picture.

She didn't care for it.

And thus, this chapter's conversation begins like this . . .

"So . . . Granita? How did you get hooked up with the

---

[60] Not at all like the butchery of consonants and vowels that is Amanda Shutter.

Terminator over here." I stabbed a thumb at Honey—Hyon Hui had been thusly christened due to a terrible speech impediment of Wendy's called indifference.

She gulped. "Well . . . I was really happy with my job at the rubber stamp store—"

I could feel the pit opening and I was ready to drop. "Wow, I'm sure that was going to be very interesting but let's talk to Honey some more."

"Ew. Burn," Wendy said to Granita. Being around these teenage girls was doing nothing for our etiquette.

"I was going to tell you that Mr. Kim, or Kimmy as we call him, seems perfectly happy now, completely at ease with his lot in life . . . or . . . death, as it were. And, there's really no reason for you to worry about him."

"I'm sure that's true, but I need to see him again. I really can't take you bitches' word for it. Uh. Uh," she stuttered. "I mean ladies."

"Oh, Honey." Wendy stood from the campfire and patted Honey on the shoulder. "You were right the first time." She slipped past Gil as he dropped out of the camper door.

"I just don't see a way for that to happen. I'm sorry." I tapped a cigarette against the metal folding chair's arm.

I really have to learn to think before I speak, at least in social settings. Back on the Ad train, I can wing it like nobody's business, but in these weird seemingly sensitive situations, I find myself at a loss. Take this response, for an example: Honey's face had gone slack. Mr. Kim's had soured into an uncharacteristic scowl. I could see it from where he stood next to the Volvo, hand anchored on the side mirror like the base for a game of tag, stretching as close as he could. Sorry, I mouthed.

"That's not necessarily true," Gil said plopping down between the girl and her pale companion. "I'm Gil, and don't worry, I'm not a glutton like those two hags, just a run of the mill vampire." He extended his hand and surprisingly Honey accepted it. Granita did not, deciding instead to go with a shocked glare followed by a stroll around the campground. This was, of course, a perfectly acceptable response to meeting her first bloodsucker.

"What do you mean?" Honey asked.

"Well, theories abound in regards to humans interacting with the spirit world. There are mediums that swear they can provide a vessel for the deceased to speak with their family and friends. Surely you own a TV."

"I'm talking about seeing Dae-Jung again. Not just speaking to someone who could very well be pulling my dick."

Despite the seriousness of her tone, I had to giggle.[61] Wendy returned from the trailer, a brown smudge staining her cheek. I motioned for her to wipe and didn't wait for a response, lest she think I was picking again. It was bad enough that Mr. Kim had outed her eating disorder in front of Honey, who had caught our exchange and was blatant with her smirk.

"Well, we could always find a mystic of some sort," Gil continued. "Some shaman or witch or kraken, I suppose."

"Kraken? Like in the pirate movie?"

"Yeah," Wendy said. "Just like it, they pop up in the weirdest places, in fact . . ." She pulled out her phone, dialed. "I think there's a hotspot on our route."

"Well." I stood up and dusted off my sarong. "On that really bizarre note, I'm going to brave the Shady Glen Shower building."

"Oh my God." Gil gasped. "Are you serious? Do you have shower shoes?"

"What are those even for?"

"So you don't get a staph infection or someone's spooge under your toenails, dumbass."

I recoiled. I hadn't thought of either of those possibilities. I

[61] She said, "pulling my dick." Couldn't help it.

just knew I needed a shower. Plus, I had to rinse out my bra and panties, at the very least. Those two items are definitely not magical. I'd just have to risk it.

I broke from the group toward the tin-roofed structure in the center of the compound. Closer to the road, Granita had stopped to chat with a couple of clean-cut guys, who were setting up a tent. Both were unreasonably thin and too well cared-for to be a possible food source, not that I was hungry, but you never know when there'll be a shortage.[62] Plus, their short-sleeved dress shirts pretty much ensured they were carrying a box of *Watchtowers*.

Up a few slots was another RV, this one a large bus-like monstrosity. Outside, a family was preparing for dinner. A plaid-shirted father-type flipped burgers on a grill, while a woman wearing capri pants and an apron opened a Costco-sized jar of mayonnaise. Nearby, a couple of adolescents dawdled on a swing set meant for much smaller children and whispered secrets in each other's ears.

I know what you're thinking. The whole scene was absolutely disturbing, like the quartet had drifted out of some 50s sitcom and landed at my campground just to taunt me with their . . . family-ness. Everything about them was foreign, not the least their consensus of smiles.

I needed a shower, or at the very least a toilet to dry heave over.

A single bulb splayed a cone of light around the wash building's closed door; a padlock dangled from a chain on the frame and a sign reported:

TOILETS CLOSED AFTER 10 P.M.
USE HONEY BUCKET.

[62] Would someone tell me why I'm explaining myself? Fuck off.

The thought of which reminded me of shakily hovering over clogged muddy holes. Something I was happy not to have to deal with again.

When I pushed the door open, I was accosted by an odor akin to aged and moldy cheddar hanging in the air like a gas attack, mingling with the pungent sourness of urine. A row of stalls lined one wall facing an oxidized mirror and four sinks that spread across the other. At the opposite end, a darkened opening led to another room, probably the showers. At least it was well lit, though the bright white of the exposed bulbs did nothing for my skin tone.

With the door closed behind me, I was taken first by the silence. Except for the occasional crane fly tinging against a light bulb, the space was devoid of sound and creepy because of it. No drips, or tanks running.

Nothing.

I crossed the space in three strides to peer into the darkened area beyond the main restroom. It didn't seem to be a large space but it was hard to tell. There were no switches on either the exterior or within an arm's length on the inner walls. From what I could see, the concrete floor gave way to soggy wooden slats a few feet in. It was only once I'd stepped onto those saggy boards that I noticed a grayed string dangling from the ceiling.

I reached out into the shadow, slipping my hand in the murky dark, for a moment. My overactive imagination kicked in and I imagined horrible creatures reaching back toward me from the soggy blackness. Quivering gelatinous digits sticky as label glue, reaching with sharp talons toward my necrotic fragile flesh.

Reaching.

I stumbled back into the light, banking that the retreat might cause the monsters to return to their drains, or at least give me a chance at some sanity. It worked and I focused on the string once more. Gathered my courage and marched straight toward it snatching at it and tugging.

It took two tries but I finally snatched it on, sending a cone of light arcing around the room as though spotlit by a cracked-out carnie. To my right hooks strung with moldy rubber sheets, themselves dotted with mold so thick it had taken on the heavy look of moss. To the left three half walls cut the area into quarters providing for a distinct area of one's own without all the pesky privacy.

"Shower shoes my ass," I said aloud, my voice played against the walls, which I could see were tiled. Flip-flops weren't going to cut it in this room.

I needed a gas can and a match.

As I was turning to leave, I heard a faint scraping. At first it seemed to be coming from the stalls, perhaps through an overlooked vent in the ceiling. How was I to know for sure—I was busy booking toward the door. Unlike so many victims in horror movies, I did not have to be told to run by the black man in the sixth row of the theater. I know what that threatening music means. I grabbed for the knob and pulled. It spun loose in my grasp, rotating in its cuff like a dial.

Broken.

I spun around and collapsed against the door, facing the shower room and the source of the odd noise, listening.

Nothing.

And then a whole lotta something.

An aching squelch that could only be nails scratching against metal flooded the room, followed by a thudding bump against the door. It jarred with such force I was scooted forward across the floor, sarong snagging on the concrete. I winced, not with pain but with the knowledge my skin was being horribly scraped. I rebounded and braced against a second assault.

"Who the fuck is it?" I screamed, forcing my heels into a couple of chips in the floor for leverage.

A low rolling growl responded and a tapping of nails scurried across the metal.

Then the door crept open, not from a ramming thud but a

slow methodical pressure. I stiffened and fought to hold my ground. There was no question the werewolves had found us, but had they found the others first? Was there anyone out there to help me?

I felt the scream climbing my throat before I even thought to do it. It echoed in the cinder block building.

The crack in the door widened and claws as black and sharp as those I'd imagined were reached for me in reality. Splintered jagged nails curving out of hairy fingers crooked around the door, where they curled the paint off with each scratch. I forced my body against it, catching the werewolf's—oh . . . what would you call that?—paw between the frame and the metal corner.

Outside a long yelping reply turned from ear-shattering to distant within a few seconds.

I flung the door open and ran like a retard in orthopedic shoes,[63] arms windmilling and feet stumbling over even the smallest pebbles, twigs and/or Idahoan rodent in my path. I'd reached the campfire before I noticed that both the heels were missing from my Manolos . . . or were they Louboutins? Jesus! You know I'm freaked out when I can't categorize fashion.

"What's up with you?" Gil asked, sipping from a red plastic party cup.

"Didn't any of you hear me?" I looked from one face to the next. Pina Colada, or whatever, had returned from her stroll with the Jojobas in tow;[64] they flanked her on a fireside bench like zealous bookends, but wait . . . these were zealous bookends with name tags—as if the short-sleeve dress shirts weren't geeky enough.

Tad and Corey.

Moving on . . .

Honey and Gil were a bit too cozy for Mr. Kim's taste. He stood on the hood of the car with his arms crossed and an un-

---

[63] That's right, a retard. You want to make somethin' of it?
[64] If only we could be so lucky to get a skin care fix out here in bumfuck.

commonly murderous glare. Wendy was licking at the inside rim of her flask.

"Wow. You guys are super helpful. I barely escaped a horrific death, and here you are chatting and . . ." I paused to point out the presumed missionaries, ". . . flirting."

"Am not!" Granita yelled and stalked off into the night, Jehovah and Witness—respectively—trailing in her wake. As she rounded the corner of the RV, the two Cleaver kids came into view, for a second—and only a second—I could have sworn they were holding hands. Maybe I'd misjudged their relationship.

Maybe.

"Good evening, folks," the boy said. His blonde hair was Swedish straight and tossed around his head like a beaded skirt. The girl stood half behind him, a mirror in female form. If these weren't a couple of Flowers in the Attic, I'd eat my shoes. "I'm Billy and this is my sister, Clare."

"Hi, everyone," she said.

His words were so measured, so deliberately polite and polished; I couldn't help but mock. "Hi, Billy. Hi, Clare. It's super great to meet you both."

"Jesus. Could you be a bigger bitch?" Wendy asked tossing the shiny Chococat flask to the ground and stomping away.[65] The kids might actually be useful. If they hadn't just come from a taboo gropefest, they might have seen or at least heard my scrap with the werewolf.

"She's right. I'm such a dick. Why don't you plant your asses?" I motioned toward the log Wendy left. The twins (I was fairly certain) both cringed—possibly due to my course language,[66] but followed the direction; Billy, producing an actual

---

[65] I won't fault her for it. There's nothing worse than hitting the bottom of the bottle, or is that 'rock bottom'? Whatever.
[66] But, really, do I seem like I'd be bothered worrying about the fragile sensibilities of the incestuous? C'mon.

handkerchief, unfolded and shook it out across the bark. Clare sat down on it, mouthing a thank you to Billy.

I shuddered at their intimacy and looked around the group for some back up. Gil's eyes were wide with horror and remarkably so were Honey's. That girl was growing on me. I had to shake off the grossness and get down to business.

"Did either of you hear that howling, a while back?" I asked.

"Wild dogs, I thought," Billy said. "But we were down by the barn, so I can't be certain."

Honey and Gil snickered.

I refrained and pounced. "So you did hear!" I pointed at the kid daring Gil not to acquiesce to the possibility. "See? I was totally being attacked and even these two—who were twice as far away, mind you—heard it. You can be so fucking self-absorbed."

"Granted." He took another sip, and said nothing more. Instead, his eyes darted from the twins back to me and then to the back window of the RV. The tin foil screen was peeled back á là Jiffy Pop, framing Fishhook as he waved his arms back and forth; his eyes bugging out like a Looney Toons character.

He got it. "Well, it's been real nice meeting you two. I'm sure your parents are worried, it being dark and all." I stood, extending my hand in the direction of the path between the vehicles.

"Well, it was nice meeting you as well, Miss?" Billy rose and helped his sister up.

"Amanda is fine. That's Gil and Honey."

"It was nice meeting all of you. Maybe we could talk more tomorrow, but if not, enjoy your trip and . . ." He curled his fingers into claws and growled. "Don't let the dogs get you."

"Yeah, okay." I followed them to the road and watched them make their way back to their trailer. I supposed I was just being sensitive, what with the guy showing up at the motel, and the more recent gunplay with Honey. Was everyone following us? It was enough to make a girl paranoid.

Inside the camper, Fishhook had calmed down considerably. He slouched into the passenger seat, the Tupperware container open on his lap. And empty. Whatever he was protecting—drugs I'd suspected—had long since been consumed. His eyes rolled up into his skull and a shallow sigh took the place of the urgent comment I expected.

"They're comin', girl," he whispered and then his head lolled against his shoulder, out. I didn't need to check his pulse to know the man had life in him; I could smell his body functioning, the various tracts filling, emptying. The bile, the food digesting in stomach acid. The blood gravy sloshing through the pipes.

I shook off the urge to devour, remembering the hooks that laced his intestines like landmines. Once you got started, it was nearly impossible to stop at one bite, and I couldn't risk another reaper bill. As it was, the abrasions from the concrete were going to cost a couple of thousand to clear up.

I left him there and joined Honey, Gil and Wendy, who'd returned from her huff.

"He's passed out now, drugs I think."

"He sure was animated a minute ago. Freaked out, even." Gil tossed the cup into the fire. It popped and curled in on itself until it was a black ball. The dense smoke it produced filled the air with that harsh chemical smell that always seems to signal the end of a fireside chat.

"What were you drinking anyway?"

Gil shrugged.

Wendy, still clearly aggravated, said, "He got some blood off of your buddy in there."

"Gil!"

"It's not like I didn't ask, first. He just popped off a scab and let it drain."

"That is so gross!"

"Yeah, right," he said. "*That's* gross. Drinking blood from a cup is gross."

I raised my palms in defeat. Better than hear him recount the litany of filth that hung out in human bowels and bladders and such. "Did we figure out how we're going to give Honey a final viewing of her dearly departed?"

Honey's voice waivered. "Madame Gloria helped us out. We're going to see the Kraken of Butte."

"Montana, then?" Wendy had her I'm sorry face on so I didn't sneer or anything.

"One problem," she said. "The Kraken won't tell us any secrets without an offering."

"Like money?"

"Like a heart," Honey said, downtrodden.

"I don't think that'll be a problem."

Wendy nodded her agreement.

Chapter 10

You Gotta Have Heart

The human population, at large, has come close to discovering our presence on a number of occasions, primarily as a result of various unchecked werewolf packs and the zombie outbreaks of 2007. The reapers counteract these events in metropolitan areas, but what if something happens in a rural community? Is it time to deputize?
—Undead Science Monitor (Fall Yearbook)

There's nothing quite like a scream to break up the pristine silence of dawn. It puts everyone on edge and really sets the tone for a busy day in advertising. That's why I have it set as my alarm at home—not that I sleep or anything as mundane as that.[67] But I hadn't brought my alarm clock, so this particular scream was a little disconcerting, plus it interrupted my reading and I hate that.

I glanced across the table to Wendy. "Could you?"

"Could I what?" Her tone dropped immediately into lazy suspicion.

"What do you mean what? Go check on that scream."

"Bitch, please." She rolled her eyes. "I need to know how *this* turns out." She snapped an *OK* magazine cover in front of my face. "Hello? Brad's leaving Angelina because she only eats toast. That's important news, no matter how you slice it."

---

[67] We've been over that, right?

"Are you serious?"

"Um. If that weren't enough, Hannah Montana has VD."

I clicked my tongue. "You made that up."

"You investigate," she whined. "You enjoy that kind of shit."

"Fine." I slapped my novel down on the table, loud enough to wake a dozing Fishhook. He swung his arm down from the bunk over the driver's seat, waved me off. His heavy-lidded eyes and groaning had me worried I'd actually bitten him on accident. Then I remembered his drug binge.

With a sneer, I slipped my feet into the surprisingly comfortable penny loafers, rolled up the pants until I'd achieved a sly Audrey Hepburn homage, or at the very least a Jet girl from *West Side Story*.

The door slammed after me, slapping into place with an echo. I stepped off the slab of concrete into the piles of dead leaves that carpeted the majority of the grounds and slipped between the Volvo and the camper to get out to the car path. On my way, I glanced inside the backseat and saw Honey crashed out asleep and Mr. Kim watching over her from behind the seat, a subtle smile played on his nearly visible lips. He didn't notice me.

I didn't notice anything weird, at first. There wasn't any immediate activity to warrant a scream of that nature, no herds of zombie mistakes shambling around, no sasquatches out hunting for the morning newspaper, and certainly no snarling werewolves. Now, *that* would be screamworthy.

The Cleavers must have been getting ready to go when it happened. Their campsite was cleaner than when they came and the father, a broad-shouldered man with a hair part as crisp as his pressed dress shirt and khakis was already ambling down the road, a look of concern slapped on his face.[68]

"Did you hear that?" he asked in a tone both friendly and

---

[68] The only things he was missing to complete the whole '50s Dad ensemble were an unlit pipe and a newspaper folded in thirds under his arm.

authoritarian; his face crinkled up in such a sincere way I was mesmerized. "A mighty loud scream. Mighty loud."

"Yes sir." The words just flew out of my mouth, like I was actually used to being polite.

He continued past me toward the cultist's tent. I followed.

"Are your wife and daughter alright?" I struggled to keep up."

"They're safe and sound in our rolling abode." He turned and gave a weak wave in that direction. "Everyone accounted for in your rig?"

I had to think. Wendy and Fishhook were in there. Gil had just tucked in for the dawn and Mr. Kim and his sister were safe in the car. That left . . . Granita. Had she not come back last night? She didn't seem to be the type to tag team the choirboys.[69] I could be wrong.

My fear was that the werewolves had really found us. I'd nearly forgotten about them, preferring to blame last night's horror on the kid's "wild dog" theory.

"Yeah. I think one of the girls is missing." Why couldn't I remember her name? "You must have seen her. *Très très* white?"

"Ah yes. I hope she's down there with those boys." He pointed down the road. One stood facing the entrance to their tent, the other squatted beside him cradling his own head and rocking.

As we approached, nothing seemed to be out of the ordinary. The tent was an average two-man number in an impractical shade of yellow with gray stripes, but other than that, nothing apparent to warrant the guy's breakdown. He sobbed and mumbled, blowing saliva bubbles like a toddler.

"It's a mess," Tad or Corey said, it was hard to distinguish them without their nametags.

Standing directly in front of the open flaps, the scene opened up like an autopsy. The left portion of the tent's internal divide

[69] Maybe she needed a little pinga in her colada.

was splattered with gore. A jagged hole intruded into its side, dripping blood from swaying nylon scraps. Entrails formed a breadcrumb trail to Granita's body—or at least her torso—heaped and broken under the empty lower branches of a dying evergreen. The misshapen squares of pale flesh that weren't clumped with wads of bloody pine needles had grown blue and mottled in death.[70] Ants marched across the pile of meat *en masse* nestling in the empty socket of Becky's neck, like the final guests to some gruesome picnic.

No sign of her head or extremities.[71]

Ward gave no indication if he was horrified at the discovery. Of course, I wasn't particularly grossed out, but you'd think I'd be the only one.

"Yep. That's a dead girl. Poor thing," he said and then with a quick smile, turned and strode back up the gravel road and out of sight. My mouth was still open in shock at his hasty departure, when the bus revved up and came barreling toward the exit, forcing the two freaked-out cultists to dive out of the way and toward the tent. Corey or Tad, one, fell across the top, collapsing the structure with a sloshing wet thud, that shot blood out the opening like a smashed ketchup packet. This caused the other missionary to weep all the more dramatically, dropping to his knees and pounding his chest.[72]

The Cleavers slowed to a stop a few feet away and the passenger window opened revealing the happy homemaker for the first time.

"Oops!" she yelled out to the splayed boy. "Sorry about that." Then disregarded the prone traumatized figure to address me. "And you must be Amanda. I must thank you for being hospitable toward my William and Clare. I am truly sorry we didn't get a chance to meet, before *this* terrible circumstance." Her blond

---

[70] Just like mine. Glory be to the Gods of make-up.
[71] Those were the most meaty, after all.
[72] Even I thought it was gross, but you don't see me crying about it. Baby.

hair was scrolled away from her pert face in a French twist, revealing a thin upturned nose and ruby lips not seen since the '50s. "You will understand if we get on with our trip. We do so hate to be waylaid. I'm sure you'd agree."

"Naturally," I said. Though, frankly, I was just happy to see the weirdos go.

"Ciao!" she yelled and pageant waved, one photo away from an antique soapbox.

As they made the corner, Mr. Cleaver gunned it sending a spray of gravel spraying across the lawn like a tacky Vegas fountain show. Billy and Clare were staring placidly from the rear window.

"Are you alright?" I took the boy's hand and pulled him out of the ruins of canvas and bent poles.

"Just a little disturbed." He kneaded his left shoulder.

"Well yeah. So . . . what happened?"

"I don't really know. We were up late talking. Tad and I had nearly convinced Becky to let us take her up to the compound, but it got late and she said she'd be more comfortable sleeping down here."

I cocked my head, wondering if the "compound" was some sort of cultist code for a little train party. I prepared for the naughty bits. Unfortunately, none were forthcoming. Fucking goody-two-shoes.

"We zipped the center wall in place and gave her one of the sleeping bags, while we shared the other."

"Oh yes?" I winked at him. "Okay. Alright. I gotcha." I certainly knew my share of euphemisms.

He flinched. Clearly, the implication of gayness passed well over his head. "The next thing we knew, Becky was screaming. By the time we got out of the tent this is what we found. Whatever did it was awfully fast . . . and quiet."

Or whoever, I thought, looking over the property. The forested areas surrounding the field were certainly dense enough to secret away an entire pack of werewolves. Markham's goons wouldn't have any problem surveying the scene from just about anywhere.

They probably were.

And they wouldn't be the only ones appraising.

Wendy and Honey were hoofin' it towards the tent. A spark of empathy ignited inside me, and was immediately extinguished upon noticing that the pair were arm in arm like sisters. Um . . . when did that happen? I haven't been overly self-absorbed, I don't think. So, when did I miss out on critical bonding time?

Somehow, it was my mother's fault.[73]

Honey broke into a skip as she approached. "Becky, let's get goin'!" Her hopeful smile drooped into a sick frown then exploded into a wide-eyed expression of horror. "Becky! Becky!" She ran the length of the carnage stopping briefly to heave up a meal I didn't remember the girl consuming, yet suspected it contained primarily Twix bars. I glared at Wendy.

She shrugged. "She didn't tell us Becky was a cutter."

"You're bad," I said.

Honey circled the torso trying to make the connection between the lump of gore and her former traveling companion.

"What the fuck happened?" The girl stomped back. She poked at Corey's chest. "What did you do to her?"

"Nothing!"

She prodded the boy, again, harder.

"Nothing!" he shouted, flinching. "We found her like that, I swear."

She poked a third and final time.

The missionary covered the spot with his hand, scowling. "Ow! Knock it off!"

I swear when Honey withdrew, I detected a hint of a smile on her lips. So mean.[74] "How much are we lovin' her?" I asked Wendy, who simply smirked. "He's telling the truth, I'm pretty sure."

---

[73] Seriously. Who else could I blame?

[74] Did I have a child and not feel it?

"I'm sure. What's the big deal?" Wendy plucked a scrap of shredded tent from a nearby branch, as though it were a used condom hung there to drip dry. "Could've been worse."

"Oh yeah? How?" Honey glared.

"She could have been horribly disfigured."

"You're a real piece of work, you know," she said.

Wendy shrugged.

The girl stepped away from Wendy, scowling. I looped my hand through the crook of her elbow and led her off toward the barn full of antique crap. "I have to tell you that you aren't the only person following us. Gil got into a bit of trouble back in Seattle and—"

"I know. I was following you guys, remember? That guy was pissed."

"Well he sent a couple of his men after us. I think they may have done this."

Honey nodded, eyes following the edges of the forest, the corners of the building. "Werewolves. And you think they're still here, don't you?"

"I'd bet on it," Wendy said from a nearby table of mismatched silverware locked away in Ziploc bags. "All the more reason to get out of here, quick."

"No doubt." I walked over to Wendy and emptied one of the bags onto the table and plucked the sharpest knife I could find from the debris. It was time to salvage something helpful from the shitstorm. "Take Honey back to the cars and get ready to go. And Honey, please tell me that piece of crap you came in was your friend's?"

"It was, but why—"

"Leave it. I'll meet you back at the camper and then we'll get out of here." I jogged off toward the tent and the two guys. "Get your stuff and go," I said. "Unless you want to be held for questioning. You do look like the only ones who could have done this."

Corey winced, but nodded, snatched Tad by the arm and led

him to their rusty Nissan truck. As they pulled away from the site, I shuffled through the grass and clumped bloody grass toward Granita's prone form.

It didn't take much effort to extract her heart, just a few purposeful cuts, a couple of ribs to crack and move aside and then there it was; cold and sunken. I severed the climbing vines of muscle, fat and arteries, dropped the organ into the Ziploc bag and gave it a shake.[75]

We had ourselves an offering.

As I stood to leave, I saw a pile of what looked like furry black balls[76] mounded where Granita's hip should have been. A quick prodding sent a puff of smoke into the air. I backed away. You never could tell what was dangerous, plus, there was something familiar about the size and color that had me thinking they might fit well inside a Tupperware container—if you know what I mean.

It couldn't be Fishhook, though. He wasn't out of my sight all night.

---

[75] Yellow and blue make green and in this case, red. Lots of red.
[76] Not those kind, you pervert.

Chapter 11

Blowing Adolf and the Rest of the Mini-Gestapo

It is every supernatural citizen's responsibility to quash a zombie outbreak in the rural territories. Nothing will expose us quicker, or diminish our cushy lifestyle more completely than a zombie apocalypse. Please do your part.
—PSA aired during *A Very Zombie Christmas*

About twelve miles out of Coeur d'Alene, signs of habitation faltered and even the cars on the freeway became sporadic. Honey tossed the last of Wendy's gossip rags and started hounding me for a beer and boy fix, doing everything humanly (or inhumanly) possible to prove her point save scooting her butt across the backseat like a dog in heat. This being a new and previously unexplored side of Honey, I figure it couldn't hurt to indulge the girl.

"Dude. The mere presence of testosterone will lighten the gloomy atmosphere you two seem to be honing," she offered as evidence. "Plus, I've got to pee and this little bathroom is *too* gross."

"Maybe if you curl up in a ball against the bedroom door you could leach some pheromones from Gil," I said.

"I'm so sure. He's gay. Don't you mean like estrogen?"

"Okay, whatever." I shrugged. She stared. Clearly the joke

was lost on her. "Fine, we'll look for a place," I said and Honey clapped and squealed in an off-putting cheerleaderish way.

Anyway, she was right, there was simply no reason not to splurge on some ogle time. Becky was gone, after all. We couldn't bring her back, and who'd want to live without extremities, or a head for that matter? There was just no good reason to mope around. The sun was another hour off before setting, so Gil could just continue his beauty sleep with the rest of the luggage. I hadn't been drooled over in nearly six hours; my quota was sorely lacking.

Wendy brightened and pointed out a smear of neon off to the right. The tires left the highway, instantly kicking dust into the air. Honey giggled. The sign came into view: THE WHITE HOUSE. An impressive enough name, though attached to it was no stately columned manor. The building, itself, was a squatty mangle of board and glass—no more thought had been put into its construction than a preteen boy's circle-jerk fort—and surrounded by a gravel lot filled with cheap domestic cars and pick-ups that wore rust spots like tattoos.

"Grim." Wendy opened the glove box and moved the bottle of hand sanitizer into her bag.

"Oh, I think it's cute."

I turned with my hand outstretched to check the girl for a fever. She swatted it away.

"Just darling," I said. Before Wendy could add to the snark, Honey opened the car door and bounded for the shack. "Let's go, then."

Since Fishhook couldn't be counted on to keep off the mushrooms, we lost valuable travel time having the Volvo hooked up to the RV, so at least we weren't involved in a caravan any longer. I waved for him and Mr. Kim to watch the Winnebago.

We found Honey at the bar, flipping her stripes of gold and brown hair for a slobbering road worker with a shaved head dimpled in three spots like bowling ball finger holes and a torso clad in dirty wife beater. The guy worked nearly as quick as the flirty girl. Honey was already nursing a pint of amber colored liquid. I shuddered to think what it might be—this being the land microbreweries forgot. I suspected something as hoity as Pabst Blue Ribbon drawn from a moldy keg.

Wendy and I scanned the remaining customers from our spot at the door. A lopsided mix of twenty or so, predominantly surly male and seemingly uniformed. The look du jour was identical to Honey's catch, crewcut to bald, dingy tank tees, stained jeans tucked into black combat boots. Familiar from afternoon talk shows that usually ended in violent confrontation. Do I have to spell it out? The place was crawling with fucking skinheads, and not a single one poon-worthy. The irony of the bar's name was not lost on me. The few females present were either as rough as their men, or bore the meek and disciplined look of domestic violence victims.

I stomped over to Honey, wrapped my arm around her shoulder, and leaned in to her ear. "Hi sweetie. Do you notice anything odd about your love shack?"

"Not a thing." Honey's hand traced a figure-eight around her particular Adolph's nipple. It poked against the tight shirt like an obscene jujyfruit. His face was pleasant enough, tan from day labor, undoubtedly, a light sanding of blond stubble across his jaw, and pale blue eyes. He might even have been cute, if you could look past the big swastika tattoo on his bicep.

Since Honey seemed to be clueless, I pointed out the offensive ink. "Are you a Buddhist?"

The pleasant face turned into a glower. He shifted his weight. His body entered my personal bubble[77]—any further and he'd have popped it altogether—and to think I even smiled at the neo-Nazi piece of shit.

---

[77] So much for boundaries, if only the Aryan Brotherhood could hold off on their busy cross-burning schedule and organize an impulse control seminar.

"What do you mean by that?"

"That symbol. Buddhist, right?"

He looked from his tattoo to me then to one of the Gestapo goons that littered the pool tables. The man was taller and built like an ape on steroids, only hairier. He wore an army green barn jacket riddled with patches that I didn't need to be able to see to tell were offensive. He lumbered toward us, the crowd parting as though the bulls had been released.

"Let's go." I took Honey by the arm and directed her to the door. Wendy was waiting there digging in her purse. As we reached her, she slapped something sharp into my palm.

"Just in case," she said.

We were in the parking lot before I looked in my hand. There sat a gleaming gold set of dentures, but not in any human shape. These seemed to mimic a full set of dog teeth; the incisors sharp from the grinding. I looked back at Wendy, confused. She merely winked in reply and turned to Honey.

"Get in the car girl, and stay there. We'll handle this." Wendy's voice was steady and serious.

"Whatever. You guys are really overreacting." The girl bounded off, shaking her head as though we'd made an undue fuss. She sat into the back and reclined, her bare legs hung from the open door, crossed and ankle popping.

"They're extra special Grillz. I picked them up and had them enchanted down at Willie's as a joke, but I think I've found a use." Wendy retrieved a pair of her own from her Coach bag and slid them over her teeth. Despite their odd size and shape, they melted into place, becoming a natural extension of her mouth, albeit shiny and gangsta. "See how they fit right on top?"

"Yeah, but is this really the time to try out a new look?"

As if on cue, Hess and Himmler stumbled out of The White House, kicking up a dust storm as they approached. A few more followed. I half expected them to goose step.

"It's exactly the right time." Wendy's back was to the on-coming hoard. She contorted her mouth and jaw into the familiar shark-like biting radius that we do so well. Inside the gold teeth grew and shifted, changing the shape of her mouth in the process. "We can't eat 'em all. This way the bodies will look like animal attacks."

So . . . they did look like dog teeth.

"Got it." I slid my enchanted Grillz on and grinned at the five skinheads stalking toward us. They stopped a few feet away. The gorilla took the lead.

"You girls lookin' for somethin'? I think you're lookin' for somethin'." His hand ran down his belly to his crotch; he pulled at the denim down his leg as if there were even the slightest full-ness.

"If you're thinking we're lookin' to leave, then you're on to something." I shuffled up alongside Wendy.

"I don't think that's it." His mouth stretched into a hideous grin. "I think you're wantin' to service the brotherhood. Eh boys?"

Honey's target puffed up his chest and stepped toward me. "This one here's wantin' to bow down in front of my big Buddha. She told me that inside." He rubbed his crotch lewdly—as if he could possibly be doing it in a refined way, perhaps with his Grandmother's silver salad tongs.

I reached over to swastika boy's groin and cupped. "It's like you've known me all my life, sugar."

He nodded—the smug bastard—showing off for his friends.

Wendy and I burst into laughter. She looked over her shoulder at the car. Mr. Kim was on the roof, waving his arms franti-cally.

"Get those motherfuckers away from Hyon Hui!" he yelled.

I almost giggled. The ghost had been around me long enough to catch my potty mouth. He was right; of course, Honey needed protection, and it was up to us. If we fucked this up, she'd probably end up wearing a white sheet instead of Dolce and Gabbana, and that was totally unacceptable.

"Is there somewhere private we can go, and by private I do mean somewhere we can fuck?" I winked at the bigger man. Wendy slid in next to him and grabbed his ass. His head jerked toward her, eyes wide.

"What about my friends?" He jerked a thumb toward Adolph and two other skinheads who'd come for the show.

I smiled. "They can come, too. Watch." I shrugged. ". . . or whatever."

They led us around the side of the tavern to a picnic table studded with cigarette butts and surrounded by a semicircle of pines that needled the ground like a carpet. Our audience took up a spot near a tire swing, sneering and trying for threatening stances while only managing to look like playground bullies.

"So what, you want us to just whip 'em out?" the gorilla asked.

"Yeah." I twirled my hair, playing the coquette to Wendy's slut. "I don't know about Wendy, but I'd like that a lot."

"Me, too." She sucked at her index finger—cuz she's nasty like that.

The two skinheads were reduced to quivering golems of pathetic adolescence; ham-fisted fumbling with the buttons on their Levis gave way to those goofy toothsome grins associated primarily with the blue balls of the AV club. They were completely incapacitated by the tangle of jeans and jockeys around their ankles—just like we like 'em.

Wendy dropped to her knees in front of the gorilla. He let out a feeble, "Woo," as her frigid breath lit on his tiny pecker; it nearly turtled in under a pocket of hairy fat—that for our purposes, we'll call a pooch, if you don't mind. Her eyes fluttered and a shudder rolled through her body. I didn't need a therapist to tell me she was revolted.

I said a quick prayer and peeked down at my guy's dick.

The horror.

Because I am who I am and not someone with actual luck, I was faced with a throbbing fleshy poultry mallet. This cock was not content to be simply misshapen in its engorgement— no—its oversized mushroom cap oozed a thick yellow discharge. Why me? Why was I subjected to such atrocities? I didn't deserve it. Yet, there it was, stretching out toward me. Reaching like those horrible claws in the shower room.

I turned away and saw Wendy positioning her guy by the hips, turning him to obstruct our audience's ability to see. They moved away from the swing, one walking in close enough to grab. I winked at the straggler, hoping to lure him in. He took another step and stopped.

It would have to do.

"Close your eyes, big boy," I said.

The snarling began before my jaws cracked open, ratcheting to shark-bite radius. The Grillz tingled, bonding magically. Gold canines emerged from my gums forcing my lips back in a way that was too uncomfortable to make a habit. I slapped at Adolph's dick and bit through his hip and pelvis, dropping him instantly. His scream was cut into a short crow-like "caw" as his throat was the next to go.

To my left, Wendy had taken out the gorilla's genitals and abdomen, leaving him looking like a cartoonish bow-legged cowboy, albeit dripping with blood. In the next instant, she tore into the closest guy, snapping his head clean off before he had any awareness of what was happening.

Impressive.

So much so, that I'd nearly forgot about the straggler. The shorter skinhead was already at the corner of the bar when I caught up to him, biting through his shoulder. His dismembered arm fell to the ground. My feet caught on it and I fell face first into the dirt.

When the man looked back I could see the bite had begun

the change. Despite my ability to breathe someone into a zombie, my bite still carried the viral load necessary to create a mistake and this guy was turning quick.

"Aaaarrrrghhhh!" he cried, which was totally dramatic since they're really fully capable of words, but seem to get lazy vocabularies.[78]

He darted through the swinging doors into the bar.

"Wendy! One of them turned mistake!"

She pulled her mouth off her prey to acknowledge me. "Let the reapers get 'em."

If only. "Hello? We're in Bumfuck, Egypt. There aren't any reapers coming. We've got to handle this."

"Shit!" She leapt to her feet and followed me to the doors.

The inside of The White House had devolved into a full-blown zombie outbreak. At least ten new zombies shambled between the tables, chewing on an assortment of limbs, organs and the ubiquitous sweetbreads.[79] The bartender dragged his legless torso from behind the bar, a swath of intestines draped from his mouth like a gory handlebar moustache—never a good look. From the pool tables, a burly woman fought off my armless mistake with a pool cue. Behind her, a blood-spattered ghoul crept up on tip toes with the child-like precision of a Santa/parent bust. I almost yelled for her to watch out.

Almost.

"What are we gonna do?" Wendy's face was smeared with

---

[78] A quick zombie primer:
- While I can breathe zombie life, my saliva still creates mistakes.
- Mistakes are your typical mindless shambler types, hell-bent on brains and entrails and not remotely interested in high fashion or skin care.
- Breathers like Mr. Kim's mother and I are the rarest type of zombie.
- There has been talk of the old school Haitian kind of zombie, but they aren't really dead and so don't count in this primer.
- Sentient zombies rot at a much slower rate and have been known to heal, but only like paper cuts and small things. Anything else would be ridiculous.

[79] What? You were expecting me to say brrraaaaaainnnnnsssss?

blood, chunks of hairy skin and drippy globs of fat. Her look of horror was sadly incongruent. Her teeth were shiny and gold, though.

I realized I was still wearing the damn Grillz, too, reached in, pulled them off and handed the sloppy things back to Wendy. She shrugged and did the same, tossing them in her purse.

I scanned the front of the building. "Maybe we could find some way to lock them in. A stick. Something." I pointed to the two looped handles on the slatted wooden doors. She nodded and darted off into the woods. I turned back toward the Volvo, considering the tire iron. That would definitely be sturdy enough to hold them back.

Honey stood next to the car, her hand dangling from the open door, pale with shock. Mr. Kim stood atop, shaking his head.

"Get back in the fucking car!" I yelled. "And lock the doors!"

My voice had a second effect, one I hadn't considered; it alerted the horde of newly departed to our presence. I turned back in time to see a pack of the mindless creatures shamble for the doors. To my right, Wendy was barreling through the dirt lot with a piece of pipe raised over her head. I pressed against the doors, grabbing the handles and evening them. I braced for either Wendy to save the day, or a zombie to bust through and make my already dead flesh unrecognizable with their fury.

Tables were upended and chairs and bottles crashed on the wood planks as the undead scrabbled toward the door. A wave of blood, bile and excrement preceded them. It washed out from the gap and splattered its warm mess on my shoes and ankles. The first zombie to reach me was a petite woman—thank God—not that I could tell that from her horrible makeup job; *that* had been stripped clean off her skull along with her scalp. The whole mess hung around her shoulders like a shawl. Her sunken lidless eyes glowered; she pushed at the doors, shaking them. Alternating one to the other. Creating an opening

Behind her a couple of husky ghouls sprang forward, tossing

the woman into an electronic dartboard and scoring a bullseye with a splinter of bone that protruded from her mangled nose.

"Wendy!" I screamed.

And she appeared, powering forward with the length of pipe, slipping it through the door handles on her first attempt. We stepped away, hugged. I nearly collapsed in her arms.

"Whew. That was close," I said, taking her arm and just turning back to the RV, when a loud crack broke behind us. We turned just in time to see the door handles come loose and the pipe fly toward us.

Chapter 12

Well Hello Love Interest[80]

*Online personals are so '90s. Coffee shops used to be
the new meet markets. But nowadays, you can't meet a
decent undead unless you're fighting beside them . . .*
— *Paranormal Star Signs*

I don't enjoy being dirty or bars where you can't get good vodka,
yet there I was splayed out like roadkill in front of a crappy
Idahoan skinhead joint. I wasn't even sure what had happened.
But, I did know two things . . . one: zombies were shambling
towards me, ready to tear me three new assholes . . . and . . .
two: I was going to need a new ensemble.

I pushed myself up out of the mud and scanned the ground
for Wendy. She wasn't wallowing like me, instead—to my horror—I spotted her stumbling toward the RV, sporting a brand
new accessory, a metal pipe piercing her gut.[81] When she
reached the door, she turned back.

"You've got a cigarette stuck to your cheek," she said, disre-
garding her more heinous accoutrement.

I flicked the butt from my face and pointed out the pole.
Wendy's gaze followed mine to flesh puckered and gray where
it protruded; a slow gurgle of puss ran from the injury like sap.

"Oh shit." She grimaced and jiggled it as I joined her.

---

[80] Or at the very least lust.
[81] Pipe will never replace a cute belt or the perfect peek-toe stiletto.

The zombies were a good fifty feet away and closing, every bit as dangerous, though slowing and losing focus. One merely sat on a piece of broken door preening and eating the bits of flesh that clung to his tattooed arms in such a dainty manner you'd think he'd stopped for a quick spot of tea and a raspberry scone.

I certainly knew where he could find some lemon curd. It was pouring from the widening gash in Wendy's gut and splattering the ground in fat plops.

"Gross," she said, as she twisted the pipe. "Could you help get this out of me?"

"Oh God. Do I have to?"

Her eyes narrowed into slits. "Um . . . yeah. Look at this shit."

I looked at the side of the Winnebago and directed her to hang on to the handle by the door. I grabbed on a little lower with one hand and with the other I gripped the pipe. One foot bracing against the side of the RV I threw my weight into pulling out the projectile, which detached with a sucking thunk. Decomposed entrails clung to my hand like gravy. I tossed the pipe away, disgusted.

"Does it look okay?" Wendy performed a poorly executed grin.

I dropped to one knee and examined the gaping hole. Its edges were ragged and drippy but the muscle behind was drier. I poked at a dangling piece of abdomen that resembled beef jerky; it gave with some flexibility. Her stomach seemed to be intact and surprisingly red. It contracted with the remains of the afternoon neo-Nazi sample menu. The pipe missed her spine, but not by much. Its knobby presence protruded into the puncture like a pair of scuffed knuckles.

As fascinating as the injury was, the scene it framed in gore seemed a far more pressing matter. Past the rusty transport of the undereducated, past the gravel and mud parking lot, past the overgrowth of weeds and wildflowers a splotch of orange was on the horizon and getting bigger.

The Mustang, barreling toward us.

Someone's timing sucked, and I don't think I need to tell you it wasn't mine.

"Oh fuck!" I yelled.

"What?" Wendy looked down, tried to press the wound together with her fingers. "You don't think a band-aid will do?"

I stood, and turned Wendy toward the approaching Mustang. It sped into the lot, trailing a cyclone of dust, swerved into a sideways slide and plowed into five of the skindeads.[82] Body parts flew like dandelion seed.

There were five left, scattered and roaming. One was still coming toward us, scratching the air ahead of him with curled fingers too newly dead to be atrophied—it took me a second to realize he'd had cerebral palsy while living, which totally explained a limp, not to mention the ergonomic crutch attached to his forearm. The legless bartender had teamed with a willing horse, hanging around the neck of a pimply teen and wandering toward the highway. Then there were the other two. A scraggly-haired woman in dingy flannel shuffled toward the Volvo while repeatedly shoving her own jawbone back into the hamburger that used to be her face.[83] Mr. Kim jumped and raised his fists menacingly—as menacing as a middle-aged Korean businessman in a button-down shirt can be, not to mention see-through. The last was a giant. A bodybuilder-type who'd let his muscle go to flab, bounded toward the Mustang, man boobs jiggling.

Zombies on the loose and threatening to spread a global plague not dangerous enough for ya? Containment a near impossibility as it is? Why not throw in a bloodthirsty werewolf hellbent on murder and mayhem?

That oughta do it.

Markham's man stepped out of the car, casually, as though

---

[82] Ding! Coined!
[83] Multi-tasking! Zombies love multi-tasking! Can't get enough of it. Multi-tasking and brains.

fashionably late for a photo shoot, six-two if he was an inch, with a mop of sandy waves flopping and the bone structure of an underwear model. I would have had to fan myself, if I'd actually been a Southern belle. Sadly, the vapors don't really go with my body temperature.

A car horn cut through the air from our right. Fishhook popped up from the driver's side window, a deranged homeless jack-in-the-box. He pointed at the man, shouted something. I didn't need to know that this was the pizza guy. Honey opened her door and ran over, brandishing the gun that Wendy hadn't hidden so well, apparently.

"I thought you hid that?"

"I did." She shrugged.

"Super job."

Honey raised the gun, aimed for my head and fired. The bullet whizzed past my ear and thunked into something behind me. I turned in time to catch the crooked hand of the palsied zombie on my shoulder; it snagged on the sleeve of my shirt, tearing it clean off. The thing's last action was to bring the fabric to its nose and breathe in; it probably smelled like wardrobe dilemma. Honey had busted a cap right through the 'tard's forehead.[84]

I swung back to find her focused on the scene in the center of the parking lot. Markham's man had gone all wolfy during our scuffle and, let me tell you, six-two is a hell of a lot of meat to work with; he'd grown three feet taller—easy—and his claws were massive, thick and long.[85] Dexterous though. He eased the door shut with such comfort in his lupine form as to seem controlled rather than monstrous. The muscle-zombie reached for him then, jaw jacked open like an alligator's maw. A warbling cry issued from its bloodied gape. The werewolf reached out and

---

[84] I understand a fragile few may be among us. Feel free to insert the politically correct phrase, "bust a capable".

[85] If you know what I'm sayin'.

snapped off its bottom jaw and then slapped it against the thing's head on the backswing. The zombie went down, tits jiggling.

The meathead dispatched, Gil's would-be executioner aimed his snout at the dead woman approaching the Volvo. She'd managed to get the door open and was garbling sweet nothings to Fishhook, who seemed to be scrambling inside for a weapon, or possibly his drugs.

The werewolf dropped to all fours and galloped across the parking lot. His blonde coat glistened and bounced with every pounding of his considerable haunches.[86] As he reached the zombie, he reared up and swiped at her head, knocking it into the side of the car and spraying the back fender with blood. He stepped back and cocked his head. The woman was still moving, clawing her way under the SUV. His claws gripped her ankles and pulled her loose, dragging her across the parking lot before swinging her body against the wall of The White House with such force, it exploded into hot dog fixin's, a veritable buffet of lips and assholes.[87]

From his spot on the bar's porch, the werewolf faced the field and snorted. The piggybacking pair had nearly made a break in the forest and were quickly approaching the freeway gulley. I snatched the gun from Honey and ran. I picked off the bartender from five yards—inexplicably as I'd never had any formal training—and somehow expected the entire thing to stop instead of just the top half slap against a tree stump and nod off.

Pimples kept trudging forward, mere feet from a break in the brush but gaining momentum. Cars breezed by on the other side, so close I could hear radio snippets. Raising the gun again, I stepped forward, pressed it to the back of the zombie's skull and squeezed. Then . . .

Nothing.

No kick. No dead zombie.

---

[86] Is it wrong that I was getting a little turned on?
[87] The principal ingredients of hot dogs, according to Billy Cumberbatch, fifth grade über-bully.

Nothing.

Oh wait. There was a chuckle. The pimpled undead glanced toward me with a lidless eye and moaned a stuttering laugh. And my phone rang again, but it seemed inappropriate to take the call so I let it go. Plus, there was a great deal of limbs cracking from within the treed area. So, not nothing.

He stepped through trees and out onto the grassy shoulder of the freeway.

"Hey!" I called and to my surprise he actually turned to face me, lips clenched in a smug little grin. I turned the gun around and raised it to bludgeon him. His expression changed. Eyebrows drooped, shoulders curled in a defeated posture.

"You're goddamn right," I said, right before I was pushed aside into the tangle of a thick-leafed rhododendron by the werewolf, who snatched the zombie in one hand and tossed him back into the woods. Pimples gave it the old college try with an attack of his own, but the wolf simply fisted the kid's head and held him at arm's length before twisting it like a bottle cap and watching the body drop away.

"That's lovely." I backed away, certain it was my turn. I thought about the hole in Wendy's stomach and imagined similar horrors visited upon my flawless skin. It was enough to send shudders through my dead frame. But, at least she could live with it. This was it.

This was my death. I closed my eyes and waited.

The werewolf didn't charge though. I heard some scrambling in the undergrowth and caught a whiff of pine rot and freshly disturbed loam, but no physical assault.

When I peeked, the area was empty. Even the body was gone. I trudged through the brush back to the parking lot to find the crew gathered and loading bodies into the tavern. The werewolf had even turned back to his human form and was chatting politely with Honey.

Hello? Was I dreaming?

Marching out of the forest, I assessed my outfit for presentability and decided that mud stains plus blood spatter equaled a bad first impression. I ducked into the camper, swiped a T-shirt and shorts from Honey's suitcase and prayed that I'd fit into the tiny scraps of fabric. It was a close one. I shook the twigs from my hair, grabbed my cell and returned the call from Marithé.[88] She answered on the first ring.

"Where the fuck are you?" she asked.

"I don't know. Idaho?"

"Jesus! I've got some guy from *Supernatural Seattle* breathing down my neck for a scoop. He's certain you've flown to Bangalore for transcendental surgery on your thighs and he says if he doesn't get the truth within twenty-four hours he's going to run that, front page."

"Tell him I'm in rehab."

"For what?"

Yes. For what? I couldn't very well say alcohol; zombies don't get drunk. Food was out of the question; nothing will kill celebrity quicker than thoughts of incontinence, just ask June Allyson.[89] We could tell him I was visiting a sick relative, but then we'd have reporters swarming Rapid City by the time we got there. Not going to happen. And then I landed on it.

"Tell that cockroach I'm providing a personal consultation to a Hollywood celebrity that may be interested in crossing over. That'll have him drooling. He'll have his reporters swarming Los Angeles before nightfall."

"He'll want to know why Wendy is with you." She filed her nails in the background.

"Am I on speaker?"

"Oh." The phone clicked. "You were saying?"

"Tell him she's my bait. Plus—and this'll really make him hard—tell him she's getting the inside story first hand. He'll cream."

---

[88] Sometimes it's necessary to look.

[89] No. I'm serious. Ask. Contrary to popular belief, June is very much alive and supernaturally rejuvenated (though deathly pale) and living under the name *******. (Ed. note: name withheld due to legal constraints.)

"Will do." Marithé hung up without saying goodbye, a less-than-endearing trait.

I slapped my phone closed, checked my face one last time and stepped out to introduce myself to the werewolf.

He was waiting and clothed. I damned my vanity for causing me to miss the full frontal nudity that comes standard with every were-retransformation. Wendy stood behind the guy holding up nine fingers and biting her lower lip in a seriously slutty way.[90]

"I'm Scott." He reached for my hand and shook it. Holding on for a moment before releasing, searching my face with hazel eyes like round cut topaz.

For a reaction? I wondered.

"Amanda."

"You don't remember me, do you?" he asked, a sly smile curling on his lips.

I had caught a passing familiarity, but if I'd fucked him, I'd surely remember, right? It's not like I was promiscuous, that was Wendy's bit. He probably wasn't one of my string of therapy dates, either.[91] What can I say, nine out of ten unethical therapists agree, Amanda is an easy mark.

"No." I smiled and touched his arm. "But, I'd like to. Do refresh."

Jesus.

Was I hitting on a werewolf? Wendy scowled over his shoulder. Apparently she had plans.

"We met briefly last year, very briefly. I'm sure you'll remember the murders at the Washington Mutual Starbucks. The majority of the staff and customers were . . . um . . . eaten?"

"Maybe."

Maybe nothing. The memories flooded back.

---

[90] That's a full body score, you pervert!
[91] You may remember my ex-boyfriend Martin (see previous memoir). When I say ex, I mean dead. Food dead. Don't judge. Anyway, he was a therapist. Number seven in the string.

I was hiding in the bathroom when the gunshots started. The garbage can was full and wads of paper towels overflowed onto the floor around it. It's funny how you remember those things. The gross things. I'd hoped the reapers would come and clean house or the zombies would simply eat themselves out.[92] Neither happened.

I counted the gunshots, ten of them, for nine zombies.

I eased the door open and peeked out.

Scott was the shooter. A cop. Gorgeous in his uniform and empathetic to a fault, he gave me a comforting hug, which rubbed my makeup clean off and exposed my dead flesh in all its veined glory—*so* not a great first impression. Memorable, certainly, but not for romantic reasons. Intellectual, maybe.

If I'd known he was supernatural, I might not have fled. But, how could I know, he looked like a tasty nugget, to me.

Must have been fate, then.

"Fate?" he asked.

Had I said that aloud? Crap.

"No way. I've been looking for you ever since we met. I guess you could say you changed my life."

His smile turned into a dark smirk I didn't care for, but I was happy to return the snark. "Wow. I'm so glad I could be of service. Care to be more vague?"

I didn't think that last sentence out, clearly, because . . .

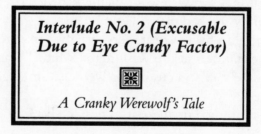

Interlude No. 2 (Excusable Due to Eye Candy Factor)

A Cranky Werewolf's Tale

---

[92] Did that sound dirty?

"After you ran, I was left with no proof of what had happened. My backup refused to corroborate my story. I knew it was zombies in that shop—couldn't be nothin' else but zombies—but all that was left was dead bodies. The kind that weren't moving. I won't kid you; I was shocked and, unfortunately for my career, too honest. My Chief put me on administrative leave when she read the final report. Said I needed R and R. Signed me up to see a shrink. What I needed was to find you.

"I started searching the following day.

"Man, I looked everywhere. From the C.D. to Aurora to West Seattle, I questioned every low-life informer I'd ever talked to and turned up nothin'. I started doing research on zombies, book research, but that was a dead end too, 'cause what I saw wasn't the kind that was still livin', like the voodoo kind. These were the flesheatin' variety.

"So I started thinkin' like a zombie, or at least what I thought a zombie would think like. I asked myself, where would I go for food? Who would I feed on? And then it was like a lightbulb turned on, just like in the cartoons.

"The homeless.

"I got my big break in the Tent City, roaming amongst the leaky tents, muddy alleys and burn barrels. It didn't quiet until about three in the A.M., so I normally showed up at two. This one night, I seen a well-dressed guy, musta been about twenty-five, tall, dark-haired, good lookin' I supposed, maybe a little pale. Completely out of place.

"I followed him through the blocks of tents, careful not to slosh in the puddles and alert him, hanging back in the shadows. He came up to an elderly man, who'd ducked out of a refrigerator box lean-to and was smoking under a big evergreen. They talked for a minute and then started walking together, down the backside of the area, toward Rupert Street, toward a long black limo. The door opened from the inside and a blond stepped out. She sauntered over to the homeless man, put her arm around him, led him to the car, and then pushed him inside with such force I could hear his body hit the opposite side of the interior.

"I didn't see any more that night. But, I did get the license plate and had a friend run it. That's when I knew I'd been looking in all the wrong places. It led me to a house in Medina. Not just a house, a mansion. Huge place.

"It didn't take long for that guy to lead me to you.

"When I saw you the second time, you were coming out of a wall into an alley near the furniture stores on Western Avenue. Not a door in a wall, either, *through* the fuckin' wall. I followed you home that night.

"During that time, I lost my job. Not that I miss it, but it was income. Like most out-of-work cops I ended up doin' security. I got a gig as a bodyguard for this big-time titty bar owner. Well, actually, they weren't titty bars.

"It wasn't long before he invited me into his 'inner circle.'

"Me and three other guys went to his new club for cigars and drinks. It was after hours and the place was smoked out as it was. There were clouds of the stuff, you couldn't even see the walls. We sat at a round table. Markham was across from me.

"He told me, 'Scotty, things are going to change around here and I need men by my side that I can trust. Can I trust you, Scotty?' 'Cause that's what he called me. Scotty.

"So, I say, 'Yeah. Of course you can, Mr. Markham. What do I look like? An asshole?'

"And that's when the girl comes, drop-dead gorgeous. I don't normally get turned on by redheads, but this one had somethin', green eyes that sparkled plus an Irish accent that vibrated through me. I could feel it in my balls, real freaky-like.

"She says, 'Alright there boys, I want you to roll up your sleeves for me.'

"Jimmy, he's to my right, he goes, 'Whatchoo gonna do give us shots?' and laughs it up.

"But that's kinda what she did. We all rolled up our sleeves, 'cause Markham was nodding and she'd asked nice, and like I said I could feel that accent of hers in my balls. She held her hand up and wiggled her fingers. They stretched and cracked until they were so long and pointy, I thought I'd scream. But, she was still smiling. And Markham was sipping his scotch like nothin' was wrong. So when she dragged that spike of a finger up my arm, cutting me right through to the bone, I wasn't expecting a thing.

"She was a werewolf," I said.

"Fuckin' A right. Didn't mean a thing to me, at first. The change was really . . . refreshing, freeing, kinda. But the other night, when we were chasing Markham's quarry, and I saw you, it got me back on track. I need to know everything. Markham doesn't tell us shit."

"What do you mean? You're not chasing Gil?"

"Well yeah. That's the excuse, but really I wanted to talk to you. I thought I'd lost your trail back in Ellensburg. It was sheer luck that I saw that ugly ass camper on the freeway a ways back."

"You're not here to kill us?" I frowned.

"Nope." He spread his arms wide as though I'd run in for a hug.

"Swear to God?"

"Yep."

Hold up. Confusion setting in.

Hold up. Hold up. Hold up.

It's terribly flattering that I've got people searching for me, and all. But if Scott wasn't hunting us, and Honey'd already revealed her secrets, then who did that leave?

Who killed Granita, or whatever her name was? Who was scratching at the bathroom door? What had freaked Fishhook out to the point of nearly overdosing on shrooms? Had he seen something?

Was it even necessary to continue driving to Rapid City? Maybe I could get out of this whole Mother thing.

And, possibly more importantly, where was I going to find a new outfit?

Chapter 13

Road Games and Gamey Discussion

Genuinely weird celebrities are rarely among the un-
dead. You'd imagine Tim Burton might be hiding a zom-
bie secret, or his wife Helena Bonham Carter, for that
matter. Not so, or, at least, not yet.
        —Celebrity Gas Chamber *with Lola LeGrave*

I tossed the bartender's torso onto the growing tangle of corpses mounded on dance floor. There were a few stragglers inside when we got the idea to burn the place down, but since their backs were broken, we just left those groaning paraplegics where they lay. Honey found a gas can near the generator and Scott did the honors of christening The White House like a priest shaking his aspergillum over sleepy parishioners. I set the blaze with the last of my cigarettes, sending flames scurrying off to every corner of the rat's nest.

A total burn was really the only thing that could be done. The grand total was twenty-four bodies—oops—but it couldn't be avoided. If those Nazis had just practiced some common decency, we wouldn't have to have resorted to our basest instincts.

The place was a dump anyway; we were doing Idaho a favor sparking it. I mean, seriously. I'm not much for college parties—though I've certainly spent enough time wiping up in strange bathrooms after frat house keggers[93]—but at least they hire maids to sweep once a week. This place was ankle deep in dry peanut shells, insects and rat poop. A fire was inevitable.

Does that sound like rationalizing?

"Rather than stand around and wait for the fire department to show up, let's think of a plan and act on it," I said.

We stood in a circle near the camper. Dusk was making its comeback and the camper door slapped open revealing a groggy Gil. He'd dragged his sorry ass outside just in time for the barbecue. He slipped between Wendy and me and whispered, "What's up?"

"Well let's see," I said. "Since you've been out that girl that was as white as poached chicken was murdered."

"Murdered!" His face went whiter than normal.

"Oh . . . hold on, it gets better," Wendy added.

"Then we swing by this shit hole to get Honey some refreshment, and the whole thing turned into a giant zombie fuck-up."

Gil eyed Scott up and down, came in close and whispered, "Who's the new yum?"

"That's Scott, he's Markham's man."

Scott offered his hand, but Gil pushed me forward forcing an impromptu brushing of my breast.

"Oh . . . I'm sorry," Scott stumbled. "I didn't mean—"

"It's fine. I suppose you'd have gotten around to that sooner or later." I winked.

"Wha—what?" He coughed as though he'd inhaled a little phlegm.

"Dirty." Wendy crossed her arms, clearly jealous that such a fortuitous mistake had happened to me rather than her. I'd seen her eyeing my trophy boy all afternoon. Sad. "I say we keep on going to Butte and talk to the Kraken. Some of us are still focused on the job at hand." She gestured at Honey.

"Well, that's fine and all, but what about Becky?"

---

[93] Sh! Keep that to yourself, please.

"Oh, I'm sure she won't be a problem." Wendy fished in her purse and hooked a lipstick.

"Uh . . . no. I mean who killed her. Is there someone else following us?"

"S o m e o n e else?" I asked. "Like who?"

"Didn't you say she was with a couple of cultists?" Fishhook had regained his clarity once more and seemed to have a knack for amateur sleuthing. "They were the last ones to see her alive. Who's to say they didn't snow you and actually cut the girl up after a double team?"

Honey flinched. "She was a virgin. I don't think—"

"Or maybe one got jealous being

Honey's Super Hot Electro Newer Wave Party Playlist

Holla!

Dragonette • *"I Get Around"*

CSS • *"Let's Make Love and Listen to Death from Above"*

Natalie Portman's Shaved Head • *"Iceage Babeland"*

Peaches • *"Fuck the Pain Away"*

New Young Pony Club • *"Ice Cream"*

Justice vs. Simian • *"We Are Your Friends"*

I Am X • *"Kiss and Swallow"*

Datarock • *"Computer Camp Love"*

Client • *"Radio"*

Fischerspooner • *"Never Win"*

Van She • *"Kelly"*

White Rose Movement • *"Girls in the Back"*

forced to watch his buddy get all the mouthwork. And I do mean the old golfball cleaner, if you know what I mean." He elbowed Scott, who gave a little snort before shaking it off for a look of disgust.

"Enough!" I interrupted. "You've made your point. Does anyone remember where they were headed?"

Gil's eyes dropped away from staring down Scott and looked at me. "Billings, I think. But they did say something about going to some kind of compound."

"Probably their cult headquarters. Somebody could try to catch up to them." I glanced at Scott. "Someone with a fast, if not entirely incognito, car"

"I like orange and I'm not ashamed of it." Scott shoved his hands into his front jean pockets.

"So?" I stepped forward close enough to embrace.

"So what?"

"Will you track down the killers . . . Officer?" I ran my fingers through my hair, lifting and letting the bulk of my waves drop in cascading layers. He was entranced. Duh.

"Yeah."

"Yeah, what?"

"I'll do it."

Wendy snorted and shook her head.

"What?" I asked her, daring her to say something to mess up my seduction of the cute werewolf.

"I'll drive the camper." She stalked off.

Honey insisted on playing her iPod over the Volvo's stereo, so for the next two hours I was transported back to the '80s through an apparent resurgence of new wave (see track listing). Everything old is new again and all that. I decided to unhook it from the camper and give Wendy a bit of breathing room.[94]

---

[94] So to speak.

Honey made the mistake of resting her feet on the dash, once and only once. The action prompted our first argument, in which I insisted that that behavior was grounds for a slow death. She had a differing viewpoint, but acquiesced when I gave her a peek at how big I could open my mouth.

"Had enough?"

"Uh . . . yeah. That's fucking gross."

"Language!" I yelled.

The word popped right out, sullying the air like a smelter. My tone was even different, like I was channeling.

Mother.

The exchange was familiar enough to remind me of Ethel, and her infamous classes on manners. Unsatisfied with scarring one person's childhood (mine, obviously), Ethel took on pupils from the neighborhood for a weekly "get-together." She called it her Cavalcade of Etiquette—emphasis on each and every one of the hard consonants. It gave her the opportunity to dress up and smoke cigarettes from long holders—throw her a full-length fur and a skunk spot and you'd have Cruella DeVille hawking deportment. Yet adults bought it, much like they do with road-side attractions.[95]

"Children!" she'd shout. "Pop quiz time!"

We stood behind our assigned dining room chairs awaiting the task. Shannon Franks shed drops of fearful tears that hung from her chin like a row of moles. Chuck Abramowitz shivered as though fresh from a dip with his polar bear club. I cocked my hip out and searched my fingernails for flaws. Those kids were amateurs.

Ethel reached around the corner into the foyer, retrieving a red velvet bag that jingled like Christmas bells. Faces changed. A small degree of hope fluttered amongst the students. I was suspicious.

"For this week's examination . . ." her voice rose with every word. "A simple matter of place settings." She marched over to the table and upended the bag sending a clanging shower of

---

[95] Largest ball of yarn? That's gotta be fun.

silverware onto the padded surface.[96] Shaking the remaining few loose, she took a long drag from her cigarette, scanned the horrified faces, turned and stalked from the room in a cloud of carcinogens, heels clicking on the hardwood like ball-peen hammers. "Formal dinner service! You have five minutes!"

Terror spread.

She might have easily proclaimed, "Medical experiments for the lot of you," from the expressions that ringed the table. There were prayers and hand-wringing and more than one suicide attempt, though I was able to wrestle the butter knife away from little Billy Armstrong before he did too much damage.

Lucky for the group, I was on to Ethel's scheme of testing us on subjects no one in their right mind would study, let alone a group of primary school children; I'd done my own homework, and this time it paid off. We sorted the various sizes of forks, spoons and knives and divvied them up evenly. We passed china dinner, salad, and bread plates, and crystal stemware with the utmost care neither to break nor leave a finger print. I held up each utensil in the correct hand and waited for them to echo before placing it. By the time Mother's heels tapped out their approaching rhythm, the table was set for an epicurean feast in the Hapsburg tradition.

Ethel was not pleased, her eyes skipped from one place setting to the next. "I see one of you is trying to be amusing." She glowered in my direction, yet refused to make eye contact. Instead, she lit another cigarette and leaned against the wall eyeing the students with the kind of loathing most often reserved for wait staff or civil servants.

"Get out of my sight," she whispered, the last syllable hissed like compressed air.

It was a mad stampede for the door. I almost made it.

"Not you." Her fingers caught in the back of my shirt col-

---

[96] You didn't really think Mother would scar the formal dining table, did you? She may have been a whore, but she wasn't sloppy.

lar, hanging me on the first button. She spun me around and drew me close. "You missed the white wine glasses."

My mouth dropped open. My hands balled into fists.

"I'd assumed you'd be having red," I said, eyes wide with defiance. "Just like every fucking night."

Smack.

I didn't even see her palm move, but my cheek sure noticed.

"A lady doesn't use that kind of language."

Language.

I shook the memory off and turned the radio down just as Peaches began a porn-as-anthem groove. "Sorry about snapping."

"Hmm?" Honey flipped her way through a *Vogue* for the third time.

"Oh . . . the comment about your language. I'm sorry. Talk how you like, I'm not your mother."

"No. No. You're right. It was rude, I apologize."

I couldn't have this girl thinking I was maternal, anything but that. "Please feel free to say fuck, shit or cooze, anything that comes normal. I'm really not one to judge."

Her eyebrow arched. "Well, I'm sorry, anyway."

"Fine." It was too late, I was stuck in the role of judgmental adult and it was all Ethel's fault. I could feel that pillow in my hands and imagine the horror in her eyes. I couldn't wait to get to Rapid City.

Ethel was a goner.

Butte sneaks up on you like a certain homeless guy's farts.

The interstate cuts through moonlit grasses, rolling across hills in dark waves. There are few homesteads and even fewer lights, bar the occasional semi speeding back to Spokane or Seattle. So, when the freeway banked, I wasn't expecting to see a glowing letter M on the hillside.

"What do you suppose that stands for?" I asked Honey.

"Montana?"

"Too easy." I grinned. "How about machete mouth."

"What's that?"

"You know. Like when someone has too many lip piercings."

"No. No. No way. It stands for . . ." She hesitated as if gauging how far she could take this.

"Go for it," I urged.

"Machine Gun Masturbation."

"What? That sounds all kinds of wrong."

"It's when a guy's masturbating and then keeps on going after he cums. Like after it starts to hurt. Boys are so fucking gross. It's crazy, right?"

"And awesome. I'm totally going to accuse Gil of doing that when he goes to sleep in the morning. We'll just pretend that everyone knows it."

"Absolutely and speaking of masturbation, Officer Scotty is certainly worthy of a rubdown."

"Did I just give you a license to be naughty?"

"Kind of yeah." She swiveled in her seat to face me. "When the two of you were talking . . . um . . . it was like high on the mack-o-meter." She put her arms together like a genie and then raised one into a rigid point.

"Do you think?"

"Oh yeah. Totally." She nodded. "I thought he was going to pop a mad boner. Maybe that's what the 'M' stands for. *Mad* boner."

I gave her a broad smile as we crested a hill and the M passed from view. There was a pleasant comfortable feeling between us; the air was warm with bonding.[97] It was nice.[98]

The highway slices Butte in two, old on one side, lounging elderly and decrepit on the hill, and the newer—but no less decrepit—spread out across the flats blistered with strip malls and

---

[97] Take that, Wendy!
[98] That didn't sound too sweet, did it? Well, don't get used to it.

fast food. I pulled into the world's dirtiest KFC to fatten up Honey—I mean feed, obviously. Despite that previous comment, I'm not my mother.

Ahem.

Wendy pulled the camper into the next alley and waved us in.

Buying a piece of chicken from an establishment that can't manage a clean floor is a big stretch for me. Factor in a brutal acne-infestation on the counter fuck, whose name tag purports "Gunrunner" and—I'm pretty sure—you're taking your life into your own hands.

"What do you want?" he asked in a monotone so labored he could have fallen over dead any second.

"A number two with Diet Coke, please." Honey smiled at the little geek. She's a much better woman than I. I could barely stomach the sight of him. Gunrunner's powder black hair hung in greasy clumps on either side of his sallow cheeks. Round old man spectacles amplified his beady eyes like marbles sitting in a couple of dirty shot glasses.

He squinted and pecked at the keys. "And you?"

"Oh. I don't eat chicken," I said, nearly just blurting out, "Nope, just human flesh, but not yours, buddy."

Honey giggled, presumably at my discomfort. My dirty high heels were sliding around on the greasy tiles and my tablecloth sarong wasn't much to look at.

She carried the tray into the dining room to find a seat, only to be found, instead.

"Over here," a voice called from the corner.

The Cleavers were huddled around a red bucket, greasy chicken clutched in their fists. Ward dipped his drumstick in the mashed potatoes and left it there to circle the Styrofoam like a chicken shark.[99] He stood and motioned for us to take the empty table next to them.

---

[99] If it moved that would make a much better simile. But, it's my memoir and you'll take what I give you.

"Please," he said. "Join us."

"Wipe your face, Billy," Mrs. Cleaver said with a smile. The boy dabbed at his chin with the paper napkin from his lap. As usual, his sister Clare was sitting so close as to be nearly on his lap. I shivered.

We slid into the plastic booth next to them and Honey started to eat.

I hadn't thought of the family since they tore out of the campground, but these people were just freaky enough to have an entire room in their tour bus devoted to weapons of medieval torture. "Sweetheart," I imagined Ward would call. "Please bring me the Mallet of Unbearable Torment and the hamburger buns, wouldya?" They were certainly as likely suspects as the Mormons, or whatever they were.

I eyed them suspiciously, then looked to Honey to see if she were thinking the same thing. She just shrugged.

"Not eating, Ms. Feral?" Billy asked.

"Not here."

"Not a fan of the fried foods, I suspect," Mrs. Cleaver said. "That's how she keeps that gorgeous figure."

Ward winked. I had to get away from this subject before I said something I'd regret. "You guys were sure hot to get out of Coeur d'Alene. In a hurry or something?"

"No. No. Just hate to mess up the old travel plan." Ward reached into his jacket and pulled out a flip book on a short spiral of wire, handmade probably, and I didn't have to guess by who. "Make these up with each trip. Clips of map routes for each day, campgrounds, restaurants, all that."

"This place is on your list?" I asked.

"Absolutely." He flipped through the little book and pointed out the KFC under the words "evening snack", but before Billings and Wal-Mart, apparently the next destination.

I scanned the floor. Chicken nuggets shared real estate with dust-covered fries and wads of greasy napkins. It was hard to believe that someone had planned to come to such a shithole, though I'd certainly need to prepare to return to the restaurant. Hip waders would have to be in play.

"I see."

"He's going to turn those little books into a million dollar idea one day," Mrs. Cleaver beamed. The rest of the quartet nodded. The same grin spread on each pasty face. These people were either too nice or too clueless to have killed that little albino girl. I didn't have the heart to tell them that AAA had beaten Ward to the punch and gave individualized flip maps out to their customers. For free.

"How did all that nastiness turn out?" he leaned toward me, a look of concern spread on his face like margarine—and not butter, nothing that real.

"We got Becky's hear—" Honey started, but I kicked her under the table. "Ow."

"Poor girl," I said. "The cops think it was a bear. Can you believe that?"

"A bear?" Billy's mouth dropped open. "But how—"

Ward kicked his son under the table. The boy's mouth snapped shut. "Imagine that. A bear. Poor thing."

"Oh my." Mrs. Cleaver gathered their trash and piled it on their tray. "Well, it's been nice chatting with you ladies. We really must be going though."

The family slid out of the booth and headed for the door.

Ward lingered. "You two take care. Maybe we'll see you up the road."

"Look forward to it," I said.

Honey rolled her eyes.

He patted the table and strode off.

Honey pointed at his back with a chicken wing. "Now those people give me the fucking creeps."

How can you not love her? Surrounded by zombies and vampires, her friend's heart nearby in a Ziploc bag and potential food poisoning at the KFC from hell were not enough to faze the girl, but the Cleavers creeped her out.

Chapter 14

The Tall and Short of the Thing

There is a multitude of supernatural water creatures in our lakes, streams and oceans. Land-dwelling undead would unlikely come across these beings without some sort of gift or offering. Take the elusive stream unicorn, for instance. An aquatic supernatural unknown until 1994, when it was discovered that a gift of red Sour Patch Kids dropped into a Northern California stream was enough to call it forth . . .
—Ominous Guides: The Redwoods and Beyond

Wendy snapped her cell closed as she rounded the dented corner of the camper—not that they didn't all have dents, they did—this one was just particularly denty. "The Kraken's at a place called the Berkeley Pit, not far from here. Madame Gloria was certain, but a little bit sketchy about directions."

"Her *moderately accurate* spirits must be acting up. What the hell is a Berkeley Pit?" I asked.

Wendy shrugged. Fishhook shook his head. Honey sucked at her Diet Coke.

"I'll run into that gas station and ask directions." Gil trotted off across the vacant main street toward the glowing kiosk beyond the pumps. It was only 8:00 at night, but he'd be the only customer. For so little to look at it was a wonder none of us had managed to see the white on brown sign that said "Berkeley Pit" with an arrow pointing to the left.

"Gil!" I yelled as the door shut behind him. "Damn."

When he returned, we rode with Honey and Mr. Kim back across the freeway and up the hill toward a dimly lit clump of buildings nestled next to a massive black hole. Wendy refused to come until someone did something about her own hole, and since no one had any idea as to how to fix it, she just sat and sulked at the camper table. Fishhook stayed, too, he had some sorting to do, it seemed.

"So this 'pit' is supposed to be the world's largest pit mine, stripped clean of copper or something, and now it's full of acid. Or at least that's what I gathered from the slow-ass clerk." Gil hunched between the bucket seats and tapped Honey on the shoulder. "Are you nervous, kid?"

"Yeah kind of, to see him again after searching so long, you know?" She turned in her seat, resting on her knees with her back to the dash. "Is he?" She pointed at the back seat.

Mr. Kim shook his head, and I thought he might be crying but I couldn't quite make out the definition of his face as his hands were in the way. I adjusted the rearview mirror. "I think we're almost there. It looks like a bigger sign and a visitors' center up ahead."

I pointed the Volvo into a space next to a trailer with the words Gift Shop scrawled over the door. There was a dim light coming from the boxy building's window, but no shadows or movement of any kind inside. Over to the right was some kind of mine entrance framed and faced in wood and topped with a chain link fence and barbed wire. An arch in the middle led to a darkened area beyond.

"This is it," I said, pointing to the routered wooden sign above the entry; a single light lit it from above.

Berkeley Pit.

"You take care of sister." Mr. Kim wrung his ethereal hands in a display of anxiety.

Gil allowed his arm to hover about Kimmy's shoulders. "She's gonna be fine, old man."

When I opened my door, a malodorous wave of rusty metal assaulted my sinuses, burning through my head like lava. I squeezed the bridge of my nose and massaged my brow, but neither seemed to be particularly effective. I glanced at my companions. Neither Honey nor Gil seemed to be having a reaction, at all. Rather, they stood side by side watching an odd figure approach from the direction of the wooden arch.

He was a giant, and not in a steroid puffed bodybuilder kind of way. He stood at least seven feet tall with thin gangly arms and legs, an elongated oval for a head and a face sheathed in darkness. You'd think he was an alien, or a basketball player, except for the tuxedo and tails he wore. And not a single gold chain to destroy the look. It was when he opened his mouth that the exotic illusion was dismembered.

"Hey, youze guys. Welcome. This here's the single most visited supernatural attraction west of the fuckin' Mississippi gash. Ain't nobody don't wanna see the Mighty Kraken. And if youze got the gift, you'll be right in there. Youze got the gift, right?"

He slinked up to Gil, knees popping sideways with every step, and glared down into the vampire's face. Gil lurched backward but was caught by the shoulder and held close. The shadow lifted from our host's face. Gil closed his eyes and started counting aloud. "One one thousand, two one thousand."

"Youze guys got the gift, right?" The guy whispered this time. The air hissed out of him like a punctured lung.

I slipped in front of Honey, who clutched the back of my shirt, and we shuffled closer to see what had spooked my friend to the point of psychobabble anxiety tricks. As I peeked around, the arc of the thing's smooth blue cheeks and a single pointy ear came into view, followed by an inky black eye and teeth to match. A cigarette dangled between shriveled gray lips. So . . . not pretty. In fact, reports of Bat Boy's death were apparently exaggerated—no wonder the *Weekly World News* went out of business. Yet, I didn't remember him being an Italian demon from New York.

I fished the Ziplocked heart from my bag and shook it over Gil's shoulder. "Right here, motherfucker. You can back off any time now."

He retreated, spreading his arms wide. "Then we got no fuckin' problem. Vinnie!" he wailed over his shoulder.

The trailer door opened and a squat brown-skinned lump, the shape and texture of chocolate pudding, but with similar ears and face to Stretch, waddled down the stairs and toward us.

"Unleash the Kraken!" the alleged Bat Boy yelled.

"Whadda you mean, Eddie?" Vinnie approached with a low stuttering roll, as though propelled by many legs, rather than the requisite two. "There ain't no goddamned—"

I could hear the tall demon whisper, "Call down to Frank and tell him we've got some fuckin' visitors, and make it quick!"

He snatched the baggie from my hand and waddled off through the arch and out of sight. I swear to God, that thing looked just like a dollop of chocolate pudding. It's probably a good thing Wendy didn't come.

"Now if youze'll just follow me we'll get on the tram for the guided tour." Tour with two syllables, naturally. He retrieved a garage door opener from his tuxedo jacket and pointed it at the side of the wooden wall. A small door cranked open with considerable creaks and whines and ejected a long, thin, wheeled vehicle with folded seats and angled footrests, a gangplank on wheels. He flipped up the front seat and punched a button on the floor. A low buzz filled the air as the contraption's engine purred.

"Well? What are youze fuckin' waitin' for? An invitation?"

Honey sat behind the demon and Gil behind me. The seats weren't uncomfortable despite being a bit rickety. I was pretty sure the place wasn't nearly the tourist draw Eddie'd suggested,

> **Leviathan**
> *The World's Oldest*
> *Aquatic Mystic*
> *(The Kraken of Butte, MT)*

until he hit another button on the garage door opener and the little Berkeley pit sign above the arch folded inward and was traded mechanically for an astonishingly gaudy hunk of neon (see inset). The garish pinks, blues and purples lit up the hole in the wall, revealing a chalky white tunnel. The effect was not un-like looking down the throat of a strep throat victim. The line of pipes that ran the ceiling even resembled the veiny stretch of fiber that connects the tongue to the base of the mouth.

Eddie pushed another button and a metal lever popped up from the left side of the tram. He pulled it and we lurched for-ward slowly.

From his right, a microphone stand pivoted from some hid-den pocket and popped up and found its way to puckered mouth. His Italian accent was abandoned for a whitewashed mid-western pronunciation.

"Leviathan, The Kraken of Butte—just like the sign says—is the oldest living aquatic mystic," Eddie began, steering us into the tunnel at a snail's crawl. "Originally hailing from the icy chop of the English Channel, Levi—as we now refer to him—sought warmer waters in the early 1900s. He traveled through the sea's deepest channels, confronting mystery and danger with the enthusiasm and strength befitting an ancient of his stature. He navigated the caves that honeycomb the earth's core and fought a multitude of ferocious battles before weaving his way to the surface of this flooded mine. Not without consequence, either. His flesh was battered and torn and he was in desperate need of rest and recuperation."

We crept into the silent tube, a pipe more than a cave, really, walls painted a hideous funereal pallor. A dim light glowed ahead, flickering occasionally as though obscured by shadows or a large enough presence to block the opening.

"So, Eddie?" Gil clutched my shoulder as he asked, leaning around to get a look at our tour guide.

"Whadda you want? I'm kinda talkin' up here, you know?"

"The guy at the gas station said this water is full of acid. Said that nothing can survive in there. Said that this one time a flock of geese landed in there and the whole lot of them died. So how—"

"Levi's different, ain't he? It'd be like someone asking you why you don't catch HIV from all the blood you gobble up all over the place. You're dead. Levi's kind of like that. He's just never been what we'd call alive."

"Huh?"

"I don't expect you to understand. No one can comprehend the majesty that is Levi. He's God-like. He must be revered."

Gil sighed. "Got it."

I yawned. The whole scene reeked of a roadside scam. We were probably wasting our time and a perfectly good albino heart for nothing more than a guy in a rubber squid outfit. Honey was bouncing on her palms with excitement. Poor thing, I thought. She's heading for a let-down.

. . . and the spiel continued.

"The Kraken of Butte rose first in the lower depths below the site. The warm pocketed eddies leached minerals from the surrounding rock, creating a healing pool for Levi's battle wounds to heal. After the mine was stripped and the pit flooded, the mighty Kraken broke through the crust, swam the shy mile to the surface and encountered his first human being, a cranky Italian named Farelli.

"Alfonse Farelli was a miner before the copper veins were worked to nothing. He had a family of seven children and an obese overbearing wife named Sofia. When Levi first set eyes on the man, he was falling through the air toward the murky waters. Being a caring sort, Levi caught him in one of his softer, less spiny tentacles and brought him close to his good eye.

"After the man stopped screaming, he asked, 'What the fuck are you?' to which the Kraken had no response, not speaking English, and all. Instead, he experienced the man's fear and granted a wish that the Italian couldn't articulate and that the Kraken didn't really understand. He gave the man the strength of the demons of the deep—"

"Bullshit," I interrupted. "Can we just skip the script and pick up the pace? I could knit a sweater in the time it's gonna take, or at least hire someone to do it."

"Sh!" Honey spun around, eyes all squinty and judgmental.

"Fine. Please excuse me." I pulled a smoke from my purse and lit up.

"There's no smoking in the pit!" Eddie yelled. He'd pulled out a hand mirror from somewhere and was eyeing me suspiciously.

I butted the cigarette and cracked my knuckles. "Go on then." Gil prodded me and passed up his flask. I don't normally imbibe on platelets but this was proving to be a long ride and, well, I'd forgotten my hooch in the car.

"Levi," Eddie continued, "Gifted Alfonse with all the strength and wisdom of the aquatic demons and for the low low price of just three of his young sons. That's where yours truly comes in. Vinnie and Frank and me were just young when it happened. The Kraken needed guards and he got 'em."

"That's sad." Honey picked at a name carved into the wall as we passed.

"No way. We was totally into it. No more fuckin' school. No more chores. No more watchin' Mom drain the bottle every night. It was good."

We were coming up on the tunnel's exit; it seemed to let out onto a platform. I could just see Vinnie waddling back and forth and another figure kneeling at the wooden guardrail. Praying perhaps.

"Here she is." Eddie pulled hard on a lever and the brakes pumped to a jerky stop. "Exit the vehicle and form a line to the left."

Honey was up and ready in an instant, while Gil needed to

be nudged awake before he scrambled from the low seat and took his place behind me.[100] The tall demon gestured for us to approach the guardrail quietly. The genuflecting figure was shrouded in a flowing hooded robe and mumbled unintelligible words. Maybe these were the basis for the Cosby Kids, I wondered. This new guy, Frank, was aping a decent Mushmouth.[101]

Lights shone down into the pit and illuminated a massive lake that butted up to a terraced hillside opposite us. A refinery stood as dark and silent as sculpture to one side. Vinnie started hopping.

"He's coming! He's coming."

Gil and I looked at each other, repressing giggles—because we're juvenile like that—and looked down the side of the pit at a mass of bubbles rising from a churning whirlpool. A mist surrounded the disturbance, as though the splashing was a result of some giant invisible waterfall.

Then it surfaced.

A slimy gray gelatinous thing.

All ten feet of it. Tentacled, yes, but—come on—so less than impressive. I expected a creature at least the size of a Greyhound bus but instead I got a Volkswagen. It clambered up the pit wall, tentacles rolling out, connecting with the rock and dragging its bulbous floppy head behind. I wished I had a flashlight to check for wires or a track.

It seemed legit, though.

It tossed loose boulders aside with ease. They cracked against the pit and fell to the water, smacking like belly flops. Occasionally it would rear back revealing a jagged beak protruding from a thick meaty welt at its center. Sure there was no way this thing was going to take down a pirate ship, but it was definitely capable of giving a human body a good munch.[102]

---

[100] That's right Gil. You need to know your place. And it will always be behind me. Snap.

[101] Noba shitba.

[102] Mmm. Body.

"Behold! Leviathan!" Eddie swept his arms wide with the pride of a religious fanatic.

"I thought he'd be bigger," Honey said

"What?" Eddie, Vinnie and Frank snapped in unison.

"I just—" Honey shrugged.

"Silence!" the kneeling brother ordered. He reached up, hands resembling flexible lobster claws, pulled back the hood— and since I'm making foreskin references, let me add—and uncovered his head, an engorged mass pitted with suckers and short stubbly tentacles where hair should be. The look was total venereal disease.

We must have looked like the row of clown mouths waiting for water stream at those stupid carnival booths, from the shock the scene engendered. Gil glanced over at me and gagged. Honey covered her mouth. An odor wafted from the thing somewhere between cheddar cheese and seaweed and I ought to know; it was so bad I sniffed it twice, just to make sure.

"What the fuck? I thought this was your brother?" I asked.

"Oh. That's Frank. He spends a lot more time with Levi than us. You get like that."

We didn't even need to discuss it; the three of us stepped back from the guardrail like pageant contestants, completely in sync and mortified. I don't take chances on blemishes let alone tentacles. Vinnie didn't seem to want much to do with the approaching creature either. He leaned against the tunnel entrance, an unlit cigarette dangling from a sucker on his face and fiddled with a Zippo, occasionally sparking it up. Eddie spun at him each time, sneering.

"You get like that?" I pointed. "Just from being around it?"

Eddie waved me off with those exceptionally long fingers. "Don't youze worry, you gots to be around it for more than a couple of minutes to notice any change."

The more I stared, the more they looked like ten tentacles hanging from his grayed hands. I imagined that slimy calamari slipping across the soft supple skin of my cheek and a shudder rolled through me that must have looked like a seizure.

Gil touched my back. "Are you okay?"

"I will be . . . when we get the fuck out of here." I forced myself to look over the edge again just in time for the Kraken to rise up and peer at us with an inky eye the size of a bowling ball. Its tentacles swirled about us and coiled around the posts.

Frank stood up and began conversing with the Kraken in a rapid-fire gibberish. The giant octopus responded in a garbled wet tone that rattled the platform and jettisoned thick ropes of spittle that splattered across the robed brother. He slipped in the puddles of saliva until finally he fell into a kneel.

"Ask your question." Frank wiped the goo from his mouth and flicked it against the wooden planks.

Honey stepped forward and spoke with uncharacteristic hesitancy. "Yes, Leviathan, er, Levi?"

"Mighty Leviathan," Eddie corrected. "To you."

"Mighty Leviathan," she parroted. "We understand you might know a way for me to see my dead brother's ghost."

The brothers looked at each other. Eddie raised an eyebrow.

Honey continued unperturbed. "It lives in this lady's car. Is that possible? For me to see him again, I mean. Even for just one time?"

Frank turned to the creature and let loose a flurry of burps and gagging noises.

The Kraken slumped back from the platform and hung from its arms, placing its full weight on the supports of the deck. It creaked and shuddered, but held firm. A long sigh gargled from Levi's throat.

Silence.

I looked at my watch, at my skin. More than a few minutes had passed, and since I already had the gray skin down under my body makeup, I wasn't looking forward to any appendages sprouting like discarded asparagus or some shit like that.

"Can we—"

"Shut up!" Eddie demanded. "He's telling Frank the answer to your query."

I leaned forward to see if I could make out a sound, but all I heard was a low hissing and the occasional spit bubble pop. The creature was watching us, but particularly Honey. Seemingly reading her. I remembered the story of the brother's father and how the Kraken had read his mind. Still, I wasn't certain the whole thing wasn't a scam. These guys came across as con-men more than confident guards of a mystical beast. Yet moments later, Frank clutched the rail and rose on slippery feet.

He turned to Honey. "Levi has spoken. There *is* a way the girl can see her brother again."

Honey clapped her hands and beamed.

"Kill her," he said.

The girl's smile disappeared, replaced by a sneer then a look of horror then a sneer, again.

Frank shuffled toward the tunnel as though our tour had come to a pleasant, mutually agreeable end.

"Hold up, Bud," I said. "We trudge all the way up to this shithole, bring you a human heart. No. Scratch that. A fresh *virgin* heart. And all we get is a curt, 'kill her'? What the fuck? I could have figured that shit out myself."

Levi let out a shriek that shook the platform and rattled the bolts that secured it to the pit wall. Someone was a little crabby.

"No. No. Levi. We got it right here! Promise! Vinnie!" Eddie reached behind him but his brother simply shrugged and backed away into the tunnel. Where he stood lay the empty Ziploc baggy, slimy with Granita's coagulated blood. Beads of the crimson goo littered the surrounding boards. Vinnie must have gotten the munchies.

The platform splintered and gaps formed between the wooden planks, already transforming from solid footholds to wobbly funhouse ride. We may as well have been standing on skateboards.

It felt like a good time to run.

I clutched Honey's arm and pulled her toward the exit, Gil hot on our heels.

"Vinnie! Get back here! We're gonna need that hear—" Eddie's voice was clipped into silence.

In the next moment, a splash echoed down the pipe followed by a warble that could only be Frank screaming and the crashing dismemberment of timbers as the platform collapsed into the massive lake of acid.

Shame.

It could quite possibly have been the most exciting roadside attraction I'd ever seen.

Chapter 15

An Expedition, Wal-Mart Style

*No. Not bondage. Silly. Bonding parties. They are all
the rage. Since we lose our families as a result of our various transformations, it's only natural to want to develop
connections with a carefully chosen few. Pharmacy is even
starting up an Evening of Speed Bonding . . .*
    —Constance Clarity on *Dark Evening with
    Cameron Hansen*

"He's not the *only* mystic, you know?" Vinnie squatted next to
the Volvo's front tire, ran his slimy mitt across the black tread.
Mr. Kim glowered above him through a cloud of cigarette smoke,
blending in at times. For a second, I thought the little creep had
shivved a knife in it, but when he stood the object in his hand
looked nothing like a knife. He noticed my stare. "Oh this? Cars
are kinda my thing. Just checking the pressure." He held out the
gauge to show me.

"I told him get away from goddamn car," my ghosty friend
said. "He no goddamn listen."

"Thanks, Mr. Badass." I gave him my sassiest wink. Mr. Kim
was still getting the hang of profanity, but he was catching on. I
stomped over and made like I'd kick him away from the car if
he didn't move.[103]

"Don't!"

---

[103] And . . . I think you know I would have.

I kicked the air in front of him, causing the little welt to flinch. It's the small things in life that make you feel good, like a hug.

"I guess I have difficulty listening to someone who'd throw their family under the bus like you just did."

He skittered away a few feet and stammered, "The-the-they'll be fine. Just a little fuckin' wet. Side effects, you know." He lifted his trouser leg to reveal a tentacled appendage. "Besides. I been lookin' for an opportunity to get the fuck outta here. This seems to be it."

Honey stepped in between and interrupted the love fest. "You were talking about another mystic."

I reached for her shoulder. "C'mon. Let's just get out of here."

She swatted my hand away. "Just wait. God." She spat the G-word out like a punishment.

"Oh yeah. Levi's not the only seein' thing around here." Vinnie shifted from one set of tentacles to the other. Comfortable with his newfound upper hand.[104] Pig. "Crow Res gots a fuckin' shaman. And he ain't no mooch like 'the Mighty Levi.' Got a job and everything."

"So where do we find this . . . shaman?" I was hesitant to give any credence to the guy's story. For all I knew this was going to be just another in a string of fabulous cock-ups that seemed to be scripted for us by some unknown writer somewhere, some overweight forty-year old loafing in cargo shorts and flip-flops.

"He sweeps up nights at the deep Crow grocers. Youze go and find the emcee. He might have your answers."

"The emcee?" Honey asked.

"You heard me. I gotta go pack. I'm fixin' to get outta this here shithole. Got a girl waiting for me in Vegas." He waddled up the steps of the trailer and slammed the door behind him.

[104] Or tentacle? Upper sucker?

Gil and I gagged, but Mr. Kim just sighed and sank to a kneel on the hood. "Honey don't look happy."

It was true. She'd been watching us interact with her brother, a solemn frown marring her pretty face like a hot zit.

"Oh Honey. It's not like we're going to go ahead with the Kraken's idea. We wouldn't do that."

"I know. It's just that you both seemed so willing to give up." She glanced off toward the lights of downtown Butte. "Maybe Wendy should have come."

Ouch. I won't lie. Those words bit into my cold dead heart like an unwelcome memory. Much like when I'd seen them arm and arm. Or when they'd been chatting while stacking body parts like firewood. I wanted to tell her that Wendy wouldn't have bothered to come even if she didn't have a hole the size of a cantaloupe in her gut. That she would've eaten the girl if any of us had turned our backs. But no. Because I'm a good friend, I bit my tongue. Not off, mind you.

"Wendy doesn't like this kind of stuff. If there were a party she'd have been all about it."

Gil glowered. I chased off his judgment with a sneer and a hiss. He clucked his tongue and swung the Volvo door open. I put my arm around the girl and led her to the car.

"We'll find an answer. You'll see Kimmy, again. And you won't have to die to do it. I promise."

She met my gaze. "You promise?"

"I promise. Now get in there and let's get back into town."

Honey hopped into the backseat with a bit more spring than I'd expected. Maybe I had some maternal instinct, after all. You'd think Ethel would have stripped any of that away cleaner than the flooded pit mine behind us. But, maybe I wasn't so much my mother's daughter. I mean. I'm not my mother's daughter. That's what I mean. If I could just stop measuring my life against that dying woman's, that'd be great.[105]

---

[105] Could someone arrange that for me? Thanks.

"You're going to have to mend this shit between you and Wendy." Gil flipped down the visor and picked at his canines.

"Why is it my responsibility?" I asked as I pulled out of the Berkeley Pit parking lot.

"Um. 'Cause you're the one being a bitch."

"How's that any different than any other time?"

He slapped the visor closed and turned toward me. "Because it's directed at Wendy. You've been bitchy this whole trip. Bickering. Snapping. It hasn't been pleasant, I can tell you. You're not fooling anyone, you know?"

Honey's eyes avoided mine in the rearview mirror. "I'm not?"

"No. This is all about your mother. Admit it."

"Maybe it is. But I—"

"Just take care of Wendy. If you're not up to it, I'll take care of your mother when the time comes."

"You'd do that?"

"Sure. I'm one of your best friends, remember? The other one's waiting for some relief from the tension."

I reached over and squeezed his hand, a rare tender moment between two friends plotting a dying woman's murder. It warms the cockles.[106]

Wendy and Fishhook were playing cards when we found them. Through the window of the RV, I could just make out his snorting laughter, between slurps of a Big Gulp. As we approached, I could see what had him so elated. Wendy's upper lip was coated with a swath of blood. The effect was not dissimilar to a bad Sam Elliot mustache, if he were a flesh-eating cannibal or enjoyed marinara in an altogether unhealthy way.

"That's attractive." I plopped down next to Fishhook.

"Body." She sucked the last bit of gristle from her teeth. "It does a zombie good."

---

[106] Whatever those are. Anyone?

"How's it working its way through?" I pointed to her stomach and the hole.

"Not good. I've had to rig up a little system." Wendy slid from the booth in a labored steady manner, opened her ratty western shirt to reveal a jerry-rigged poop bag attached to her severed intestine with twist ties and hair scrunchies. "The gas station guy was really helpful.

In more ways than one, I suspected.

I stood up and hugged her. "Oh sweetheart. Let's get back on the road. The next big store we find, we'll patch you up good. I see where you're going with that, though." I pointed at the self-colostomy. It seemed to be doing the trick since the shopping bag was nearly full. Wendy held the crinkly plastic like a bowling ball-sized tumor. It was not at all cute. "Nice work. Really."

"Shut up."

"Sorry."

"Yeah, right."

"No I'm serious. Sorry."

"Okay."

A quick phone call, 200-some miles and we located Scott in a Wal-Mart parking lot in Billings. The chain store seemed to welcome overnight camping and an armada of recreational vehicles was already moored around its atolls of light posts. Fishhook, who'd become a proficient driver and ad hoc member of the ghouly gang maneuvered the Winnebago into a space and I pulled in beside him.

Scott rang my cell phone as I did.

"We're here. But I don't see you." I scanned the lot for the god-awful orange sports car.

"We're near the front of the store."

I opened my door and stood to get a look above some of

the other cars in the lot. Despite it being nearly 10:00 at night, the store drew hundreds of customers. But there, near a corral of shopping carts, stood the hot ex-cop. Beside him the two decidedly luke-warm missionaries kicked the ground, their heads hung low.

"There you are. I see you. Be there in a second." I waved and hung up.

Wendy watched me from the camper's side window. I wondered if I'd shown too much excitement at seeing Scott again. I waved her out and grabbed my purse from between Mr. Kim's legs, or within actually. He raised a transparent eyebrow, making me giggle.

"Honey? Wendy and I have some shopping to do, right after we talk to Scott about this whole shaman thing." I wondered if the words were too flippant, then added, "Which is totally my main priority. I'd like you to stay by the trailer."

The girl pushed her door open and bounded off around the front of the RV. I heard a few raps, followed by the sight of Wendy slinking toward the door.

I'd expected Wendy to be a bit brighter, more effervescent. Despite all my friends being dead, I credited Wendy with expressing a certain *joie de vivre*. Even her killings are executed with gleeful and guiltless exuberance.[107] Yet, when she rounded the back of the Winnebago, she appeared sullen. Her shoulders curled in; her back was hunched—while unquestionably a high fashion pose, it did nothing when highlighting a grubby Dukes of Hazzard ensemble.

"I know what we're going to do." I slung my arm around her shoulders. "We're going to do some shopping. I don't have much hope for the quality, but if I can do anything it's put an outfit together. That ought to cheer you up."

She patted her stomach and scowled. "Not with this."

"Oh that. I've got some ideas about that."

---

[107] And that's the gold standard.

And I did. Or at least I figured they'd come to me once we rolled through the automatic door.

Scott's eyes prowled my body as we strode toward the men. He met my approaching gaze without apology and extended his hand to greet us. I wasn't sure how to read the gesture. A business-like sexual interest? Horny yet gentlemanly? I shook anyway, half expecting to be pulled into his arms and ravaged.[108]

"Did you get what you were after in Butte?" He attempted to shake Wendy's hand as well, but she withdrew, turning her nose up as though she'd encountered bad meat.

"Not really. We got a lead on a shaman on the Crow Reservation that sounds promising, though." I aimed my chin at the cultists. "How about you. Anything?"

Tad and Corey began to protest.

Scott waved them off. "These boys didn't have anything to do with that girl's murder, anymore than I did."

"Oh . . . hold on." I stepped away from him, pointed at my eyes with my middle finger and then at his, just like a movie I saw once.[109] "I haven't excluded you as a suspect either, Officer Scotty. I'm watching you."

A half-smile arched at the corner of his mouth, which he then wet. "As I am you." He paused, scanned my body. "But, these boys just don't have it in 'em. You and I know what it takes. Just look at 'em."

They weren't particularly threatening—true—gangly-limbed and bad haircuts both. The two of them together probably weighed only slightly more than Scott, though muscle weighs more than fat, and don't think I didn't notice the ex-cop was toting some guns and I don't mean the kind you shoot out of, except maybe that one, *you* know, the one that actually does shoot.

The one down there.

Only not bullets.

---

[108] This ain't that kind of memoir. I do the ravaging. I think you know that.
[109] 'Cuz I'm a bad ass, like that. You know.

Jesus.

Am I rambling? I sound like a retard.

Anyway, the conversation continued.

"Granted. Tad and Corey don't look like your traditional albino killers, but—"

"She was just pale, she didn't have pink eyes or nothin'," one of the guys said.

Scott glowered at the kid. "But?"

"But," I reiterated. "That doesn't mean they didn't do it."

"We're bound—" one said.

"Shut up, Corey," said the other, presumably Tad.

Even Wendy cocked her head at that remark. Until now, we hadn't learned much of anything from the boys, simply assuming a wide range of possibilities as to their identities (I've made you a little list in the footnote; won't you meander?).[110] So this remark caught us off guard a bit and smelled suspiciously of witchcraft. I was intrigued and that's a tough response for a human to get that wasn't bound for my stomach. There's that word again. Bound.

"What do you mean . . . bound?" Wendy stepped up. Her arm touched mine.

---

[110] Who were Tad and Corey, anyway?

1. *Mormons or Jojobas?* They both wore short sleeve dress shirts and everyone knows those are restricted to mathematicians, teacher's assistants and those who interrupt Saturday morning television trying to get you to read magazines sans gorgeous cover models—what were in those pamphlets, anyway? Words?

2. *Kirby salesmen?* I hadn't checked in the back of their truck but couldn't it be filled with vacuum cleaners and dry shampoo? It was a possibility.

3. *Gay lovers fleeing persecution?* There had been just the one tent. Were gay lovers even persecuted anymore? It seemed a useless enterprise, unless they were on the run from a gang of homophobic truck drivers with those metal testicles hanging from the hitch. Almost plausible, eh?

4. *Vicious traveling serial killers with a penchant—pronounced with French accent, s'il vous plait— for albinos?* Hmm. Intriguing but not likely. That sort of pigment deficiency is quite rare. Plus, weren't serial killers supposed to be charming? I think I've made my point.

5. *Other?* This seemed the most appropriate, given the newly revealed clue and the vibes Officer Scotty was getting. Back to it . . .

"Uh." Corey looked at Tad, who only shook his head. "We're not at liberty to say."

"But not bound from saying so?"

"Huh? What?"

I simply nodded. Sometimes a quick play on words could trip up a hambone like Corey.

"We're bound from doing physical harm, by the Maha," he said.

"Why'd you tell her that?"

"Why'd you let me?"

"I didn't. Wha?"

Back and forth they bickered until they realized we'd continued to focus on them, then they turned back, frightened. "You won't tell will you?" Tad said, or it could have been Corey. I'd forgotten again.

"Not if you tell us who or what this Maha is," Scott took on the stern look of a police officer shaking down an informant. The boys were instantly talkative.

"The Maha Durgha is our guru," one said.

"She knows everything," the other said.

"She probably knows we're talking to you."

"She's powerful."

"She's awesome."

"Okay," I interrupted. "Got it. She's a superstar."

"She'd probably know how to fix the girl's problem. Help her see the ghost," said Tad, we'll say, for the sake of time. In fact, from now on, I'm just going to use their names arbitrarily, because honestly, does it really matter?[111] The kid had won my attention, though.

"Can we talk to her?" I asked.

"No," Tad said.

"Nope," Corey mimicked.[112] "But maybe one of you could."

---

[111] No is the answer you're looking for.
[112] See how this can work?

"How so?" I glanced briefly at Scott, whose eyes had narrowed to suspicious slits. I knew what he was thinking. This was either a tactic to get one of us alone and do fun things with our severed appendages or a legitimate attempt to help. My instincts told me it was the latter.

"She'll only accept one audience per month. It may have already happened this month for all we know, but there's a fairly good chance it hasn't. Honey can go with us to the compound. It's not too far from here. We'd have her back by morning."

Wendy laughed, but a sloshing sound echoed from her gut silencing her. She held what must have been her do-it-yourself colostomy bag until it quieted. I gave her a wink, mouthed, "We'll fix that," and turned back to the boy. "If anyone's going it's me. 'Cause, newsflash you little fucker . . ." the boy flinched, ". . . we don't trust you."

"Okay, then. We'll take you."

That was easy.

"You're goddamn right you will, right after me and my girl go shopping." I reached around Wendy's waist and led her into the discount store.

We found some batting in the fabric section and after holding up a bag to Wendy's midsection, decided on two and tossed them into the wobbly-wheeled cart. A few Ace bandages would hold it all in place, so we rolled off to Health & Beauty.

"Do you ever think about what binds us, Amanda?" Wendy rested her hand on the cart as we navigated the aisles.

"You're getting philosophical on me or is this because of those boys?"

"I'm just wondering if the only connection we have is our food. Or this." She gripped the cart and stopped walking, forcing me to do the same and raised her shirt to reveal the hole. Dark gray tendrils etched into the surrounding skin. The rot was escaping her insides and infecting the surface somehow. Maybe it was mold—I'd have to remember to get some Pine-Sol—or it could just have been the store's horrendous lighting. Either way, I couldn't stand looking at it for any length of time.

I scanned the aisle for witnesses, clutched Wendy's hands and pushed them down, covering the source of our joint horror. "No baby. Not just *this*. You're like my sister. Gil's our brother. Like family. That's why we argue. It's just banter."

Her eyelids dimmed, but she nodded as we shuffled past pots and pans and through the linen department, where a grungy girl with a bad haircut was fondling terrycloth.

"It's changing me, you know?"

"No. I don't."

"This hole. It's letting the monster out. I can feel the need to eat all the time. I used to be able to control the hunger pretty well, but now it's slipping away. We call the bitten *mistakes*, but we all are . . . really." If her eyes could produce them, she'd have cried.

I'd have cried, too. None of this was normal. We shouldn't exist, at all. But what good was dwelling on the fact? We were here. Sure, Wal-Mart isn't exactly living, but it was something.

"If you want to see it that way," I said. "Even the humans are mistakes, then. This whole planet's a mistake."

Wendy stared holes into my forehead.

I looked away, plucked the bandages from the shelf and pushed off to makeup. "Come on. We've got work to do. Can't spend all night sinking into depression, save it for drive time."

She shuffled behind me. It really was just going to be a matter of fixing her up. There's nothing like a makeover to change irrational thought patterns. At least that's what Oprah's taught me.

Wardrobe was the tricky part and required trips to women's, men's and boys' clothing to come up with an outfit worthy of emotional confluence. By the time we stood in one of the two excruciatingly long lines, Wendy had begun to act like herself again.

"I can't believe those bitches closed their lanes on us. Sorry! Break." She aped the girl's waddle.

"Oh God and when the other one pointed at me with those curly long fingernails, I felt like one of Gil's bottles of celebrity plasma. Note the celebrity part."

"Of course." Wendy poked at the batting. "Are you sure this'll work?"

"It'll do the trick until we can get back to the reapers for a freshening."

"It's gonna cost a fortune." She sighed. "I don't think I have it."

"Don't worry. I've got some copy you can freelance for me."

"Serious?"

"Absolutely."

"Thanks, sister."

Like a fucking Hallmark card.

Chapter 16

What's the Maha You?

The tropics are a great location for a supernatural get-away. Nothing beats Malaysia in piercing season. The Gods and Goddesses turn out in full force. Good times. I'm telling you.

—Letters to the Editor, *Travel & Creature*

"That's not too tight is it?" Tad asked. His voice was a bit gravelly, not froggy per se, just scratchy. Clearly the phrase wasn't one he'd used before.[113]

"It's fine." I patted the blindfold and shifted my hips around on the flip-down seat in the truck's cab. I guess I should have been happy that handcuffs weren't part of the deal, or worse yet, duct tape. As it was, all I could see was a thin sliver of my new blouse, and only if I strained my eyes. Not that there was anything to look at.

"You comfortable?" the other one asked.

"It's like a fuckin' spa day back here. What do you mean, 'Am I comfortable?' Of course not!"

"Now Miss. That's naughty talk and we don't naughty talk in this truck."

I decided not to respond. One, I couldn't tell what exactly

---

[113] If you know what I mean.

had been "naughty" about what I'd said and two, why bother? Clearly Maha had these guys brainwashed.[114]

I already liked her.

My cell phone rang and I had a hell of a time digging it out of my skirt pocket. Why didn't I just carry my purse? I damned myself to hell for that with every contorted twisting metal-rod-in-the-back movement it took to get the goddamn phone.

It was Marithé.

"That guy keeps callin'."

"Tell him to fuck off."

"I don't think he'll go for that. Besides I already threatened him with a restraining order. He responded by faxing a copy of an article that was so heinous, there was nothing I could do but tell him you were tending to family issues."

"Oh my God. You made up a different location, right?"

"Of course."

I hung up on her. Disgusted.

We drove for close to an hour, on a paved road for most of the way. But in the last fifteen minutes the smooth surface gave way to gravel and potholes, bouncing me around the cramped compartment like change in the bottom of my purse, without the soft buffering of tampons, 'cause really, why would I need those? The old uterus doesn't really function anymore.

I don't bleed. If you must force me to spell it out.

And . . . since you're on to me.

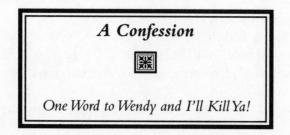

A Confession

One Word to Wendy and I'll Kill Ya!

---

[114] 'Cause who talks like that? Seriously? Who?

Yes. I have some tampons.

I know I get on Wendy for her Twix habit, but I can't give up coffee. How is it even possible to do that? And really, it's Wendy's fault for getting me back into it. She's the one that told me about using Depends to eat whatever we want.

I just took the idea to its next logical step.

Of course, there is the pain to deal with; undead diarrhea is a bitch. But for a quick caffeine fix, an OB Ultra does the trick quite nicely.

Don't tell.

I'll only deny it.

"You can take off your blindfold," Corey said. "We're almost there."

"There ain't nothin' to see anyhow," Tad finished.

But there sure as shit had been something to smell. During the entire ride, the driver's window had remained cracked, flipping my hair into a bramble of knots—a hair don't, no matter what Vivienne Westwood says—and filling my nose with blatant notes of manure and an acrid hint of smoke.

Montana's ranch land was proving quite quaint.

I slipped my fingers between the fabric and my cheeks, pushed it up and fashioned it into a cute hair band—if I was going to meet their messiah I would damn sure be presentable.

As we crested a small hill, the truck came upon a remarkable structure. A glossy black wall rose from the waves of moonlit grasses, high into the night sky. Tad slowed to a stop a few yards away from it and put the car in park.

There didn't seem to be a gate or door or anything. The dirt road just butted right up to the thing. Nothing interrupted the finish except an occasional etching, which seemed to be written in Sanskrit.

"What does that say?" I pressed myself between the front seats.

"It says, 'Know thyself and enter, know nothing and perish. The truth is all around you.'" Tad opened his door with a creak that shattered the silence. He stepped out and walked up to the wall, pausing for a moment and then passing into it. The obsidian material became liquid, sliding around his flesh like quicksilver. He spasmed a bit and then disappeared. The wall solidified.

Corey opened his door and left me sitting in the back.

"Wait!" I yelled. "Where the fuck are you going?"

But it was too late. Corey didn't hesitate at all. He walked straight into the wall, again with the creepy spasm and then he was gone.

With not much room to maneuver, I banged around the cab of the truck until my foot finally caught on the lever for the seat back. I triggered it and it slid forward unexpectedly, leaving me wallowing on the floorboards, searching for purchase to pull myself up. Not since prom night had I been so contorted.

Prom night.

I'd seen the aptly designated Dr. Crooks in my senior year of high school, after being caught shoplifting high-end cosmetics. Mother made me, I'd have preferred a male therapist—as some of you may know—but the bitch was paying, so . . .

Meander with me, won't you?[115]

Her post-therapy homework assignment had been helpful and forced Ethel to fork out $200 on a facial, new skin-care regimen and a hairdo to match. It hit the mark, and I managed a prom invite, despite my less-than-sunny disposition.

Gary Lortner—oddly hot band geek, but not my first foray into the submissive male specimen (Ethel had paraded enough of those through her bedroom)—made the first move of his life in a shaky one-word question outside the girl's bathroom.

"Pro-o-om?" He studied the industrial tile floor while he asked, kicking the water fountain with a dusty Doc Marten.

I pinched his chin and forced him to look at me. Training

---

[115] It's like a little trip through my mind. You know you want to.

puppies is quite similar; eye contact is key. "What was that, Gary? Full sentence, please."

"Woo-would you go with me to the pro-o-om?"

"Of course, I would and don't looked so shocked. You're pretty hot and a girl has needs."

Gary blushed for the rest of the day. Probably analyzing that last sentence through several bathroom pass masturbation sessions. The idea of that made me feel powerful, in a way that a previously disclosed molestation did not.[116] I'm talking about one of Ethel's boyfriends, not my real Dad. He ran when he could and I certainly don't hold that against him. He saw his opening and darted. I'd have done the same if I'd been given the latitude. I'm not talking about a rape or anything just some over the panty fumbling. I'll survive.

Oh . . . wait.

Anyway.

The prom was magical, and all. But I was looking for the payday, and I don't mean to reference a peanut-studded candy bar as a phallic image. I was talking about losing my virginity. Some of you want to imagine that every girl's fantasy is to do it with someone they love, hand the pussy over on some buffed and shiny silver platter, or some shit. Well, it isn't *every* girl's fantasy.

If I learned anything from Ethel it was that a woman can want and enjoy sex without love entering into the equation.

So . . . later.

After Carly Bookman had snagged her crown—duh—I took Gary back out to his ratty old Volkswagen Rabbit and fucked the shit out of him—to put it nicely. For all his bellowing cries to God I was surprised we didn't get a visit from our Lord and Personal Savior right there, or at least a cum-stained reliquary

---

[116] I know. I know. It's really terribly cliché to have so many family issues. But what can I say? I guess it really does take a village to raise a child. One great big fucked up village.

out of the deal. I bet to this day Gary still has the belt buckle dents in his back as a memento. Maybe one is even shaped like the Virgin Mary.[117]

We never spoke again but he lost the stutter in those back seat screams and became quite the ladies man around Barnaby Ridge High. What can I say? I'm like a social worker for all my good deeds.

Hmm. Yet no one was there to help me in my time of need.

The grass slapped around my new sweatshop heels and bare ankles. There didn't seem to be any alternative but to follow Tad and Corey and step right in. But where to do it? Was one place as good as the next? And what about that ominous Sanskrit message? A little over the top, if you ask me.

I mean "know nothing and perish." C'mon, what does that even mean? And who reads Sanskrit in Montana? I was pretty sure the ranchers aren't writing their grocery lists in the ancient language.

I marched up to the wall and touched the surface, expecting mercurial liquid. Instead I was confronted by a cold solid construction. I walked along, trailing my fingers across it.

"The truth is all around me?" I wondered aloud. There was grass all around me, sky, air and one big impossible wall.

Impossible.

Or maybe that was the answer. The wall's existence was impossible. How did it even get built? The thing was massive. Everyone would know about it if it were real. My eyes followed the swirls of Sanskrit and I bounded forward, head held high and eyes open.

There's no wall, I told myself. No wall.

But there was.

As my face connected, the material splattered across it like mud. Cold and wet and not at all like the kind that Helga

---

[117] Too far? It felt like I was skating on thin ice with that one. Oh well. Hell it is.

spreads on at the supernatural spa, Riyadh Morte, which is—in a word—delightful. The feeling spread down my body until I was interred inside it. I hesitated for a moment, expecting the spasm to come. When it didn't, I pushed further in and popped out the other side into a sopping humidity. The temperature was so hot that moisture rose to the surface of my dead flesh.

Around me stood a lush forest of palms and banana trees so dense I was reminded of Vietnam War movies and gangrene and sweat. The scent of night jasmine hung in the air, and orchids grew from creases in the tree trunks. Either it was all an illusion or that wall was a door to a land that hated straight hair. Off to my right a raised wooden boardwalk meandered into the jungle, illuminated by the occasional metal fire pot.

Tad and Corey hadn't bothered to wait.

I stepped off a slight grassed incline onto the boards and creaked through the jungle, half expecting to encounter a hungry tiger, or some psychotic aging Vietcong to roll out of the greenery in a viney wheelchair, clueless as to the end of the war and the fact that Vietnam was the new Bali. But the most perilous obstacle proved to be a dense clumping Bird of Paradise grown up out of the jungle floor and into the rotting damp boards; spiky flowers pecked at my blouse as I tried to give it a wide berth.

As the jungle thinned, I came upon an arch with a scrolling pagoda roof. A bell hung from its ornately carved post. Beyond this rose a vast complex of Oriental architecture—Thai salas and pointy wats shared space with blue Chinese tiled mansions and many-storied Indian palaces. Wherever I was, it was not Asia, but some sort of recreation, without the massive population and third-world smells. An idealized version, like Epcot or restaurant row near the opera house.

I reached out and grasped the pull in the center of the bell. Debated a moment and then clanged the bronze fish that hung there against the interior bowl. The sound echoed across the plaza toward the massive buildings in the distance.

And, I waited.[118]

The boardwalk snaked over canals dotted with water lilies, past little houses on stilts, with fabric for doors and stairs leading to sagging longboats. The roots of mangled trees wrapped and grew around golden idols, some Buddhas, others Hindu gods, a Quan Yin carved into the bark of a cypress. Near the end of the raised path, I noted movement.

A dark boxy shape navigated the curves of the walk accompanied by a clopping and popping of wheels on board. A rickshaw as wide as the path was approaching, wheels teetering precariously, with Tad between the lead poles bearing the weight.

"I see you made it though fine." Tad was out of breath but jovial.

"No help from you. That's for sure."

He flipped the handles over the top of the seating compartment and climbed over the tiled roof. "It's a little sketchy getting around but, if you get a good fingerhold here . . ." he pointed at a spot below the roof line. "You shouldn't have any trouble. C'mon now, hop on."

Again, no help. Why is it I have to do everything myself, lately? I stomped up to the edge of the boardwalk, glancing briefly at the murky water and noting a gathering of very large koi swarming the area. Insanely large. As I watched one broke the surface and snapped at the air with row upon row of razor sharp teeth.

Lovely.

I cringed and searched the side of the dark wood box until my fingers hit on a gap above the opening, made sure I had steady balance on my left foot and then swung my weight around. I aimed my foot for the floor of the carriage, caught it for a second

[118] Manners are very important.

but then the cheap Wal-Mart sole skipped across the threshold like a stone on placid water. My shins scraped the edge as I dangled from my grip, pendulum-like, losing one of my shoes to the snapping mouths below. Small sacrifice.

Bringing my left arm around I was able to wedge my body in through the hole and skid across the floor on my knees. Lucky for me it was polished or I'd have had a mess on my hands.[119]

I struggled to find a place to sit as there were only a few loose pillows and Tad had begun to pull. By the time I came to rest, we were already careening around the curves of the boardwalk, winding back and forth toward the complex.

"You okay, back there?" he shouted.

"Perfect," I said, stripping my other foot bare and tossing the shoe out into the canal.

"That's awesome. The Maha Durgha is known for her hospitality."

The rickshaw hit some loose boards, bouncing me around the cabin. "It shows," I called out. "I'm super comfortable."

"Great!"

Sarcasm was wasted on the brainwashed, it seemed.

We rolled onto a hard surface, past a stone gate, and through the center of a black field. Figures roamed the dark rows of the expanse, squeezing powders from bellows they carried under their arms. The air was dense with smoke and shit.

"What the fu—"

"Language, Miss. That smell is the mushroom field. It'll dissipate. Remember, no cursing. The Maha hates potty words."

Fuck, I thought.

This really was going to be an adventure.

Tad stopped the rickshaw in front of a high peaked pavilion, shingled in crimson tiles like fish scales, the edges burnished in gold. He helped me exit the carriage—the first time he'd offered

---

[119] You get skinned knees, I get *skinless* knees.

assistance the whole trip, I might add—and led me through a massive arch and down a center hall lined with potted tea trees and eucalyptus. The fragrance so filled my head that I swayed. Tad steadied me, laying my arm across his, and guided me past doorways expelling the waller of hundreds of voices. He sat me at a bench.

"Wait here. I'll see if she's ready for you." He jogged off toward the arch at the opposite end.

I couldn't resist the call of the voices. I stood, balanced myself against the wall and teetered across to the first doorway. A maze of office cubicles stretched out for hundreds of yards, each occupied by a young woman wearing a telephone headset. I couldn't make out the conversations and to get any closer would surely alert them to my presence.

A call center?

What was going on here?

Were they dealing in mushrooms?

And then it hit me. Fishhook wasn't just addicted to inedible sharp objects, but those little black mushrooms in his Tupperware. The last time he'd taken them he was so fucking high he could have entered pilot training.

So that's what was going on here. Drugs.

I swiveled around and wobbled across the hall to rest on the bench.

The boys weren't cultists at all—they were drug dealers. Their guru was the mastermind. It all seemed logical.

"The Maha will see you now." Tad slipped his arm around me and helped me up. "She's very excited about your visit. I believe she's making tea for you."

"No, no. I really couldn't possibly." I thought of the tampons, briefly, and then excused the idea. It would be much easier to simply decline than to excuse myself to shove a wad of cotton up my ass. Why couldn't she offer up a servant, even a very small one, something I could digest? I eyed Tad. He'd do.

"But you must. The Maha will be very upset."

Once in the open air, my head cleared and I was able to stabilize my legs. Whatever fumes filled that hall were potent as Hell.

A low table was set under a gazebo in the center of a formal garden, with dense strings of Chinese lanterns hanging from the ceiling casting a warm glow over a silver tea service. Again, no chairs, but pillows stacked neatly beside the table.

"Have a seat. She'll be with you in a moment. You may want to gather your thoughts, she won't have long to chat." Tad scurried back toward the pavilion.

Surrounding the garden were three single-storied structures draped in silks that fluttered in the breezeless night. The panels were drawn back from the furthest, and a tall woman approached, flanked by two men each carrying a tiered set of fringed parasols, one in shades of amber, the other vibrant navies—the umbrellas, not the servants. She stomped at the ground in drool-worthy high heels that were visible only as she lifted the front of her gown's weighty skirt. The bodice was covered by a Victorian men's coat in jet, fitted at her waist, open and turned back to reveal the voluminous skirt underneath. White lace trailed from her wrists and décolletage, and she wore a top hat at an angle over dreadlocks, some woven with wire and black pieces of plastic straps.

The walk itself was totally Tyra. I nearly yelled out, "Bring it, bitch," but thought better of it.

Corey brought up the rear, arranging her train like a handmaid. The servants stopped at the edge of the gazebo and the Maha Durgha stepped forward, waving off Corey before he could introduce her.

"She knows who I am, boy. Run along and . . ." She paused as she glanced at my feet. "Bring this girl a pair of shoes." She angled her head and squinted. Her face scrunched up on one side like Nancy, from PBS's *Sewing with Nancy*.[120] "Size 7."

---

[120] Damn you, Bell's palsy—what with all those appliqués to talk about. Slurp.

Impressive. I nodded.

"Yes, Maha." Corey scuttled away, bowing with each step and stumbling.

"I'm Amanda Feral." I reached for her and then withdrew my hand when the gesture was not reciprocated.

"This I know, as well. You've come for answers. But I imagine what you've witnessed here has only aroused more questions."

Her skin was dark, stretched across a thin face without blemish, her pinched nose puffed at the nostrils like a goblet base and her eyes were large, brown as Belgian chocolate and wide-set. The woman's presence calmed me. Charmed me. Mostly.

"Yeah. I'd originally come to ask whether it's possible for a human to see a ghost, by whatever means that would entail. You see. We picked up this girl—"

"Yes. Yes. But, you already know the answer to that. In fact, it will happen soon enough as it is."

"What do you mean?"

"The Korean girl will die. Soon." She smiled broadly, as though delivering happy news. "And then she'll see her brother. Problem solved."

Everything but the fucking hand brushing.

If it was possible, I'd have thought my shriveled heart sunk at the comment. Honey was going to die? How? And how could this woman be so sure?

"How do you know that?" I asked.

"It's a gift from the gods. Does my name sound remotely familiar to your Western ears? No. Well no matter. I've been around for a long time, girl. I took my name in India, where the Hindus call me the Maha Durgha. It was pleasant enough to the ears so I kept it. My skills of premonition have waned like that moon over there. But, I'm still the best mystic I know. As for the girl, I'm only moderately accurate, but I'm fairly certain we're talking about days, rather than weeks."

I tilted my head at the phrase "moderately accurate."

Someone else I knew was "moderately accurate."

"Moderately accurate?"

"I see you've put it together." She reached for the silver pot and poured a dark tea into my cup. "For you to smell. I know you won't be drinking it."

She nodded and I took the cup. Its warmth spread through my fingers. The scent was everything I'd smelled so far, rolled into one—though the field of manure was thankfully absent.

"The operators you saw are my business. You see, I still like to help mankind and as Madame Gloria I can do that. The mushrooms help them to see what I do. Spread the visions around. You may have noticed the fragrance, felt the lightheadedness?"

"Oh yeah. It was fu—." I cut the word off, remembering Tad's multiple warnings. "Awful. Just awful."

"The ladies offer up their bodies as conduits for six weeks at a time—any more than that and there are side effects—the rest of their year is spent in this paradise."

I looked around at the menagerie of tropical plants, lined up neatly in rows and berms. "Is this even real? It's just so . . . magical."

Corey tiptoed up to the gazebo, leaving a pair of Nike running shoes, Air-something-or-others, and backed away. I slid them on my bare feet with a nod to my hostess.

"Of course it's real, just embellished a little. The farm, the buildings." She swept her hand across the horizon, "all very much real. The décor is a bit of glamour, a bit of the old world. I can't seem to enjoy the metal valley of city. It's just not my style."

I let my eyes wander over the goddess's eccentric ensemble. While outlandish and over-the-top, there was richness in the layering. A depth to the fabric. The more I examined it, the more detail was revealed.

Human forms. Curling and contorting around one another. I saw myself in the folds, clinging to them. A man's face emerged from the shadows behind mine. His arms next, slinking about my torso. We were naked, grasping at each other, grinding. Fucking. He was familiar though I couldn't see his face. Strong. Then the fabric darkened to black. Chilled. A cave entrance loomed. A small figure, huddled on his knees crying. Shoulders heaving. Mr. Kim.

She shifted and the spell was broken. "A vision for you. I'm sorry. Only part of it was pleasant, I'm afraid."

Was I supposed to be thankful?

I shook off the fashion trance. "Tad and Corey?"

"Also real, though not drug dealers as you suspect—just loyal penitents. They're particularly helpful to me." She leaned across the table and grinned. "This is going to drive you nuts. That you are here at all is a complete coincidence. I didn't even put it together myself. Corey filled me in on the murder. I hope you don't suspect my boys, they just aren't capable."

"Of course not." I held the cup in front of my face, hiding behind it. Madame Gloria's proximity was a little threatening for my taste.

"Still, we can't just let someone go killing your friends." She sighed. "I suspect one of your traveling companions."

I immediately thought of Fishhook and his visions. I suspected him briefly but he was always so cracked out, he didn't seem capable of wiping himself let alone a strenuous dismemberment. But he'd definitely seen something at the campground, right before he got loaded and he did act more like a zombie than Wendy or I ever did. Unless he was being controlled.

"Is it possible that someone outside your compound could access your mushrooms? Are they for sale or something?"

"They are. But they're very expensive." She rose and crossed the small space to glance at the descending moon. "I'm afraid that not all of my worshippers are as loyal as Tad and Corey. Some parcels have gone missing. I've heard that unscrupulous individuals have used the crop to control human beings, to make them a bit like zombies, the classic variety, not a mistake and certainly not in kind with your evolved species. More like a weapon."

"Terrible."

"Isn't it? I advise that you watch for these mushrooms. Assuming you haven't already seen them." She spun to face me. "Have you already seen them?" Her eyes narrowed to slits.

Was she fishing? I felt like I was being manipulated for an answer. I don't like to be manipulated, so it's no surprise that I reverted to my normal turns of speech.

"What are you gettin' at, Gloria? You think I'm swiping your fuckin' mushrooms?"

"Aw no." Her fingers worked the puzzles of her Victorian jacket buttons, unhooking them one at a time, her body puffing out between the lapels as though the jacket had corseted a much larger woman. "You were being so polite. I'd never expected to hear potty language. But now I have." As she undid the final button, the jacket was flung away by seemingly hundreds of appendages. They snatched at the air furiously creating a shimmering fan of anger. "Too bad. I do so love visitors."

Madame Gloria took a step forward, but I was already moving, darting from the gazebo and through the pavilion. The goddess was hot on my heels, her presence announced by the buzzing of her many arms.

"Stop girl, I'm just going to strip those words out of you. Strip them right out."

I didn't like the sound of that. "The hell you are!"

But worse than losing my ability to cuss like a sailor was the thought of those arms coming down on me, tangling in my hair, picking at my flesh. I ran with sloppy abandon, back down the dirt road we'd come in the rickshaw, slipping through the fields of excrement and the path over the canals.

Serpentine! Serpentine! I commanded myself to weave as I ran, mimicking those commando movies. Fast and low, Amanda.

I barely escaped her crazy puritanical grasp as I breezed through the jungle and straight into the wall of obsidian.

I expected her hand to grab hold of my hair and pull me back into her tropical illusion, but no.

In seconds I was out the other side and the buzzing was gone. I fell to the ground and rubbed at my arms. So close. So very close. But I'd outrun the bitch. Thanks to my Nike Air-Somethings.[121]

I never thought of myself as much of an athlete but I'd definitely proved myself capable of a sprint.

"She let you go," a guy's voice said.

I jerked my head towards the sound and found Tad waiting by the truck, the back of which was laden with sack upon sack of mushrooms.

"Wha-what do you mean? I outran her."

"You mean in those new track shoes she gave you?"

I shot a glance at the sporty kicks and glowered at the kid. "Bullshit. She was going to strip me of my ability to curse. And believe me, in my social group, that would have hurt."

"Okay. You're right. She wasn't fucking with you." The boy laughed then, as though freed of some big lie, or at least of a witness.

I gasped. "You're a pottymouth?"

He opened the passenger door. "I hope you don't mind the smell. I've got a shipment."

Apparently Madame Gloria was not only "moderately accurate" in her visions, but in her judge of character.

---

[121] Dear Mr. Nike,
Please send me much free swag, c/o Feral Inc. [Editor's note: Address withheld], Seattle, WA
Sincerely,
Amanda Feral, Celebrity Ghoul, Nike endorser

Chapter 17

On the Hush-Hush, the DL, or the QT[122]

Looking to spice up your supernatural relationship? Why not treat your lover to some Aural Sex. That's right, dead things, envelope your sex partner in a shimmering miasma of ecstasy, courtesy of Wicked Wishes (the people who brought you Bunghole Calliope and the Wand-o-Plenty).

—A paid commercial seen on early morning *Supernatural Satellite*

Upon returning, Wendy noticed my distress and darted into the store for chemical refreshment in the form of a gallon jug of rubbing alcohol. Strong shit but effective. The Cleavers had arrived in their gaudy traveling palace and the twins were chatting up Honey, hopefully not discussing a three-way—'cuz . . . ew, really. Fishhook and Tad took a walk somewhere and Gil found a lonely runaway sleeping in her car and took her behind the store.[123]

Scott, Wendy and I went over the incident from beginning to end.

---

[122] Depending on your demographic, of course.
[123] . . . If you know what I mean. No. Not that. No. The other thing. Yep.

"So she's gonna die?" Wendy stole a glance at the trio and shuddered.

"Apparently. Don't tell Mr. Kim. We'll try to prove the bitch wrong." I followed her gaze. Honey was regaling the little pervs with an undoubtedly fascinating tale, as Chris and Cathy warmed themselves under a blanket—or something . . . else. Probably daydreaming about attics.

"We really ought to ban her from talking to those two," I said.

"I agree," Scott said. "I've done a lot of safety checks for Child Protective Services and those two reek of mental institution. I wouldn't be surprised if that whole family was one big incest factory. Too sweet. Too normal. I've been watching."

"Hmm. Your cynicism's making me horny," I joked.[124]

His laugh was deep and guttural, akin to a guffaw but without any of the associated bumpkin-ness that word seems to engender. Wendy rolled her eyes, patting me on the shoulder and wandering off to check on Honey and dinner, presumably.

A blessing.

Madame Gloria's images played across my eyelids in a loop, like a radio station on holiday, only with full-frontal nudity and body fluids. I caught myself running my fingers across my cheek, chasing a rare warmth I didn't think the rubbing alcohol was entirely responsible for. I was so rapt in the memory, in fact, I didn't notice the man, himself, until his fingers curled over my shoulders and began to knead where the tension settled. He swept my hair aside and ran his thumbs down my neck and inside the collar of my blouse. The pressure was exquisite.

"I was worried about you." His voice was close. The bass tones caught on the tiny hairs of my neck, sending a vibration that echoed through my body; it elevated to a quake as it found its target. I slid my hand from my stomach to my thigh, clawed at thin cotton.

---

[124] Kinda.

Scott wore the same cologne as the male body in the vision.
Grassy. Fresh.

Clean.

Everything that the parking lot lacked was in that scent. I
closed my eyes and let it carry me away from the painful straps
of the lawn chair, away from all the drama of the past few days.
The conflict. The bloodshed.

The discount clothing.

"Mmm hmm. But I'm here now. I'm fine." The words
stretched out in a sleepy tone I didn't recognize, or maybe I did
but from long before my death, from a time when I could relax
and rid myself of all the self-critique and just be.

"Yes, you are." He knelt beside me then, I felt the soft pressure of his lips on my eyelids. Heard the tiny pops of the smallest kisses. His hands traced the geometry of my throat, the swell
of my breasts. His fingers lingered on the soft tents of my nipples, until they were hard enough to cut diamonds, or at least
fabric produced by 10-year-old Guatemalan seamstresses.

Scott slid his arms around me and rested his head on my
chest. "Do you want to find somewhere . . . quiet?"

I held his lightly stubbled face and pressed it to me, nuzzling
and kissing his warm brow through the soft blond curls. He
tilted his head back and searched my face with those sultry eyes,
bloodshot and droopy from not enough sleep. His lips seemed
swollen from this angle, pillowy soft. They parted in that instant,
a question forming.

I answered with slow sweeps of my lips across his warm
mouth, our supple skin barely touching. His warm breath sparked
against my cold dead flesh, carrying all the scents I expected and
would have to struggle against. If I ever wanted to devour anyone so totally, it was this man. He clutched me to him as our
tongues twirled and withdrew, thrust deeper, exploring and
then. . . .

A snort.

Scott's breath had lost its comfortable warmth. Our lips

parted and I noticed a fire dancing in his eyes. In fact, fire was an appropriate description, as steam forced itself from his nostrils; they flared with each exhalation.

"Just a second." He took some deep breaths, rolled his head from side to side and rubbed his palms against his jeans. When he looked back at me, his eyes returned to the deep amber that entranced me so.[125] "You want to get a room or what?"

"Oh . . . yeah," I said. "Four walls and roof will do. Just so you know, I'm no innocent farmer's daughter. You were turning wolfy just then and I saw it."

He raised his hands in surrender. "Caught."

"Let's just be clear from the beginning. This is going to be more than just exercise. We're both going to have to control ourselves. At least in the supernatural sense."

He grinned, thickened canines retracting into his gums. "I can do that."

"Well, I'm not going to make any promises. If you hear my jaw popping, you better head for the door, or at least spin me around doggy style."

He laughed. "You're a naughty one."

"You bet your ass."

In the distance, Wendy seemed to be carrying out her reconnaissance of the Cleaver camp. The mister and missus had joined the fun and brought out a triangular box that could only be that horrific determiner of IQ, Trivial Pursuit—hate that game. Unless the questions are about fashion, fads or celebrity faux pas, I'm shit out of luck. They seemed to be accepting of Wendy's presence. If they weren't careful with their hospitality, we wouldn't be worrying about them as suspects so much as how to get their remains out of Wendy's batting-packed gut.

I had little hope that sex with Scott would end up in a relationship, but he was warm—so warm—and it had been forever since I'd had a decent lay. Granted, that last time with Martin

---

[125] Yeah. I can say things like 'entranced', but don't get used to it.

didn't end so well—unless you're looking at it from the perspective of a black widow—but the couple since then had turned out to be horrible lovers. I mean really bad. So can you blame me if I wanted to get a little action, particularly with someone so animalistic? Didn't think so.

I slid my hand into his and led him to the dented Winnebago, looking around to make sure the others wouldn't made a quick return to catch us at it. I left the lights off. No sense in worrying about gray mottled skintones ruining the mood, or worse, reminding my suitor that he'd be experiencing the joys of a taboo.[126] As it was, the light through the window cast a shade of pink across my pale flesh that was quite attractive, if I do say.

He spun me around, lifted me onto the counter and spread my legs with his hips. I clawed at the buttons on his shirt, caught hold of the yokes and tore. A button fired off the fabric and pegged me in the eye—sexy, right? I rubbed at it and decided to spare him the same indignity by tending to my own shirt.

"You look so hot in this light." His breath curled hot around the shell of my ear.

The scent of meat rose off him, nearly sending me into that manic zombie feeding frenzy. I needed to break away.

"I know, right?" I pushed him back to shake off the tendency, focus and admire the light dusting of golden fur on his pecs, the trail leading south over the hills and valleys of his taut abdomen. I ran my fingers around the tracks of his nipples, coaxing them to points. His body erupted into a shudder, heat rising to his flesh again. He inhaled. Exhaled. Struggled to keep the beast inside.

I scooted off the counter and slid down his body, lightly teasing his chest with kisses, flicking my tongue against his nip-

---

[126] I've tried to avoid the necrophilia commentary. No one wants to get the image of some greasy perv hittin' it with a corpse on a mausoleum slab—I know I don't. But I'm different, right? Right?

ples, trailing it down his stomach until I was in the promissory
position, head to hip.

. . . and on that note: a quick word on dick.

Chest hair trimming usually means that you're not going to
come face to face with a big '70s bush, which is entirely unacceptable. No one—and by no one, I'm talking about me—wants
to unzip a guy and come face to face with Barbara Streisand in
A Star Is Born. You get me? Of course, there is the issue of find-
ing no patch at all. I don't know about you, but twelve-year old
boys aren't sexy, no matter what your neighbor's pregnant daughter says. As for the big reveal, I'm concerned with two things
and two things only:

1. That I'm not dealing with a micro-penis. Seriously, it's
   going to take more than the eraser end of a pencil to get
   me off. I don't mean to be harsh, but I'm pretty sure that's
   a medical condition. Men, please consult your physician.
2. That the sheep's been sheared. If your weiner's got a
   hoody, it's not going anywhere near my mouth, let alone
   the other two spots.

Are we clear?

Now, from the bulge in Scott's jeans I could tell we'd be
working with some decent-sized equipment, but you never
know about the other concerns until the boxers are down, or
briefs, as the case may be.

I slid his jeans down his legs, helped him off with his shoes—
but not socks, the trailer floor was too nasty—and ran my hands
up the architecture of his legs, the thick cords of muscle flexed
under my grip. Scott grinned above me, clearly proud that his
message had reached me. I shook my head and went for the
business, the head of which was already peeking over the elastic
band of his shorts, straining for relief, and without a turtleneck,
I might add. With the briefs down, I could finally get a good
look.

The assessment: a little on the long side of average and veinier than a designer dildo. A trimmed patch completed the look.[127]

"Are you sure?" I asked. Sex is a huge trust thing for a woman, but a blowjob from a zombie has to be the biggest act of trust ever. He nodded eagerly.

I was fairly certain I wasn't going to chew off his dick, so I went down on him.

Scott closed his eyes and let out a low moan as I toyed with his manhood, rocking it across my tongue, the insides of my cheeks.

That's when I heard the first clue of what I was in for.

"Oh yeah," he said. "Suck it. Suck that big dick."

I should have stopped right there, and I did pause. Nothing is more distracting than porno talk. It's laughable in the movies, but when you hear it in real life? It's just weird. But, I didn't stop; I kept going. In fact, I even took off my bra while I blew him. Quite a feat, considering I was in a squat rather than on my knees—um . . . did I mention the floor?

Rather than wrap it up with a quick summation, like I'd normally do, let's stay with this. Play it out. I'm gonna need some advice when it's over, anyway.

Scott guided me up by the shoulder, wrapping me in a tight embrace and pressing his lips into mine. His fingers dug in the band of my panties, pushing them down and searching my folds, exploring.

His eyes were red with passion or transformation, one or the other, but they locked on mine as he whispered, "You want it baby? You want it deep inside you?"

"Um." I did, yes, however, to say so might reinforce his potty-mouth. In the end I just let him guess and it didn't take him long to make a decision.

---

[127] You'll note I'm not talking about balls. I just don't care for them. The only sacks I'm interested in have leather handles and Italian labels. Thank you.

His cock slipped between my lips, the tip gliding against my engorging clit. He tried to open me up with his other hand, withdrew from the arid hole and, unperturbed, spat into his palm, greased up his dick and tucked it inside of me in a graceful fluid movement.[128]

He started thrusting, deeper, grinding his hips against me. He lifted my thighs, forcing me back onto the counter. I met each push with a lift of my pelvis, rising up, forcing him further inside of me.

"Unh-unh. You feel that?" he asked, teeth chattering between the words, canines longer and thicker than before.

"Um . . . yeah? Of course I—"

"Yeah? That's me fucking you baby." He cut me off, lifting my knees higher, directing his cock like an orchestra. "Fucking you wide open. Getting in there good."

"Okay?" The talking was really turning me off, and I was almost there. Something had to be done.

"Am I hittin' your spot? I mean really hittin' it. Hittin' it right?"

Enough with the porno talk, I decided. I pressed my hand across his mouth. He mumbled into my palm.

"Just fuck me," I said.

He did. And for the first time since I died, I had an orgasm. The muted throbbing from our rhythm gave way to a rolling shudder so intense that I curled over and screamed, heaving an unconscious lungful of *the breath* from my mouth. It scrolled through the air, tendrils seeking the warm dampness of human lungs. Scott's lungs. I pinched off his nose, and sucked as much as I could of the virus back in—the rest would need some time to dissipate. My little porn star was going to have to hold out for air.

His thrust became more fervent, his fiery eyes widened and

---

[128] No lubrication pun intended.

his breath blazed against my hand. He seemed to be enjoying the experience a bit too much. When he did come, his body convulsed as though a grand mal seizure was passing through it. He shook and his jaw slackened. He slid out of me and onto the floor, unconscious.

I prodded him with my toe, fearing that I'd been too slow in shielding him from the breath and half expecting him to turn zombie on the spot.

And then I realized what I'd done.

I remembered the kid on the news that died strangling himself for a high when he masturbated. I thought of the lead singer of that band, rumored to have done the same.

Erotic asphyxiation.

That's what I'd done to Scott and the freak had truly gotten off on it. But I'm pretty sure that wasn't on the books as a method to kill a werewolf.

"Wha-wha-what was that?" He twisted on the floor. Writhed might be a better word. It wasn't at all sexy as chunks of filthy moss stuck to his naked skin with each roll across the disgusting carpet. His socks were similarly spotted and streaked; all he needed was a frame and an art critic.

"Oh God. Are you okay?" I reached down and helped him to his feet. Settling him in to the booth before hunting down my underwear.

"Are you kidding? That was awesome."

"Awesome? Are you nuts? Do you even know what happened?"

"Sure, we made love and—"

"Made love? That's debatable. Let's just call it sex, shall we?"

"Fine, we had *great* sex. Risky sex, sure. Because of the whole zombie—werewolf thing, but when you pulled your little kink move at the end—God it was awesome. Now . . . I'm your slave, baby." He reached for my hand, tried to pull me into his lap.

I swatted him away. "Ew. No. You're super gross from being on that floor. And it wasn't 'a move,' I was trying to save you from my breath."

"It didn't smell *too* bad," he said.

My mouth dropped open, purely instinctual response to the stupidity of the male animal. Did he just say my breath stunk? "You can shut up any time now."

I turned away from him and slipped on my panties, just as the camper door swung open revealing four shocked faces. It was really a crap shoot as to which was the most horrified, Wendy or Honey. Gil simply covered his mouth and chuckled, while Fishhook openly drooled. It's not enough that I'm clearly a kinky pervert, now I have to be a slut, too. The evening had been nothing short of magical.

"You should probably put your bra on," Wendy said. "There's been another murder."

Of course.

Chapter 18

As the Mothafuckin' Crow Flies

Serenity Forever Wipes are a zombie's best friend. Just ask Velma Carruthers of Omalika, Arkansas. Ms. Carruthers left her usual dining spot, the Last Chance trailer park, at 2 A.M. An hour later, those unfortunate and pesky leaks kicked in sending a dribble down her thigh. Not one to be unprepared, Velma pulled out her Serenity Forever Wipes and stopped that dribble in its tracks. Serenity Forever Wipes. They really are a zombie's best friend.

—Commercial, *Supernatural Satellite*

Tad's body was strewn across three parking spaces in a gory smear as brown and stringy as a discarded diaper after an unfortunate tire spinout.[129] His head was missing, like the albino's, though large clumps of hair don't normally sprout from concrete curbs, so it might have been smashed into the mess somewhere.

Dawn had brought a shimmering glow to the scene—we all know how important good lighting is, particularly for us innocent bystanders. But it also lit up a particularly obvious claw mark that grooved the concrete paving in five distinct lines, a pile of collected stone at its ends.

---

[129] I hadn't seen one yet, but you know Wal-Mart parking lots. There's bound to be one mining the cement somewhere—guaranteed to be explosive.

Werewolf. No question.

The police cordoned off the area and were questioning the bystanders too curious to witness the atrocity from their cars. One cop unleashed a tirade of judgment on a stringy-haired youth holding a tree branch. A gray bit of gristle hung from the end—I didn't even need to take a whiff, to tell you the globber was brains. What a waste. Perfectly good brains rendered inedible by hardened wads of chewing gum, cigarette butts and oil-soaked kitty litter.[130]

We settled in behind an ever-expanding ring of gore hounds.

"Alright, this is getting ridiculous," I said. "It's been what . . . an hour since we saw the fucker last? And now he's been pap-smeared by a werewolf. Who was with him?"

Scott shrugged. Wendy pointed at Honey.

"Dude! Was not," the girl recoiled, crossing her arms.

"Where's Fishhook?" I asked.

"Oh yeah. Fuckin' Fishhook." Wendy's eyes widened and she started searching the crowd for the scraggly blood tap. "He took a walk with the guy right when you guys got back."

"No. Where's he now? He was just with you guys."

"Was he?" Honey looked confused.

Had I been seeing things or had the shock of being exposed like that made me fill in the blanks with just another face to horrify. He'd been drooling, though.

"I was sure he was. I meant to talk to him first thing when we got back, too. Particularly after Madame Gloria told me that bit about the mushrooms. Shit, and then it turns out Tad is his dealer. That's got to be it right?"

"Who else could it be?" Scott asked. "You and I were . . . um . . . busy." His face changed as though he'd thought of a rational alternative. "Gil *was* off feeding—"

"And *then* he joined Honey and me with that weird family. Plus, he's not big on unmaintained body hair." Wendy headed

---

[130] Let's observe a moment of silence.

off any insinuation of Gil's involvement, slapping her hands on her hips—a Nancy Drew pose that really didn't suit her. Though, if she hadn't done it, I probably would have.

Scott shrugged.

I scanned the parking lot for the massive RV. "Where are the Cleavers, anyway?"

"They were there an hour ago when we left them." Honey jumped onto the bumper of some domestic piece of crap to get a better look. "I don't see it now."

"When you left them?" I asked.

"Oh yeah." Wendy nodded. "Couldn't put up with their charades, and I do mean the stupid game, not their obvious attempts at presenting themselves as the perfect family. You don't think they're were, do you?"

"We definitely can't rule 'em out." Scott wound his arm around my waist, an action that caused Honey to roll her eyes and Wendy to flinch.

I twisted from his grip. "Yeah, but doesn't Fishhook make more sense? He was with the guy last, after all. Now, where's Tad's truck? I bet his mushrooms are gone."

I meandered back to the RV, the others following. We walked in a slow and deliberate manner, not to attract attention from the cops who'd surely be getting information that Tad had been seen with a certain gorgeous brunette.[131]

I was right. The mushrooms were gone. So was the truck. So were the Cleavers. Leaving us the only possible suspects in the parking lot. We didn't even need to discuss it, really. We were outtie.

"Anyone need some groceries?" Scott asked.

"Dude!" Honey exclaimed.

We dispersed to our respective vehicles, cranked up and sped out of Billings.

---

[131] That'd be me.

★   ★   ★

Newsflash: There is more than one grocery store on the Crow Reservation—and I'm not including the Custer's Last Stand Gift shop, Café and Quick Mart—but not a single road-side casino, as far as I could tell.[132] I don't know why I was surprised at this; perhaps I'd gotten used to the glut of neon rising on the sides of the Western Washington interstate, or the billboards for Gamblers' Anonymous.[133]

The grocery store in question was as far from civilization as is humanly possible. The cut-off from the main highway promised to shave an hour off the drive to South Dakota, but miles of grassland, rolling hills and abandoned houses lay in between, so reaching the shaman and our final destination was as tedious as a televised cheerleading competition.

"This is boring, dude." Honey flung her Chuck Taylors up on the dash. The skin-tight jeans she wore made her tiny feet seem larger, flatter. The girl needed to be introduced to the world of high-end heels.

I cringed but didn't chastise.[134]

She turned in her seat, eyes wandering over the back seat. "Where is he?"

I scanned the rear view. Kimmy was sitting on the hump between the back seats, grinning. "She want to talk?"

"He asked if you wanted to talk."

"Dude, totally." She faced the general area where the ghost sat. "What's it like? Being all ghosty, I mean."

Mr. Kim chuckled. "Tell her it not so bad. Get to see people I like. Go places. See things."

I did.

"But you're always stuck with her."

---

[132] There might have been one, but unless it's right in front of me, or properly advertised, I'm not going to go looking for it.
[133] Particularly funny is the one with the little girl crying into an empty Christmas box. Sorry little Missy, Mommy loves the slots, now.
[134] Progress!

"Hey! I'm right here. I can hear you."

Honey ignored me. "You can't move around. Do as you please."

"I can't?" Mr. Kim seemed to be genuinely surprised.

"I don't know." I stopped directing the conversation back to Honey. "I'd always heard that you'd be stuck where you died. But maybe that's not the case. Maybe you just stick around because I'm the hottest person you know." I winked and could swear a light pink tinged his aura.

"Yeah, that's it." Honey rolled her eyes.

"I wasn't always here. Before I somewhere different. Right after get shot."

I thought back to the vision. Mr. Kim standing in the cave entrance, the car nowhere in sight.

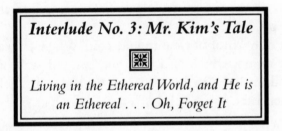

Interlude No. 3: Mr. Kim's Tale

Living in the Ethereal World, and He is an Ethereal . . . Oh, Forget It

"After get shot," he said, "there was time where I could no see anything. Just black. More black." He paused, waited for me to interpret before continuing.

"When lights came on, was in room, like waiting room at doctor's office only big big. A beautiful girl with gold hair and blue eyes like ocean sat behind desk. In front there was long line of people. Ghosts like me only solid. Understand?

"There we all solid. No see-through. I got in line behind old woman with cane carved like horse head, hair like steamed bun. She very nice, ask, 'What are we doing here?' I say, 'Don't know, thought maybe you know.'

"She did not know, but ask man in front of her. He wear

white construction hat and mustache like '80s television star Magnum P.I. He say, 'I don't know, either.'

"Line move slow but could tell that once ghost talk to pretty lady behind desk, then go to one of two doors.

"Macho construction guy answer questions and go to door on right, steamed bun lady go through door on right, too.

"Then it my turn. I expect to go to door on right.

" 'Natural causes?' she ask.

" 'Not really' I say.

" 'What was it, exactly, sir?' she ask.

"When I say, I no remember, because I didn't, then, she grab up big stick like office light bulb. I think she going to hit me, so I put up arms to protect—like this—but she waves over my body, sits back down and say, 'Gunshot. Left door, please, thank you, next.'

"I no see anyone go to left door before, so I scared. Little bit. Little bit.

"The door knob it's damp and cold. When I turn, it open into dark tunnel which also cold and damp. I walk down and get to end, realize I'm back in Ms. Amanda car. Lickity split. Only much later."

"That's so weird, dude," Honey said. "It's like all those shows and movies about the afterworld are right. It's like dying is no different than going to get your driver's license or a smoothie. Kinda sucks dog weiner."

"No shit." I slowed to a stop for a roadwork flagger. "Of course, death can go in other, more bizarre directions. Just look at me, or Wendy, or Gil. You never know what's going to happen, but it's always exciting."

"That's comforting." She smiled then and bit her lip. "I guess."

The flagger, a barrel-shaped Native American woman with a smooth smiling face spoke to Scott, ahead of us, and then approached my window. I hit the button and the glass rolled away.

"You gotta slow down through these parts for the construction. Gotta drive no more than 25 miles per hour, and there's the cops, so you know."

"Thanks."

"Gonna add about an hour to your drive, I'm afraid." So much for shaving an hour off the drive time, I thought. The woman moved on to the camper. Wendy was visibly scowling as she struggled to crank down her window.

An hour into the drive, we rolled up to our first stoplight. A thin strip of town bled off to the right. I didn't have much hope that this was the place, but there was a gas station and on the post in front a sign for a grocery. Scott had spotted it, too. The orange monstrosity turned.

Three buildings down the dirtiest street in America stood the Crow Valley Shop Mart. A single picture window next to a glass door were both obscured by so many flyers, it was impossible to see inside. I parked around the back of the building between a dented dumpster and a broke-down Chevelle with a fuzzy purple steering wheel cover and one of those air fresheners shaped like a king's crown attached to the dash.

"Let's do this." I grabbed my bag and we were off.

Scott stayed outside but Wendy joined us. We opened the door into a vision of hell not often seen outside of war-torn third-world countries. The once-white linoleum was scarred by embedded dirt and a smoggy haze hung in the air like a crack house. I half expected to see ratty sofas with the legs busted off sitting under the list of names of people that could not enter the store without paying their bills. The poverty was palpable and yet I couldn't help but wonder how the zombie tourist board hadn't found this gem. That list just screamed menu and just like the fun runs at the welfare office, no one was going to go looking for some fiscally irresponsible Native Americans, any more than they would a down-on-her-luck single mother fresh from a weekend tweak binge.

But. And there's always a "but."

The girl at the cash register was pleasant enough looking and so I approached. "We're . . . uh . . . looking for the . . . um . . . emcee?"

She threw back her head and let out a snorting laughter that could have easily chortled from a pig's snout. "You mean M.C. Shaman?"

"I guess?" I shrugged.

"Master of the mike?" She giggled. "Duke of dope rhymes?"

"That's him," Wendy added. "He around?"

"He's down cleaning the piss pit." She poked her thumb over her shoulder at an open staircase leading into some kind of a basement. The sign above it read: "Restrooms locked for OUR safety." Quaint.

"Should we just do down—"

"Gilbert!" the checker yelled, cutting off my question. "Give these people the keys to the piss pit."

Do you see how those two words just don't sound good together? The imagery conjures up summer camp nightmares and German kink nightclubs. I was left queasy as though I'd turned a corner and sauntered through a lingering fart or opened *Grave and Country* and found an unflattering picture in the society section.

An elderly Indian man, skin as wrinkled as ribbon candy, creaked into view from behind stacks of yellowed paper, from a raised dais that must have served as the office-slash-security lookout. He shuffled toward the rear and then out of sight. A full minute later, he rounded the corner, baggy trousers dangling off his skeletal frame from a pair of suspenders fashioned from electrical cords. A look NOT from the resort collection of any major house, I assure you.

He scraped across the floor, dragging two scuff tracks in his wake. It took him a full five minutes to reach the cashier, and I oughta know; I checked my watch about eighteen fuckin' times during the old man's trek. He came right up to the girl, reached past her and underneath the cash register, moaning with the effort and retrieved a ring of keys attached to a two-by-four.

I was outraged. "What the fuck? Why didn't you just get us the keys," I asked the checker.

"Policy." She shrugged, and pulled an emery board from the cash drawer and began filing the chipped nails at the end of her stubby fingers.

Gilbert handed Wendy the keys and shuffled back to his post.

Where any normal store that locked its facilities would simply tag the keys, "Ladies" or "Gents," the Crow Valley Shop Mart proprietors felt it necessary to mark their bathroom keys thusly . . .

●   Key to the PISS PIT. Enter at your own risk and clean as you go. Watch for needles, broken bottles, and loose stool.

    Please alert the cashier of empty chip bags and meat packs. Thank you, The Management!

. . . in Magic Marker no less.

Do I need to tell you we were horrified?

In fact, we were the ones shuffling now, each of us alternating pushing the other toward the grimy stairwell, the base of which seemed to vanish into a black hole that could only be the opening of some septic tank or heroin den.

"You go." Wendy prodded me toward the first step.

"Mr. M.C. Shaman? Are you down there?" I called. I heard nothing in response but a dull thud and some distant clanging. The first step was the hardest.

Wendy and Honey clung to my shoulders, fighting for the full use of me as a shield, as we descended into the piss pit.

Despite looking like a cave, the base of the stairs was dimly lit by a single overhead bulb, a dimple of grunge dead center like a dirty nipple. The sign on the door simply read: PRIVATE, and the key was not to a knob but to a padlock. Apparently the Duke of Dope Rhymes enjoyed absolute solitude while cleaning up piss, or whatever. I slid the key into the slit and turned. It popped open with a click and we were in. A gust of stagnant urine caused my eyes to bulge, Wendy to gasp, and Honey to shout, "Dude!"[135] The door opened on a hall of other doors; the two on the left shared the international symbols of laying cable, the other, at the far end, was cracked. The floor was cement and wet brown stains ran in rivulets from the toilets to a rusty drain in the center of the hall.

"Mr. M.C. Shaman!" I called again.

"Yo?" Wendy added.

I grimaced.

"What?" She shrugged and looked down the hall, eyebrows raised.

The cracked door opened, filling the murky hall with a blast of light bordering an angelic—dare I say—shaft. I had to squint to see the approaching silhouette—a man, not tall, but wearing some sort of cape and leaning on a cane. As he came into view, it dawned on me that he was dressed in full-on pimp regalia, from the insanity of a purple zoot suit down to the jewel-studded chalice he held in his hand like a brandy snifter. If you could just frame out all that fabric, he wasn't half bad looking. His skin was the burnished brown of years in the Montana sun. He had sleepy bedroom eyes and a nose like a small winter squash. It was the hair. You might expect a couple of braids falling from a feathered headband.[136] No. Not M.C. Shaman. He was rockin' it old school in a larger-than-life afro.

I swallowed a laugh. I wish I could say the same for Wendy and Honey, who giggled openly. Pointing.

He rapped the cane on the cement like a gavel and stepped closer. "There you is, I been waitin' for y'alls dead asses. Where you bitches been?"

I for one was appalled. Not at his deft use of ebonics, but at

---

[135] As opposed to the farm fresh scent of newly expelled urine, of course.
[136] You, being a racist and all. I won't tell.

the Grillz he wore. I'd initially thought they were gold teeth. But as he entered our comfort bubble, I noticed that the word "shaman" was spelled out across his teeth in diamonds—er—cubic zirconia.

"Dude, you talk just like Davonne Graham." Honey grinned.

"Thanks. You the girl with a question to ax. Get yo ass ova here." He gestured for her to come forward.[137]

She slipped passed me, but I held onto her belt and dropped in behind. "That's right. I—" she began.

"Oh I already knows the question." He tapped his 'fro with the tip of his cane. "And it's a sad thang. A sad sad sad thang."

"Well if you could just—"

"Shit. You know what it is?" His eyes widened.

"What *what* is?" I asked, unable to hold a fashion comment back any longer. "And why are you dressed like a—"

"A mothafuckin' white tragedy, that's what."

Honey's mouth dropped open, she glowered. "But I'm Korean."

"Don't matta none."

"Listen. Don't you think you're being a little racist?" Wendy pointed out, literally.

"I can't be no racist, bitch. I's a minority."

I pushed Honey behind me, the logistics of which were becoming increasingly difficult, as the walls were smaller on one end of the hallway than the other. "Not where we are, you aren't. The way I see it we're the minority and you're being offensive." I felt a knuckle in my back and looked back at Wendy. She mouthed, "You're offended?"

I shook my head, mouthed back an exaggerated "No, of course not," and went back to work. "We've driven a long way to meet you, and this poor girl just wants to see her brother again. The least you can do is drop the bullshit posturing and give us an answer."

---

[137] In case you need some interpretation. I'm ashamed of you, really.

"You gots the answer. Bust a cap in the bitch. She'll be eyein' her brotha real quick." He jutted his jaw, pursing his lips.

Wendy must have sensed my anger, as she grabbed Honey's hand and stomped off up the stairs.

I twirled toward M.C. Shaman. "Okay Mr. M.C. Wannabe Gangsta. I'm gonna need another answer before I leave here or I know one racist Indian that's going to go missing." I cocked my jaw open, clicking at the man until his eyes were saucers and he'd begun to back away into the bright room.

"No. No. No. Don't do that. I got tons of answers. You just don't know the questions."

I followed him in. A card table sat square in the middle of the room under a pendant lamp, a label-less bottle rested on the motheaten green felt, a glass next to it; stacks of cellophane envelopes sat awaiting sets from a piles of Grillz.

"Holy shit. Those aren't by any chance enchanted," I asked.

"Now there's a question. Hells yeah. They all gots the mag-ixes. I see you familiar with my product."

I thought of The White House, the mistakes, the cluster-fuck. "Not really. So, how about we start with a way for Honey to see her brother again?" I asked.

"Well, sure. There are tons of ways. An ocularis, for instance. Drink?"

"What's that?" I pointed at the bottle.

"Alcohol. Whatchoo mean what's that?" He poured a shot and slid it toward me.

I sat down and fondled the glass. "No. What you just said. Ocularis?"

"Just like a telescope only different. You don't see no stars, you see spirits. But it don't matta. Her problem ain't about see-ing her brother. Her problem about dyin'. Bitch is gonna die soon and there ain't nothin' you can do about it."

"Why? How?" I reached for the shot glass, tossed it back and whistled. Rotgut. Probably made it himself in a rusty bucket. Still, I needed a little pick-me-up. His words were hitting hard.

"Don't know why but seem to me she get beat to death. Nasty way to bite it, you ask me." He poured me another.

"Who?"

"Don't know that, either."

"Jesus, can't we go do a sweat or do some kind of vision quest or some other Indian shit and figure it out?" I rolled my eyes.

"Who's being racist now?"

"Well you are a shaman, aren't you?"

"God, no." He stood up and snatched his pimp cup.

"What?"

"I'm a psychic . . . and a pimp. I just like the name M.C. Shaman. Helps with my street cred."

I imagined the sad little patch of cement outside. "Don't you mean 'road cred'? There's not even enough pavement outside to call it a street."

"Whatever. All I'm sayin' is your girl's gonna die. Or supposed to."

"Supposed to?"

"Sometimes you can stop these things."

"I can?"

"No."

"Jesus, you just said—"

"I know. I thought it'd make you feel better. Kinda don't wanna go down your food hole." A series of giggles erupted from M.C. Shaman, nervous as hiccups.

"I see." I stood up and walked back into the hall.

"Wait. I do see one more thing."

I stopped but didn't turn around.

"Caves. Lots and lots of caves."

Caves. Yeah. I got that one already.

I was done with M.C. Shaman. Done with mystics, psychics, seers, whatever. If there was a way to save Honey it was going to come from good old-fashioned ingenuity or perhaps a big mouth, and I'm pretty sure you know I'm not talking about a snappy comeback.

Chapter 19

The Worst Realization Ever, Seriously

Travel is the bane of a vampire's existence. For the most part, the big freeway chain hotels are full of families and people that will be missed. If, say, you have an early morning craving you end up having to drive to some downtrodden neighborhood to feed, and then you run the risk of dawn. The best course of action is a downtown hotel. But that has its own series of risks; you'll likely have to valet, so there goes the getaway car. Now, bed and breakfasts. There's a solution.

—Gary Smagille's *Budget Travel for Bloodsuckers*

As the Crow Reservation gave way to Montana ranch land, the horizon flattened out paper thin and wind swept off the snow-capped Big Horns like a frigid hurricane. Scott's Mustang, arguably the most aerodynamic of the three vehicles, rocked with each gust and I ought to know; I was spread-eagled in the passenger seat, clutching the headrest with white knuckles, Scott's hand searching for the sweet spot between my legs.

"The way I see it . . ." He drew languorous circles around my nasty nugget.[138] "We've got three likely scenarios."

---

[138] You don't mind if I call it my nasty nugget, do you? Normally, I'd come right out and say clit before I call it something like love button. I guess I was feeling romantical.

"Uh huh." I tensed my thighs, trapping his fingers in place for a moment.

"One—the most likely—your boy Fishhook has been up to no good. He killed Tad for the mushroom haul."

I slid my hand across his thigh groping the bulge he'd cultivated.

"Aah . . . or two. The weirdo family shapeshift . . . *and* are killing off perfectly good white people."

I hummed a response. His fingers moving faster now, crossed and trapping my clit like a wish. I played my fingers across the fly of his jeans, teasing with the idea of springing that bad boy from its cell.

"Th-th-three." He stuttered. "I haven't mentioned this before now, but there's a strong possibility that Markham's onto my little defection and he's sent Randy or Darryl to follow up and finish the job. At least we know for sure they're werewolves. What's worse, I've got a pretty decent nose and I didn't catch a whiff of werewolf ass on anyone in that parking lot last night."

That last sentence killed my libido. I left his cock struggling, reached for his wrist and gave it a pat. "Yeah, I'm done down here, let's pick that back up later."

"Are you serious?" He watched for me to shift into a grin, gestured at his lap, and then shoulders slouched, pulled his hand away. He wiped off what little moisture I was able to manufacture on his pants leg. "You're gonna give me blue balls, you know?"

I lifted my hips off the seat, straightened my panties and pulled the discount skirt out of my ass. "So when were you going to tell me about your new theory?"

"I just thought about it on the drive from Billings."

"Okay, smart guy, then get this shit. Who killed the albino girl? That was only two days out. Markham couldn't have found out your plans that quick, unless he's got you LoJacked or something. Do you remember that wereslut shoving an electronic tampon up your butt?"

"How'd you know?" Scott asked with a wink. "Did you ever think maybe he didn't trust me to begin with?"

I hadn't. "That would definitely make it plausible. But why would they kill that girl?"

"A warning?" He shrugged.

"To whom?"

"To me. To let me know that they're out there and watching me *not* do my job." As if to drive his point home, he fiddled with the rearview mirror.

"Why not just put you down?"

He cringed at the lame dog reference.

"Sorry. But, well, you know? Why hold back?"

"I guess they should have really. I would have in their position."

"So maybe that's not what's happening."

"But just in case, when we get to Rapid City, we'd better build a fort and hunker down."

"That's all very frontier, stud, and don't think I don't appreciate the image, but I can't."

"What?"

"I've got plans."

"What the hell are you talking about?"

"Okay." I held up my hands in surrender. "My mother's about to kick it. She's in some hospice center as we speak. As wonderful as it's been having this whole adventure to take my mind off her, time's up. I can't put off the inevitable. Gil's agreed to go with me, just to help me through it.

"Oh. I'm sorry, babe. Must be horrible for you."

"Oh no no no. I mean yes." I shook my head. "Oh yes. It's horrible, but not for the reasons you're thinking. Ethel's totally getting what's coming to her. She was a real asshole. Gil and Wendy were the ones who talked me into getting closure." Complete with air quotes on "closure." "I was just going to let the issue die."

"Jesus."

"What?"

"It's just . . . That's a little harsh. She is your mother."

I could feel my mouth contorting into a cat's anus. How dare he? "How *dare* you make judgments?" I asked, swiveling in the seat to face him.

"I was just saying—"

"I heard you. I'm just not in the mood to take criticism from my own private stalker."

"Also harsh."

"It was meant to be."

"Listen. Wendy and Gil are right in some respects. It's important to clear the air before she dies. But you also need to understand that—"

"Don't say it." I couldn't bear to hear it spoken.

"We all take after our parents in one way or another. In a sense, you owe a lotta what makes you so cool to your Mom. Sure there were bad times. We all had those, but there were good times, I bet. Fun times. Times where I bet you even admired her."

I seethed.

But didn't have to cover his mouth. Scott knew enough to keep quiet this time. We sat in silence as we crossed the border into South Dakota. His words echoed in my head the entire time, mixed with my own in a symphony of shame.

Just like Mom.

It was true. God it was true. The bitch had worn off on me like a red shirt dropped in with the goddamn whites. It was in my freshman year at Seattle Community College that I first noticed the similarities and began to shove the reality down as deep as Wendy could a Twix bar.

Take a look. . . .

Jordan Lamb-Corey was a 14-year-old advanced placement student working through a tough social challenge and not just a premature hyphen. The girl was a legitimate genius, SAT scores off the charts, president of the Honor Society and a complete social reject. It didn't help that her parents cut a deal with her high school to split up her time between college coursework and age-appropriate social activities (lunch, sports, dances).

The way Jordan's days were scheduled you'd think she was a CEO or a Hollywood actress on a press tour, and not the shy bookworm. Which is why I found her in the college library, reading Candace Bushnell in a study carrel.

"The thing about that book . . ." I flicked the cover to see Sarah Jessica Parker and the girls stepping out.

"Huh?" She shuddered with surprise, sheepish eyes peeking over metal-framed glasses.

"The thing about that book is that it makes you want to live it, right?" I squeezed in between her and the carrel and sat on the desk, crossing my legs.

She scanned my look. Head-to-toe afternoon glamour complete with pearl drop earrings, a stunning up-do and the finest Edith Head knock-off lunching suit I could find. Heels of course. Pointy as hell.

"You're really gorgeous." Jordan pushed her glasses up the thin bridge of her nose, revealing a startling red indent. The girl's lips were thin and nearly as pale as her pasty cheeks.

"I know, right? Sadly, you're not. But you can be. I've seen you hanging around here and you look a little out of your element. Though . . ." Her clothes were mildly grungy, flannel shirt over a Screaming Trees T-shirt, holey-kneed jeans with words doodled on the fabric in ballpoint pen. ". . . you might want to hook up with the potheads in the teachers lounge."

"No!" She yelled. Heads poked up from their studies. She dropped to a whisper. "I don't do drugs."

"Of course not. Who said you did?"

She shrugged.

"The trick is to run with it and never let them know they fazed you." I breezed over the fact that I'd been the offensive party and reached over and took off her glasses. She squinted, grabbed them from my hand and slid them back on with a grimace.

"I don't have any friends around here. In high school, either, really. Everybody sucks."

I hatched my scheme right then and there.

"Isn't that the truth?" I assessed her hair, thick, shoulder-length and not at all scraggly. I could work with it. "Let's do a makeover. What do you say?"

As her thin lips stretched into a smile, they flattened a bit becoming almost plump. Almost attractive. Workable.

"Meet me after school. I'll be at the Starbucks."

"Which one?"

"Duh, the new one."

She nodded and so began my gracious tutelage of the poor girl.[139] If I had my way, Jordan would be the most popular girl in her school by the end of the week. I could dream, right?

Now, It's important to note that I, myself, was not particularly popular—nor was I a geek, mind you. I was feared and that's nearly as important.

"So. Do you at least know the Five Deadly Digs?"

"What? Like slams or something?" she asked.

"Something. Let's practice." I stepped away cocked my jaw and looked from her shoes, up her legs to her eyes, cringed and shook my head.

"Oh my God, what?" Jordan brushed at her top, prodded her hair, for debris, presumably.

---

[139] The makeover included:
  1. *Choppy bitch hair and hot new face* (care of the inattentive ladies at the Chanel counter and a five-finger discount.)
  2. *Contact lenses.* Coaching on parental manipulation was necessary, and since the girl had never caused a problem in her life, this one was a cinch).
  3. *Dietary restrictions and a harsh workout regimen.* Because, honestly. I saw the girl eat a muffin. A fucking muffin.
  4. *Fashion advice and shopping tips.* You simply can't rule a school in holey jeans. It's just not possible.
  5. *An attitude adjustment.* For Christ's sake the girl didn't even know the Five Deadly Digs.
  6. *On-call consultations.* I was like a saint, right? Saint Amanda of the Chronically Unpopular. Alert the Pope.

"*That*, bitch, was number one, The Look. It's an up and down perusal followed by the slow shake of the head. Non-verbal critique is essential for diminishing your adversary to a miniscule blithering idiot." I gestured to the girl. "Case in point."

"Gawd. Nice."

"It's not about nice. It's about winning. Two. Metaphor. See that woman over there?" I pointed to an overweight thing stepping out of a city bus, at least five children in tow and lugging a sixth in a car seat, likely named Sciatica. "Like so." I yelled across to the woman, "Bitch, it's a vagina not a clown car!"

Jordan's head sunk into her shoulders. "Holy shit! That was evil."

"No. That was number two and not the freshest comparison, either. I think I picked it up from my mother. By making an intellectual connection between one thing, the vagina, in this case, to a ridiculous comparison, we gain a significant advantage on our opponent, in this case, the lovely Welfaria over there. Which brings me to number three. Renaming. Don't ever call someone by their proper name. It's like giving up your power and people with high self-esteem don't do that. Got it?"

Our high heels clicked in tandem.

"Next up. Superficial agreement. Let's try. You ask me to do something."

Jordan thought for a moment, then asked, "Could you meet me after school today?"

I laughed. "Uh . . . yeah." I nodded. "I'll totally do that. For sure. Whatever. See? How'd that feel."

"Crappy."

"Excellent. Last one. The truth. Get to know people's secrets. Nothing cuts a person off at the knees like a well-timed revelation. Since I don't know any about you we'll forgo practice, but keep your eyes open and listen."

Within weeks, like magic the girl developed quite a following amongst the other students. By homecoming, she was a princess, by holiday break banging the quarterback, by prom the first sophomore queen. She was unstoppable. We'd meet in the library and conspire.

"The other day, Heather Gill came begging for a spot in my clique." Jordan exaggerated a yawn. "She used to be *très* popular. But now, sadly, she's fallen to the wayside. I, of course, let her in on some bad news. Her time was over. A new era had begun. She cried until I was forced to toss a Kleenex at her feet."

Maybe I was ill, but her words seemed cold.

"Jesus. Don't you have feelings?" I asked.

"None that I'm aware of. Should I be concerned? Oh . . ." She reached for my lapel and a blurry-edged spot—had it been on skin would have been a melanoma. "Is this mustard? Some-one sure likes their food."

"Wow. You're a nasty bitch."

"I don't make the rules, Angela." She looked me up and down, shook her head. "You did. Has your brain turned into those condiments you're so fond of?"

She sounded just like Ethel. Exactly, in fact.

Our interaction turned Jordan Lamb-Corey into a real cooze and yet she was so familiar. Nothing compares to the first real-ization that you're just like a parent. In fact, the experience is like a punch in the gut followed by a kick in the ass, as all the mem-ories of telling yourself you'd never be like her, or him, or them. And then you are.

When I realized what I'd done to Jordan was exactly what my mother had done to me, I shut down. Didn't even blink. It was shock. It was simply better not to think about it. Move into denial and stay there like a comfy cottage.

At least I thought so at the time.

Of course, it makes for a lonely existence never growing to any level of emotional maturity, but you play the hand life gives you. Even in death.

Or not.

★　★　★

"You're right."

His head snapped at the sound, mouth agape in pseudo-disbelief. "I'm what?"

I sucked at my teeth, while Scott grinned wildly and beat out a rhythm on the steering wheel. He was really pushing his luck—cute—but not enough to save him from the inevitable smack down.

"I said, 'You're right.' Now shut up about it."

A stuttering chortle erupted from the driver's seat. I chose to ignore it for a moment and then reached across the gap for a titty twister. He yelped like the mutt he was.

"Quit it!" he yelled, voice raising an octave as he shifted out of my reach. The car lurched to the left from his effort to escape my torturous fingers.

"Mmm. Not so kinky now, are you?" I crossed my arms and watched low hills rise out of nothing and a town out of that.

It was called Belle Fourche, and, though there was certainly nothing "Belle" about it—the highway did "Fourche" if that's what the town founders meant.[140] I kind of doubt it. It didn't take much longer to reach Rapid City and the cheesy Raging Rapids Water Park and Family Suites, a catastrophe of architecture not often seen outside nightmares or kindergarten art hour. Tubes of every color darted in and out of holes in the three-story center tower, like maggots threading a giant block of blue cheese. One tube expelled waves of water into a giant clear funnel; human children swirled inside like living turds, flushing into yet another tube that probably wasn't bound for the sewer, though had every right to.

"Maybe we could find somewhere else," I said, but Scott was already out of the car and heading for the lobby.

While he checked us in, I scanned a rack of local attractions. Mt. Rushmore, the Black Hills, the Jewel Caves.

Huh?

---

[140] I apologize for the lapse into cheese. Please keep your groans to a low level. Thanks.

What?

I snatched the brochure from its slot and scanned the information. About an hour away and massive, though sadly not full of diamonds, rubies or sapphires, the Jewel Caves may actually stretch out over a three-state region. Scary. And quite possibly what the vision and the freakin' shaman had been referring to. At least I was fairly certain until I looked back at the display and noticed the twenty *other* cave brochures.

Yeah, that's about right, I thought. Why make it easy?

"You ready?" Scott brandished the room key, fluttering it between his fingers.

"Yeah. Just let me grab a few of these . . . or all of them." I slipped a dozen of the brochures into my bag and followed Scott back out to the cars.

He stopped briefly at the Winnebago to tell Wendy to follow, and again at the Volvo to get the message to Honey.

Four wings spread from the water park, housing the guest rooms. Scott earned brownie points by choosing one of the furthest. Number 184 was in the far corner of the property, nestled snug against and comfortable . . . oh who am I fooling? The place was a wasteland, a flat rectangle of a building with outward-facing doors rising from a cement patch in a barren prairie.

It was all just so . . . beige.

So we drove the obstacle course of happy families dragging their luggage like disobedient pets, marauding hoards of children, SpongeBob SquarePants towel capes flapping in their wake and packs of sullen teens comparing self-mutilation trophies. Our convoy spilled into the last three spaces, the RV jutting into the parking lot like a hernia.

Two beds, a desk, a dresser with a TV on it. Standard motel room but with the edgy addition of a glass-based lamp, pseudo-Warhols and a carpet straight off a Vegas casino floor. While I filled in the girls on the possibility of Markham's guys swooping in for a massacre, Scott made quick work of the mattresses, doubling them up in front of the window.

"Where's your gun?" I asked Honey.

She reached into her backpack and pulled out the shiny black thing, slid out the cartridge, fondled the top bullet and slapped it back in.

"Okay. So that's one." Scott stood with his hands on his hips à la Superman. "I'll get mine from the car. The bullets won't stop them if they come, but they'll surely slow them down."

"Dude. What if it really was Fishhook, though?" Honey asked.

"Then he's probably long gone." I patted her shoulder on my way to the door. "Gil and I won't be long and then we'll get out of here and head home. There's got to be something we can do to patch things up with Markham."

Scott shrugged. "Doubtful, but it's worth a shot."

So, as dusk took hold and Scott battened down the hatches with Wendy and Honey, Gil and I drove off in search of Passages Hospice Center and . . . ahem . . . closure.

Chapter 20

Checking In on Those Checking Out

The elderly may be an acquired taste, but in some of our "edgier" circles, senior citizens have replaced the homeless as the entrée of choice. Late-night dining clubs are cutting deals with human "partners" at nursing homes for access to their financially "unstable" clients. It's all in good fun. The cherry on this bloody sundae is usually . . . the "partner" himself.

—Graciella Meeks, Food Reporter,
Goodnight, Undead

Rapid City, South Dakota is not a big place.

So why, I ask, did it take Gil and me three hours to find the place? We drove through downtown three times, passed by what seemed to be the hospital row at least five, even stopping once to fill up with gas and a shabbily dressed pedestrian with a shopping cart nowhere near a grocer.[141] Gil insisted it was one way, I the other.

Bicker, brake, accelerate.

We ended up having to ask the gas station attendant for directions. Bob, I believe his name was, stared at us like he'd never seen anything but twelve-dollar haircuts. Sure enough, Passages

---

[141] And if that doesn't scream "fair game," nothing does.

was right there near the hospital, only slightly further up the road. Neither of us had been correct, which is a shame, because the banter would have been much more lively.[142]

"Is that it?" Gil pointed across the bridge of my nose at a darkened lawn between two rows of poplar trees; it meandered down a gently sloping hill toward a single story building, overly columned like every other memorial.

"It's gotta be. I feel the rest of the life draining out of me the closer we get." I glanced at his normally handsome face; it took on the worn boredom of a daycare worker. Maybe I was laying it on a little thick. "Looks like a mausoleum, though. Huh?"

He grinned, nodded. "No doubt, only darker. The sign is even off. Maybe they close up to visitors after a certain hour, you think?"

It was difficult to make out the swirling ethereal lettering of the word "Passages," but "Hospice" was clear enough even by street lamp. The big black lettering was ominous and blocky as though Death himself—or herself—had done the job.

I grimaced. There weren't any cars lining the drive down into the place, so I shut off the headlights, just in case we'd need to get in there unnoticed—and by unnoticed I do mean breaking and entering.[143] "The workers probably all park in the back."

"Yep. Probably smoke back there, too."

"You think? Even with all the cancer patients and shit."

"Oh yeah. Addicts don't have those kind of boundaries."

I passed the facility and spun the SUV around to the opposite side of the street, coming to rest in the deep shadow of an overgrown lilac bush. Too deep, apparently. Gil struggled to open his door and grumbled as the branches slapped at him as he made his way around to the back.

"Jesus Christ!" He stumbled through the last bit, a stray branch dragging across his cheek like a claw.

---

[142] See? I'm looking out for you and me, but mostly me.
[143] You really don't expect me to come back, do you?

"Shut up," I whispered. "We need to be quiet. I've got no intention of waiting until morning for visiting hours. Let's just keep to the tree line and get a look around first, see if there's an easy entrance."

As we neared the center, stumbling nearly the entire way over roots like rude feet, the windows only appeared darker, even less occupied than was suggested from the road. The main entrance was a black pit and the glass transoms were barely visible in the moonlight.

There were quite a few cars in the back, mostly older model domestics, but a few Japanese cars dotted the rear parking lot, right up next to a low fence. Beyond this was a vast panorama that had it been daylight might have stretched out across the fabled Badlands and the Etch A Sketch doodles of residential streets and block houses between. A Mercedes as black as ink gathered moonlight and my attention—would there even be an import dealer in this shitty town?

Must be a doctor, I thought.

The back door was nearly as dark as the front, but propped open with a wooden wedge. But, that wasn't nearly as interesting as the one brightly lit room shining on the far right like a beacon. The curtains were closed and the light snuck around the edges like a copy machine.

"Well, someone's home," I said, then pointed and darted across the gray lot, careful not to crunch against stray gravel or break an ankle in a pothole. Gil followed, close enough that when I paused, his hand rested on the center of my back, urging me forward, up the short set of stairs, and he crouched with me to listen at the crack in the door.

The soft strains of some easy listening, horns like Lawrence Welk dancers would spin to, sweeping the floor with gauzy chiffon gowns and patent leather nightmares floated toward us. But the sound was not my concern.

It was the smell.

A dense iron-filled stench crept from the building. Gil caught the scent too and his nose crinkled with interest.

Blood.

Not the luscious flowing vibrant crimson that we crave, either. This was spilt blood, coagulated and congealed on floors thick with wax buildup, reeking of bleachy cleansers and artificial pine.[144]

Gil's cheek pressed against mine, nose jutting toward the crack. "That's different types. Way more than just one vein is open in there. I don't like this."

Before I'd really thought about it, my hand was reaching for the door pushing it open into a scene from a horror movie. Bodies were strewn everywhere. Bloated corpses in white uniforms shared floor space with cancer-riddled shells in thin cotton robes, overlapping legs and arms woven together as they fell or were linked purposefully into one disturbing game of Barrel of Monkeys. A sweep of bloody gore like a red carpet stretched out to an open door at the end. Light flooded from the room and shadows danced in the glow.

So much for closure.

I won't lie, the thought of my mother's body being strewn amongst the rest of the victims, indistinguishable from the crowd, made me smile. Just a little one, though.[145] How ironic that Ethel expended so much effort to be a unique individualist, and here she was just some stray flotsam, a bit of goo on the floor.

Still. It would have been nice to see her off.

I scanned the floor as I stood, Gil rising with me. I knew who'd done this. Somewhere in my scattered mind pieces of phone calls were surfacing, moving forward. Someone had wanted to know an awful lot about me, capitalizing on my—how shall we say—penchant for celebrity. That someone could have been

---

[144] What a waste.*
*This footnote sponsored by Gil's Luxury Vamping, creating quality bloodsuckers since 2007.
[145] I'm not completely insensitive.

Jack the Ripper and I'd have fed him information as long as he said he worked for Rupert Murdoch. That someone had probably arrived in that Mercedes. If that someone turned out to be Markham, I wouldn't forget that Marithé had been the middleman in the whole fuck up, or middlewoman. Middlezombie?

Either way, she'd be dealt with. Oh yes.[146]

I slipped my feet out of my heels and gestured for Gil to do the same. Probably not a good idea to knock at this point— once you've decorated a hall with dead bodies, you pretty much don't want visitors.

The linoleum was cool under the pads of my feet, so it must have been freezing in there. I'm not such a good indicator of climate, being roughly room temperature, myself. I was careful with my footing, though. Cold or not, blood was slippery and it webbed across the floor like Italianate marbling.

The closest body was a chubby nurse splayed like a broken doll with her skirt bunched up around her waist and granny panties dotted with old menses. And something else, or lack there of. I held out my arm to get Gil's attention and pointed to where the woman's head should have been. The vampire's nose curled in disgust. Gil never even left a drop of blood, and some of the time his victims gave it up willingly.

A palsied hand clutched the dead nurse's wrist like a talon, a patient obviously, and probably near death, but again, no head. I examined each of the dead by turn, breezing over the particulars of the remains. Looking for that singular indicator, that calling card.

No fucking head.

None of them.

We crept with our backs to the wall, stopping at each open door to listen, peek around the corner. And in each instance, the same thing, white sheets, stripped and cascading from hospital

---

[146] It would probably go something like: "You told him where we were!" "Did not." "Okay." I'm not saying I'm scared of her. I'm just sayin'.

beds like winter waterfalls. Dragged from their beds in the middle of the night. For what purpose?

"It's a fucking massacre," Gil whispered.

"No shit. It's pretty bad."

We didn't say any more. We're used to death, but this was different. There was a glee in this, a blatant wastefulness. It was almost too much to take.

At the midpoint of the hall we found the heads. Lined up two deep on the floor, spanning the entire distance of the entry hall and facing the door, ready to greet those first horrified pioneers.

"Look at that," I said.

"It's shocking. I think we should get out of here." His eyes were wide and fear played across his face in spasms. "Like now."

"Hold on." I stepped over the rows and squinted at the heads in the dim light. Face after unfamiliar face. Men, women, young, old, mostly thinned out to gristle and leather by a lingering death. But no Ethel. "She's not here." I grabbed Gil's shoulder. "It's Markham."

"I know it is."

"How?"

"We don't have near enough time for that story. I'll tell you later, once we're out and safe." He slid his hand into mine and pulled me toward the exit.

"No, Gil. I can't." I jerked my hand from his. "Not until I see."

Now I know what you're thinking, this is the stupidest, horror movie victim bullshit I've ever read. Why would she keep walking toward that door, when he's obviously down there, waiting? No. Unh uh. Don't go down there, bitch!

But here's the deal: I had a plan.

"Wait for me in the parking lot. This won't take too long."

Gil lingered.

"Just do it, Gil. I know what I'm doing. He turned and tiptoed over the carnage, slipping out the door without a squeak.

The same lilting strains whispered down the hall. A radio station might have broken in with a call sign, so I suspected someone was listening to a CD. The music was familiar, too, like a memory.

Like Saturday night at the Frazier's.

Mother loved Lawrence Welk, but that was a secret, punishable by death and/or public humiliation, of the verbal sort, since Ethel couldn't legally employ a front yard gallows. She used to dance with me, spinning me until my robe would twirl.

Mother.

Markham was listening to my mother's CDs. Probably dancing with her dead body, her head lolling and arms and legs flopping around like a rag doll. That sick fucker.

I crept down the hall, the music's volume increasing with each step. He was definitely in there. Dancing. The shadow stretched across the linoleum, across the bodies, like a De Chirico study.

I stopped in my tracks.

It was time for the plan.

Markham has a thing for bottomless girls? Wait until he got a load of me. I'd show him bottomless—the hottest piece of zombie ass around, guaranteed. Wendy was out of service, after all, and this was Bumfuck, Nowhere. How stiff could the competition be? Once I'd lured him in with my perfectly trimmed patch and badonkadonk, I'd have him near enough to blow the life right out of him. Just one quick exhalation into his unsuspecting mouth and those lungs would turn to sponge and suck the life out of the vamp.

I slipped out of my skirt and panties, letting them drop to the floor in a rare patch of blood-free linoleum. I took off my blouse, hung it on a doorknob and sauntered into the shaft of light, posing with my hips twisted outward and a pout on my perfectly toned lips, playing the slut for all it was worth.

And that would have been great. Demeaning, sure.

But, it would have worked perfect.

If only it had been Markham.

"Amanda!" The voice exploded from the figure in the center of the room, as though shouted into a microphone, and blood swirled in between us, curling away from the vile creature's lips.

It couldn't be.

It just wasn't possible.

I could feel bile, or bits of skinhead rise in my throat along with the dreaded words.

"Hello Mother."

She stood in the center of the room; hand on her cocked hip and a look of condescension on her bloody face. At her feet lay a desiccated Markham, looking a lot less threatening in a sunken colorless heap. Dead. Again.

"Where are your clothes, girl?" she asked, followed immediately by the look and a slow condescending shake of her head.[147] Blood dripped from her chin, down the front of her hospital gown.

I covered myself with both hands. "What the fuck?"

"Well, I'm alive, obviously, get some clothes on, you're embarrassing me." She stepped over Markham's body and then stopped, head snapping to the right. "Avert your eyes boys. I'm not kidding. I'll do you like I did the rest of these shitheads."

Two burly guys, one red-headed and freckled as Becky Thatcher, the other black and shiny, but with unusually thin lips, covered their eyes like a quick salute. Turning and facing the wall, apparently under my mother's spell.

Did she have spells?

I was even less prepared than I was clothed. The words wouldn't come. All that practiced hatred seemed inaccessible. I slipped out and put my clothes back on.

"What the hell happened here? And why aren't you dead, Ethel?" She wasn't, that was clear. Wasn't even dying. She looked healthy, in fact, glowing, gorgeous, even youthful, by twenty years, at least.

---

[147] Yeah. That one. The first Deadly Dig.

I always knew I looked like my mother. But seeing her like this made me realize it again. We could have been sisters.

"Mr. Markham here . . ." She kicked the body. ". . . was waiting for you to get here with someone named Gil. Oh-ho-ho boy did he want to kill that one. Who is that, by the way, boyfriend? Husband?"

"Oh no. God no, just a friend. He's outside." Why was I even responding? I should have turned and walked out the moment I saw her. Abandoned her to figure all this shit out on her own.

"So our dead friend here got bored and thought it'd be fun to bite your old mom. Pick on a dying woman, can you imagine? Well, that was just rude. So, I bit the fucker back."

"More than just bit from the looks of it."

"Oh well, the blood sprayed in my mouth and at first I was disgusted. Then something odd happened. It started to taste good. So good. It's been a long time since I've even tasted anything, what with the fluid they keep pushing here and the medication. Might as well have been in a coma, for the treatment. So, I kept drinking and drinking. He did, too, I guess. That's what vampires do. But, I was thirstier. By the time I was done, so was he." She jerked a thumb at the pile. "Passed out a little bit, but then felt this amazing strength. Like rage. It's what I've been missing all my life, Mandy."

"Don't call me that."

She ignored me and continued, "When I walked out in the hall, these two hambones were making a real mess. I gave them quite a talking to, I can tell you. Ask them, if you don't believe me."

"It's true," Darryl or Randy said, still facing the wall. "I'm guessing we work for Ethel, now. Your mom, I mean."

I rolled my eyes.

"I should say so." She strode past me and snapped her fingers. Inexplicably, I followed. "I finished off the rest myself, took off their heads because some of the skinny fuckers were starting to turn into wolves." She plodded through the bloody mess in the hall in fuzzy slippers, soppy with gore, kicking cheerfully through the deceased like new snow. "Sloppy boys. Couldn't tell if the others were going to so I thought it would be prudent to even it up."

"God. Why'd you line up their heads like that?"

"Seemed like the right thing to do. Plus, you know how I like to be organized. This way they can be easily identified. Now." She turned and smiled, fangs bared. "Where's that boyfriend of yours? I owe him a great big hug for sending me the cure."

"Sending you the . . ." I slapped my forehead with my palm. "Mother. You don't need to meet Gil. You need to get outta here, figure out what you're gonna to do. The police are eventually going to show up."

"Oh." She reached for my hand. "Silly. I know exactly what I'm going to do. I'm going to follow my girl back to wherever all this magic comes from and live happily ever after. That's what I'm going to do."

I groaned. This wasn't how it was supposed to go at all. I couldn't even tap into the anger. It was all just so weird. Maybe Gil could just take care of her, like some vampire Big Brother program.

"Amanda!" Gil shouted from the rear entrance. "Are you alright?"

"Ooh." She clapped her hands once. "There he is now. I can't wait to meet him."

"Is someone with you down there?"

"Um . . . yeah."

Chapter 21

The Water Park
Runs Red with Blood

Werewolves are unfairly targeted as the most overtly aggressive species on the planet. The assumption is simply ridiculous. With their penchant for wars and covert military actions, high crime rates, and even violence within their own packs—I mean families, of course—humans are by far the most vicious, dangerous, and deadly species. At least werewolf governments function adequately.
—Interview with Angela Coltrane, Were Advocate
and Separatist, *Undead Science Monitor*

"Darling?" Ethel asked. "Who's this glassy Asian gentleman sitting next to me?"

Mr. Kim gave my mother a suspicious glance and with good reason. Not only did she not care for strangers, she wasn't a fan of Asians. Never had been. I cringed at the thought of her calling him a gook or chink or some other more offensive derogation.[148] You should have seen her toy with the delivery boy when I was a kid. Horrific.

"That's Mr. Kim and that's *exactly* how you'll refer to him. Understand?"

---

[148] Oh yeah. There's lots.

She sneered and held out her hand as though he'd gladly kiss it. "The pleasure is all mine, Mr. Kim."

He simply stared.

I slammed her door and we were on our way back to the hotel. Randy and Darryl followed behind in—oddly enough—a bright yellow Volkswagen Bug, looking very much the couple. Where did they go to henchman school? Fire Island?

"It's been quite a while, darling. We've got some catching up to do."

"Is that a threat?" I glanced over at Gil for back up. He hid his eyes behind his hand like a Venetian mask.

"No." The word spilled out of her in two long venomous syllables, the last one pitching upward, ever so slightly, like a shank under the ribs. "I'm just trying to reconnect with my long-lost daughter, after what? Ten years."

"Wow," Gil mumbled. "That's a long time."

My mother nodded her agreement, dramatically.[149]

"I gotta tell you, Amanda. I'm kinda lovin' your mom. Saving me from that psycho, and all."

Ethel winked at him, beaming. "And you're a wonderful boy, Gil. A shame I weren't twen—uh . . . ten years younger. I'd change you back to our team in a heartbeat."

Gil chuckled. "I just might let ya, you minx."

"You're a naughty one, too." They were both laughing. Even Mr. Kim giggled a bit. I, meanwhile, could have chewed the insides of my cheeks off.

Thankfully, Rapid City is a small town so the lovefest and the ride were cut blessedly short. I pulled off the highway and the hotel rose ahead of us like the world's largest fantasy bong. But that's not what caught my attention first. The Cleavers' RV was barreling through the parking lot toward the exit and us. Ward drove with a face full of rage, scrunched up like one of Grandma's pantyhose dolls.

---

[149] Of course. Do you hate her already? Please say you do.

"Jesus!" Gil yelled, clutching the little handle over his window as I swerved to avoid a head-on collision.

A victory cry echoed from the monstrous vehicle (The Cleavers were not at all subtle) and the creepy boy gave us the finger from the back window. So much for the happy family—these Cleavers were driving like methheads fleeing a lab explosion. The RV took the curb like a stunt jump, scraping the ground and sending a fantail of sparks into the waning night.

If that weren't enough of a scene, close on their tail sped an oddly familiar white truck, its driver shouted obscenities from the window. "Goddamn ass lickin' pigfuckers!"

Fishhook was mad.

He careened after the RV out onto the main road and west on the freeway, the crappy Nissan truck coughing black smoke that shadowed the streetlights like a low budget Eastern European vampire movie.

Meanwhile, the Volvo ended up wedged between a dumpster and a horrified family of four, interrupted while packing their car full of luggage and miniature Mount Rushmore figurines.

"Well what was all that about?" Ethel straightened the raincoat she'd swiped.

Whatever it was, it wasn't good. I'd completely downgraded the family's threat level from "oh crap" to "eh" on my personal security advisory scale, but now we were going to be moving them up into the highest category, "holy shit." Fishhook's behavior defied proper classification. But it begged the question . . .

What the fuck was going on?

I backed the car away from the frightened family and crept toward our room in the far wing of the hotel. The camper was still there, ditto the orange Mustang. But, I felt an anxious stitch spark in my stomach when I saw our supposedly barricaded door hanging open.

Have you ever known a cracked door to spell anything but trouble? I wished we hadn't snuck into the Passages Hospice

Center, 'cause look where that got me. Now we were faced with what I hoped wasn't another murder, or three.

I pulled into an empty spot a few doors away.

"Wait here. Gil and I will go check it out and see what's happening."

"I'm perfectly capable of taking care of myself."

"I realize that. It's more so I won't be tempted to toss you in harm's way."

"Oh. That's pleasant. Thank you." She eyed her nails and then motioned behind us at the Volkswagen. Darryl and Randy stumbled out and joined us in the investigation.

I plodded down the walkway, followed by the two goons. Gil took the rear.[150] At the doorway we stopped. "Wendy? Scott? Honey?" I called.

No sound. But then, a grunt.

I pushed the door the rest of the way open to see a battered Scott dragging himself across the carpet, eyes black and swollen closed and a trail of blood leading from each pant leg.

"Oh shit." I ran in and knelt beside him. "Don't move. Jesus."

"Mama," he said. So not endearing, I can tell you. "Maaa."

The blood poured from two gashes above his feet. Severed tendons dangled from the openings and his feet flopped at weird angles. All I could think was: those better heal, wolfman, because I won't be carting you around in a wagon to social events. Callous, perhaps. But, in my defense, a handicap really doesn't go with my wardrobe. Seriously, he's a werewolf and he'll heal. Get over it.

"Get those beds back on the ground and get him comfortable. Gil, check the bathroom and that goddamned closet. Make sure we're alone."

The two goons helped their former coworker onto the mattress. He screamed as one of the guys tried to position his feet. I

---

[150] I'm afraid the pun was entirely intended on that one. Tee hee.

sat at the head of the bed and brushed the damp curls from his forehead.

"What the hell happened, man?"

"That family. They're bad. So bad."

He drifted into a pseudo-sleep that didn't seem to break when I slapped his cheeks.

"He's in the healing sleep," one of the guys said.

I looked up. It was the black one, Randy.[151]

"He'll be out for hours while those wounds and muscles stitch themselves up and heal."

"Great." I stood and wheeled around at Gil. "Now all we have to go on is that the family did this and they're 'bad.' Where are Wendy and Honey, for Christ sake?"

Gil stood next to the dresser lifting a Juicy Couture bag resembling Wendy's. He unzipped it and pulled out a handful of Twix miniatures, the husks of several wrappers spilled out on the floor. "Does this answer your question?"

"Oh shit. Kidnapped." Do I need to tell you Wendy wouldn't go anywhere without her stash, let alone her hobo bag? Those bastards took them. This was it. This was what the mystics were talking about. They were going to kill Honey. But why take Wendy? "Why would they do that?" I asked aloud. "I mean do they enjoy the smell of diarrhea?"

"Beats me but we better get after them," Gil said.

"We're not going anywhere." Ethel blocked the doorway. Behind her a hint of dawn tinged the sky a hazy pink. "Unless you're in need of a tan."

I'll give her this, the bitch caught on quick.

"You two." She pointed at her new playtoys. "Go with Amanda. She's gonna need your help."

They followed me like imprinting ducks. I looked at the

---

[151] Or would you prefer thin-lipped. Those were the only two characteristics that were even notable. Maybe I should ask my mother to describe him. Would you like that? Didn't think so. Lightweight.

Volvo, realized we were going to need a little more speed and ducked back into the room to find Scott's keys. They weren't lying around anywhere so I ended up fishing them out of his pants. He tossed on the bed, grabbed my wrist. "Fishhook," he mumbled. "Pink cave." And then he passed out.

I wasn't sure what Fishhook had to do with all this but I was certain what 'cave' meant, though the word 'pink' tossed in made me raise an eyebrow. I snatched the gun off the nightstand, darted out to my car, snatched my purse and all the brochures and scurried around to the Mustang. Randy and Darryl were still waiting obediently between the passenger side of the orange heap of metal and the Winnebago when I hit the unlock button, but instead of jumping into the car, Darryl dropped like a sack of potatoes, screamed for a second and then went silent. Randy was next.

I raced around the back of the car to see Clare Cleaver stabbing Randy, over and over in the chest. She must have crawled from under the RV, slitting their Achilles tendons just like Scott's. Her mouth stretched into a hideous grin and her eyes were wild with the kind of excitement I can only generate over a sale rack at Barney's.

The whole scene was grotesque. Not only had the emaciated little thing taken out my two assistants, she'd likely been the one to disable my lover with her duo of butterfly knives, now, pumping in and out of the gore of Randy's chest like a praying mantis.[152]

My eyes darted from the vicious little brat to the gun in my hand. I was less than enthusiastic about using the thing, it would wake everyone up, plus this assault screamed for something more physical and pure.

Brutal.

The girl was so involved in the act that she didn't notice the pointy toe of my cheap stiletto whizzing through the air towards her ear. It impacted with a wet thud. Clare seized violently, gargled and frothed with blood and eventually went limp.

---

[152] Yes. Yes. I said lover. But that's ownership in that tone.

I shook her carcass off my foot, scanned the horizon for the first real rays of dawn and, not seeing them yet, yelled, "Gil get out here."

The door to the room opened and the vampire stood there shaking his head. "Jesus. This is a mess."

"No doubt. Get the bodies inside the room before people start to wake up."

He glanced off into the lingering twilight and raced into the parking lot, dragging the two werewolves inside. With any luck, Randy and Darryl would heal—they were, as a breed the most hearty stock, so, chances were good. Clare they could flush down the toilet for all I cared.

When I turned back to get into the Mustang, Mr. Kim stood next to the Volvo, his hand clutching the door handle. "I go with you," he said.

"Oh Kimmy." I shook my head. "I've got to take the Mustang. The Volvo's not gonna cut it if I hope to catch up with them."

"I know. But I still go. Must help you find Hyon Hui. I have no choice." He seemed to breathe in deeply, his aura deepening in color to a vibrant purple.

Then, Mr. Kim stepped away from the car.

"I was sure he said pink cave." I shuffled through the brochures, my eyes shifting from the steering wheel to the rectangles of paper, weaving through the early morning traffic south, to where the majority of the tourist attractions clumped. Jewel Cave, Wind Cave, Rushmore, Crystal, Bethlehem, Wonderland. You'd think we were sitting on top of a giant anthill for all the freakin' caves.

I stopped shuffling at the Jewel Cave pamphlet. What caught my eye was a sticker on the back.

Closed for Routine Maintenance
Reopens: June 7th

A closed facility would be much easier to hide out in or kill people or whatever they had planned for Wendy and Honey. I showed the brochure to Mr. Kim.

"That look like good choice. Go."

We curved through the Black Hills at top speed. It was still too early to come across many cars; even the employees of Rushmore and Crazy Horse weren't hitting the roads before 6 A.M. An hour later we had to slow down coming into a sleepy little burg named Custer. The buildings were low and mainly catered to the tourists. Mr. Kim pointed out the replica of the cartoon Flintstone village.

"Caves?" he suggested.

"I don't think so."

Right after the attraction, as the buildings began to thin, I noted a white-steepled church off to the

---

First Methodist of Custer

Open to all who believe!
(Even the heathens next door)

THE PINK CAVE

We'll raise your steeple!

ADULT TOYS
AT ROCK BOTTOM PRICES!

---

left. Next door stood a ramshackle clapboard building, painted a garish pink. Two signs at the road battled for driver's attentions (see insets). Do I need to mention which was the winner?

"Well look at that."

"Who go to porno store next to church?" Mr. Kim grimaced.

"Doesn't make sense, right? Still we can't pass this by, look at the name." I pulled onto the gravel drive and around the back of the store, where our question was answered.

The Cleavers' RV sat idling at an odd angle. Behind it, blocking its exit, was Tad's white truck.

Chapter 22

Mr. Kim Cuts Loose

Some mysteries remain unexplained. What are the mechanics of zombie infection? How does the blood of the living give vampires such a healthy youthful glow? Why are wood nymphs so goddamned horny? Who knows? I'm just trying to have a good time up in this bitch!
—Cameron Hansen, Actor and Supernatural Celebrity

I backed away from the two vehicles and hid the car on the other side of the closed Methodist church, where I grabbed the gun and left Mr. Kim stretching away from the front fender and toward the metal stair railing of the nearby building. He tapped the ground with the precision of a tightrope walker, as though he weren't on sturdy ground at all.

"Sorry, Kimmy. I can't wait for you to get your footing. I've gotta go."

"Go. Go. Save Hyon Hui. Wendy, too. Only Hyon Hui first." He waved me on.

At the back corner, I scanned the adult store parking lot. Fishhook was nowhere near the truck, nor was there any movement inside the RV. That didn't mean that someone wasn't sitting behind the wheel. I couldn't see that far from my position. I ran in a crouch, ducking behind the truck, and inched forward toward the back window. I figured I'd step on the bumper and peek inside, only there wasn't any bumper to speak of, just a smooth plastic shell. I pushed myself up onto the hood of the truck, slipped out of my shoes and balanced in a dent. It provided a decent enough vantage, albeit a bit slippery.

Shadows oozed across dark fabrics and sleek plastic cabinets, from lights recessed under the bed like a Japanese street racer. Fancy inside as it was out, the outfit must have cost a fortune. Clean and no one around, nothing of interest except a row of drawers that might produce a clue. As I hunched to slide down, I noticed movement behind me. No sound attracted me, only the soft shifts of light and dark you notice in your periphery. I dropped to my knees and crawled around the front of the truck.

Mr. Kim.

He'd somehow navigated the church building, possibly by simply passing through it, for all I knew. His eyes, it seemed, were trained on the Pink Cave. He shifted and started, straining against his grasp of a loose wooden shutter. Stretching as far across the gravel with a pointed toe. The decision suggesting he intended to traverse the open expanse. It might have been ridiculous, had it not been the first time a ghost had successfully separated from their earthly boundaries.

I crammed my feet back into the heels and crept around the side of the camper, listening for even the slightest hint of a black-and-white television family folding aprons or arranging corn holders.[153] Despite the grumble of the engine, and the frequent stirring of tree branches from the wall of forest that butted up against the parking lot, there was no sign of the creepy clan.

I reached for the door handle. The cool metal vibrated under my touch.

Just the engine, I told myself. Just the engine.

I expected the picture of cleanliness, a sanitary space straight out of the '50s, complete with an altar to Mr. Clean.

Not so much.

In fact, as I stepped up into the trailer I was instantly taken

---

[153] With a "D"!

by the stench of rotting meat. Blood ran down the cabinetry in rivulets, pooling on the thin carpet. Rubbermaid containers like spilt Kool-Aid. The sink was full, but not with dirty dishes.

With claws.

Severed werewolf claws lay haphazard in the metal basin, clotted with the crimson syrup and strips of rotting sinew. Thick handles protruded from the furry wrists, makeshift weaponry. A ruse. The victims of such horrendous things would look exactly like werewolf victims.

Like that poor albino girl.

Tad.

Who were these people?

Who would create such devious contraptions? I thought briefly back to the magical Grillz we'd employed so unsuccessfully at the skinhead bar—where had Wendy even found those? We had no choice but to do something, right?

Skinhead rape? Uh . . . no thank you.

These people, on the other hand, seemed to be murdering willy-nilly, with no rhyme or reason or any other clichéd thing you want to call their random acts. I may be a flesh-eating zombie that eats three times per week, but that's just food chain shit. When I died I took a step up on the evolutionary ladder. Ward and June and the Beav were simply murderers.[154]

I felt a moment of pride knowing I'd already taken one of them down, and stylishly so.

Turning my attention to the rear of the RV, I passed a dining booth, similar to our own camper's, only this one was stacked with transparent Tupperware containers. Each filled with a wad of black mushrooms. I rummaged through the lots, figuring on, at least, forty different stashes. Each one labeled exactly the same way.

A single piece of masking tape bore the word "TAP" and a number.

---

[154] Do you see the distinction?

Do I even need to tell you the containers were just like Fishhook's? The Cleavers were his dealers. I didn't have to think twice about that. Who else would package drugs so fastidiously? Normally, you'd be lucky to get a Ziploc baggie.[155]

But why the word "TAP"? The only people that used that term were vampires, plumbers and alcoholics. It certainly was an apt descriptor for all the scars on Fishhook's body. The memory of his naked flesh crept back into my head like a leech. But what did the Cleavers have to do with vampires? They were humans as far as I could tell, didn't mind sunlight, nice and pink.

What would they be doing with . . .

It was almost too much to wrap my pretty little head around.

Removing the lid and sniffing brought me right back to the Maha Dhurga's field. The dense smell of shit overpowered my dry sinuses—totally nauseating but mildy pleasant. I flung the toxic fungus across the room, before the fumes took hold and disabled me. Each piece stuck like tar and slid, smudging a poop streak on the cheerful pink and tan striped wallpaper.

The juxtaposition turned my scowl into a smirk.[156]

I turned my attention to the rear room. The door was shut. Locked. I stood back and kicked at the thing, hoping to break what I assumed would be a shoddy lock. I was denied. I didn't dare use the gun for

Prospective Bait	
1.	~~Missy Sawmiller~~
2.	Todd Thomas (in service)
3.	~~Cherry Dale~~
4.	~~Synde Korman~~
5.	Beth Petri (in service)
6.	Renee Sweet (in service)
7.	~~Virginia Hendricks~~
8.	~~Carrie Zimmerman~~
9.	~~Becky Garretti~~
10.	~~Tad Turner~~
11.	*Hyon Hui Kim*

fear of alerting the Cleavers of my presence. The last thing I

---

[155] Not that I know a lot about drugs, but I do own a TV.
[156] I live for those moments. Well . . . not live, exactly.

needed was the All-American Family to come running out of the sex shop, with bags of vibrating projectiles. I scoured the kitchen area for something to jimmy the lock, anything, a butter knife a . . . werewolf claw.

The handle was wood and the appendage surprisingly heavy. But as I slashed it across the metal, the silvery tips sliced right through the door. A few well-placed strikes and it swung open on its own, the handle still clutching the jamb. I went straight for the drawers, pulling them out and dumping them. Papers parachuted to the floor, revealing some 8 x 10 glossy photos. Ten of them, in fact, paper clipped together with a precisely typed inventory card, only the last name was written in a scrolling cursive (see inset).

I thumbed through the photos until I found the last one. Honey smiling at the Cleaver boy, an evening shot, the gaudy RV in the background. The next two photos were Tad and the Albino girl, both posing happily for whoever took the shots. What the hell? I snatched the card off the front, zeroing in on the heading.

Prospective Bait.

I threw it down. Backed away.

Bait for what? Taps, drugs, werewolf claws? What the hell was going on?

I left the camper shaken, but when I turned the corner, my mouth dropped open.

Mr. Kim bounded across the gravel lot, feet breezing a foot above the ground as though he might lift off and spin into the atmosphere, which certainly was a possibility considering the vague physics of the ghost world. His arms pumped at the air and a boyish yowl screeched out of him like an American Idol reject, and then was clipped to silence as he slipped through the Pink Cave's walls.

I bolted for the door, ankles rocking on shifting gravel.

The Pink Cave was Hollywood-set bright when, really, most of the merchandise screamed for shading. The walls were lined with various DVD titles in categories not often seen at your local Best Buy. Rentals clearly and well used, so despite the guilt from the Methodists, someone in Custer was enjoying a little visual . . . um . . . assistance. On the right, a half wall separated the cashier from the customers and a swinging door led to a dark hall, the sign above it blinked, "Booths." But no one seemed to be manning the store.

The back wall was all about toys. Row upon row of dildos, vibrators, weird rubber sea anemones, things that looked like the spades you find on playing cards, some of them with long manes of hair protruding from the base. Mr. Kim roamed that aisle.

"Enjoying the selection?" I asked as I rounded the corner. "That was quite a show out there."

He didn't respond, instead just pointed at the floor. A pool of blood the size of dinner plate was smeared in a grisly streak that ended abruptly at the wall of sex toys, as though it continued past it into some secret passageway. Not Wendy's blood obviously—that would have dropped out like chocolate pudding. No. This was either Fishhook or Honey and the odds were not on the girl's side. She might be right on the other side of . . .

A door?

"Good work, Sherlock. Now we just need to figure out how to get me back there."

I ran my fingers across the wall, feeling for a crack or an indent, something that would give away the location of a door.

"I go through and see if I can help from other side." Mr. Kim leaned into the wall leaving his hips and legs on my side.

I cringed, fearing the worst, and eked out a quiet, "Do you see anything?"

"Very dark. But, look like lever right here." His hand poked back out of the wall and through a particularly heinous looking sex toy called the Oatmeal Scotchie. It was penis-shaped but its surface was mottled with a grey and beige oatmeal texture that looked suspiciously like vomit. The figure of a kilted bagpiper protruded from the base, pipes rigid and ready to stimulate some other area. The box read . . .

The Oatmeal Scotchie (Just For Men)

A churning molten oatmeal just below the silicone skin of this amazing vibrator hits all the right spots, while the generous Scotsman engages the erotic sensitivity of your throbbing perineum with his pulsating pipes.

Oh. My. God.[157]

If this was the hidden lever, whoever had designed the secret door had made the perfect choice; I felt dirty just touching the box, which depicted the act in Technicolor detail, the model in full Scots regalia, bent over and gasping. But, it indeed unlatched the door and it swung into a cold, black tunnel—somewhat appropriate considering the method of its revelation—revealing the top half of Mr. Kim and the continuation of the blood streak.

"We going to need light."

"True." I scanned the store and in the "novelty" items section happened upon a "Fleshlight" but that didn't seem to have anything to do with illumination. Behind the counter I found what I was looking for, matches and a box of candles. While not ideal, they'd have to do.

---

[157] Gil has some explaining to do.

Chapter 23

The Dark and Intimate Secrets of the Pink Cave[158]

Spelunking is quickly becoming a favorite supernatural pastime and not just with our red-winged minions. Vampires, were and zombies are all jumping on the cave exploring bandwagon. Tours to various caverns are available and most are over-day with a camping component for our light-challenged friends.
— *Supernatural Seattle* (May 2008)

It was all so Nancy Drew and the Secret of the Pink Cave, except for all the granny porn and dildos shaped like farm animals, you really wouldn't know the difference. I wished I'd been wearing tartan plaid and knee socks, maybe a soft cardigan. The candle was the topper and while the cave wasn't particularly windy, it flickered as we made our way down a steep set of uneven stairs carved into the cave floor.

Mr. Kim floated ahead like the gentleman he was, scouting out crevices and sharp turns where the Cleavers might be lurking with their claws of doom. I descended sideways, one step at a time. I couldn't very well save the day with a broken hip, and despite revolving credit with the reapers, I didn't relish the thought of physical deformity.

---

[158] Don't judge. A little innuendo never hurt anybody.

The blood trail thinned and the temperature dropped the further I climbed down. When the stairs became no more than foot holds, I was forced to break the heels off my shoes to keep moving. I freed my hands to balance, by holding the candle in my mouth and stretching my arms across to the craggy cave wall, suspending myself above the tightening shaft. The cave funneled downward, tightening with each step, as though we were dropping into some kind of tank.

"How much further down?" I called.

"Yards, maybe two."

I couldn't move much further. My arms felt like spaghetti from supporting my upper body, my legs were quivering, as well. I let the candle drop, praying it'd stay lit.

It did, illuminating a gravelly floor that seemed level enough. Just a few more feet and I could jump without hurting myself.

I pressed on.

Gripping the tiniest cracks with fingertips singing with pain and searching for juts of rock with my toes, I managed to get a little closer before losing my holds and dropping like a side of beef onto the stony floor, putting out the candle and plunging the space into darkness.

A searing pain wrenched through my back and I wondered if I'd be able to move, let alone continue searching for my friends. But Mr. Kim hovered over me, a gentle blue glow surrounding me.

"You okay?" he asked. "Not too bad hurt?"

I tried moving my arms, which although sore didn't seem to be broken. My legs worked, too. I must not have been that far off the ground, after all. Standing, tentatively, an awful crunching sound echoed through the space, followed by a wet sucking sound. One of my lungs had been punctured. When I looked down I could see a thin piece of bone protruding from my shirt, surrounded by a thick yellow and gray ooze. Zombie breath glowed white against Mr. Kim's luminescence, snaking out of the hole moving back up the cave vent and dissipating. Despite the obvious horror of this, it didn't feel too bad. The rib ached, sure, but had I been alive that lung would have kept me down.

I reached up and slid the rib back into place, cringing at the sloppy goo that dropped out in the process, but otherwise proud. A quick unbuttoning of my blouse and tying it off just under my chest seemed to do the trick.

"Yeah," I told Mr. Kim. "I oughta be. Let's go."

The cave sloped back up toward a dim light; it reflected off pockets of crystals embedded in the walls and provided enough light to traverse the path without another cosmetic tragedy. As we reached the top, I crouched and peeked around a sharp turn where cave gave way to cavern. It spread out in nearly every direction to a level floor lit by strands of light bulbs. Stalactites or mites or whatever stretched from floor to ceiling in columns resembling streaked bacon.

In the center of the room, Honey was splayed across a raised platform, arms and legs akimbo. Next to her, a machine beeped and churned, tubes feeding it the girl's blood. Mr. Kim sped forward into the room and hovered above the girl, weeping. His moans echoed through the cavern.

I caught a whiff of something fetid, dead and soiled.

"Mr. Kim!" Wendy's voice hissed from somewhere. But he disregarded it, fixated as he was on his sister's prone form.

I started toward them, tripping over something soft in the dark, coming down on top of it on my knees.

"Oof," someone groaned. "Get the fuck off me, you little bitch."

It was only as the cursing began, I realized who it was I'd stumbled upon. I lurched backward. "Fishhook?"

"Who the hell do you think it is? You been following me, right?"

"Well, yeah. No need to make me feel stupid." I reached into the band of my skirt and tugged out a candle and the matches. "What the fuck is goin' on? This cave? Those people? Honey?"

I struggled to light a match but the man's hands covered mine extinguishing the only one to catch.

"You'll show 'em where we're at."

"Where's Wendy?"

"Down there . . . somewhere," he whispered. "With them."

There didn't seem to be anyone around the pit, at all. No movement as far as I could tell, but still, it was certain that the family was lurking.

"Who are they?" I asked.

"They're business people, that's all they'll say. But it's what they sell . . . that's the sick part." He turned and took my chin between his fingers. "People. Blood."

Everything came together in those words. People. Blood. The family was providing vampires with taps—convenient fresh blood at reasonable prices and right to your door. The mushrooms must keep the taps in line.

"They keep you drugged so you won't resist," I added.

"Yeah. It's horrible."

I thought of the men that Gil kept, men who'd willingly give up a pint for a night with my homeboy. It couldn't be that bad.

"Aren't you being a little dramatic?" I asked.

His mouth dropped open, snapped shut. "I wouldn't expect you to understand. You're just like them. Monsters."

"There's just no talking to you when you're like this." Dismissing his words, I swiveled to get a better look at the table. "What are they doing to her?"

"Running tests, looking for rare blood parasites. They fancy themselves vintners. Specialists. Masters of their trade. Their clients pay millions for just one tap, and they expect the perfect bite."

"Well, yeah. For a million, sure."

His face pickled, disgust spreading across it.

"So why would they kill Becky and Tad?"

"Simple. Wrong blood type."

"How would they know?"

"Those awful kids of theirs approach prospective taps and lure them back to the trailer. At least, that's how it happened with me. While there, they slip you some black ones—mushrooms—and while you're out they check your blood type. Too common and you're out of the running. But you also know too much, so they kill you. Do you want to know how?"

I thought of the werewolf claws, the bodies. "No. I think I got it."

"They must have found a gold mine in that little girl down there. Just like me. This is where I come. They picked me up off the highway in Denver—cold as hell as I remember it. The rest went all blurry after the mushrooms kicked in. You get addicted, you see?"

"Is that why you stole Tad's truck?"

"The way I see it, that truck was in need of a new owner. Plus, I had to get me some leverage. Tad must have been their dealer. I don't know why it is they turned on him, but they did. Anyways, I got that stash hid away real good. They're going to have to do business with me now."

Just then, the boy, William, I guess, passed through the room, checked something on the machine and sauntered over to a fissure in the cavern wall.

"Sh," I warned.

The boy was saying something to someone, but the distance was too great to figure out what. He punctuated his communication by spitting in the direction of the fissure. I had no doubt a loogie was dripping down Wendy's face. He turned and bounded off in the direction he came.

"Let's go." Fishhook moved forward scrambling low over the rocks until he reached the level of the pit. I followed, darting toward the crack in the wall as I made the floor.

Wendy seethed with anger. Her face was, in fact, dripping with the boy's spit.[159] Her wrists were bound to a hook in the

---

[159] Don't these kids learn anything from *Flavor of Love*?

wall by what looked to be a man's belt, but could likely have been some sadomasochistic shit from the back room of the Pink Cave.

"Oh thank God," she said as I worked at the buckle. "I thought we were dead for sure."

"Well Honey might still be, but you my dear are . . ." I loosened the strap and she wriggled her hands free. "Stinky as hell, but free."

She threw her arms around me then and squeezed, sending shivers of pain throughout my chest, down my spine. Fucking everywhere. I had to bite my lip to keep from screaming.

"Thank you. Thank you. Thank you." She jumped up and down shaking my cracked rib all the more.

I pushed her away. "Knock it off, you're fuckin' killing me." I opened my blouse and showed her the wound.

"Oh sweetie." She cocked her head, smiling. "That's nothing a pitcher of martinis and twenty grand won't fix." And then her face changed. Shock spreading.

I turned in time to see Mrs. Cleaver pounding toward me with a claw raised over her head. I reached for the gun in the waistband of my skirt and felt nothing. It must have come lose in the fall, I thought, and ducked. The claws whizzed by slicing through several locks of hair, at least six inches long each. They floated down in front of me like a slow motion nightmare.

Oh no. Bitch didn't just cut my hair.

Instead of standing, I dropped all the way to my hands and lunged forward, ratcheting open my jaws and chomped off the woman's right leg at the knee. She teetered for a moment, a ghostly white pallor spreading across her skin, and then fell over onto her hip, screaming. Her wails echoed through the cracks and fissures, alerting the men. Wendy sprang for her, then, chewing through the woman's neck, sending an arc of blood high in the air, and her head scooting across the cave floor. The silence was immediate.

From the corner of my eye, I saw the boy moving in the

shadows, heard the scuffling of his feet. He was following the curve of the wall toward something. A glint of steel in the darkness.

A gun?

I decided I'd best beat him there and bolted, snatching his mother's weapon from the ground. He started to run and we came on a small table set into a niche in the wall at about the same time. I slashed at him and his arm went flying. He pivoted blinding me in arterial spray. The prick.

I backed off and wiped at my eyes. When I opened them, I had only a second before the boy was on me, pummeling me with his fist before stabbing me with a hypodermic needle.

Silly kid.

He screamed. I grabbed his throat, shutting him up. He kept plunging the needle in pricking at my flesh over and over.

"Those veins don't really work anymore." My face shook as I spread my jaws.

"No!" Another voice screamed. His father.

I had no sympathy or nostalgia for family, not while my friend was watching his sister bleed into a machine in a secret cave lair. I dropped the boy with one swift bite to the head. He fell to the ground with a thud and half his brain rolled from his skull, tracking black and wet across the ground.

Mr. Cleaver dropped to his knees, his head thrown back and howling as though tortured.

"Do you expect us to feel sorry for you, man?" I walked toward him. Wendy flanked me. "With what you've been doing to these people?"

"It was for the good of mankind."

"What? You gotta be kidding me, right? It was for the good of your bank account."

"No." His voice was soft now, measured. "That was strategic."

"What are you talking about?"

"We were hunters. Slayers. Vampire killers. The taps were our bait. The best blood around and once the vampires got a taste, were they ever willing to pay for it. We knew they couldn't afford our prices unless they went in together on the bill. It was always going to be a large coven that kept a tap. After the deal went through we'd stake out their spots and take 'em out one by one. Made it look like werewolves were doing it, had to keep up the stereotype that those fuckers were uncontrollable."

"Well that's just sick," Wendy said. "A bunch of crazy-ass Buffy's probably killing just as many people as they did vampires and calling it noble. I've seen it all now." She walked over to the table and started checking out the machine.

I pointed at Honey's body. "What do I need to do to let the girl go?"

He looked up from the floor then, sneering. "Perhaps you could eat shit."

"Uh . . . only as part of the whole package, but not separately, that's just gross." I kicked him in the head and he fell back, scuttling off into the dark like a crab. When he reemerged he brandished werewolf claws in each hand and a triangular bruise from my shoe on his forehead. He snarled, as if he were an actual werewolf. The effect would have been laughable—particularly in the light of his olive sweater vest and dress shirt—had the light not glinted off those terrible nails.

He lunged and I fell back, turning, readying myself to run.

A shot.

And then Ward's body hit the ground next to mine, blood and gray matter pouring from a tennis ball-sized hole in his forehead.

Fishhook emerged from the darkness, Honey's gun in his hand. "You ruined my plans, you know?"

"No we didn't," I said. "We just changed the buyers. Seattle has plenty of lowlifes that will be clamoring for that stuff. You could probably cut a deal to keep a supply coming from Madame Gloria's place."

He shrugged. "Maybe."

I half expected some sort of attack, but the man just spun the gun around and handed it to me.

★ ★ ★

Fishhook took Honey's pulse, as neither Wendy nor my fingers were sensitive enough. "It's there, but fading."

Wendy had disconnected the girl from the machine during the final showdown with the insane dad. Blood still dripped from the various tubes into little puddles around the cart. Honey was pale as death and Mr. Kim wailed in pain.

It was too much.

I seriously liked Honey, the girl was tough, didn't take shit from anyone. And we all know I love her brother. But could *I* do it to *her*?

It.

Could I force this undead afterlife on a nineteen-year old girl? Might she not be better off passing on to wherever it is dead people normally go? Mr. Kim's eyes suggested that was the right course of action. He met my gaze and darted away, only to come floating back.

Just let her go, I thought.

"She fit in so well," Wendy whispered.

"She did."

Before I'd even made up my mind that I was going to give her the breath, my hand was moving to her face. For the second time this trip, I was asphyxiating someone, this time someone I'd grown legitimately close to.[160] Her body began to convulse, her throat constricted.

I leaned down and let my lips hover over my hand and let go. Honey gasped with every bit of strength and will to live that was left in her.

I exhaled.

The tentacles of white smoke filled the space between our lips, lapping at her cheeks like tongues before forcing their way down her throat. I clutched my sides and squeezed pushing every

---

[160] Don't worry, I'm not through with Scott, yet.

ounce out of me with such force that another rib cracked, or simply moved—the bone was probably already broken in the fall.

When it was over. Honey lay there still. Fishhook checked her pulse again, but this time there was nothing.

I was beginning to think I was too late when . . .

Honey's eyes snapped open and a pink flush burnished her skin, probably for the last time. She sat bolt upright on the slab and stared into the dark.

"Dae-Jung?" A tear rolled down her cheek.[161]

"Hyon Hui? You can see me." Mr. Kim's eyes darted toward me, but did not meet my gaze. Ashamed that he'd gotten exactly what he wanted.

I suspect.

"I can see you. I can totally see you." Honey beamed.

Fishhook climbed up the rocks toward the cave to the surface.

Wendy and I hung back, opting for a view of the reunion.

"If my damned tear ducts worked I might actually be crying right now," I said.

She scowled at me. "Well you are weeping from all those needle jabs, that's gotta count for something."

"Totally."

"You *were* pretty bad-ass," she said, brushing my now shoulder-length hair away from my, apparently, injured face.

"Self defense is for pussies. I prefer a good old fashioned offense."

"Mmm hmm, girl."

"Hey, no one cuts my hair, without giving me a mani/pedi first. It's just not right."

"Amen."

---

[161] If that were the only fluid she secreted in her death, we'd all have been very lucky. Sadly this is the real world and . . . well . . . you know what happens when you die. Don't make me say it. Oh. Okay. Piss and poop. It's not dignified but, hey. We all do it. Now. Back to our poignant moment already in progress.

Epilogue

Postcards from the Road Trip

Supernatural or not, it is always important to practice good etiquette. Travel is no exception. When you're winding down after a busy night visiting haunts, feasting on local delicacies and sidling up to the bar for a horse cocktail, why not do the polite thing and send your loved ones postcards from each locale you visit? Death is not an excuse.

—Ethel Ellen Frazier, *A Manners Guide for the Afterlife*

So, you're probably looking at that chapter title and thinking—or possibly even saying aloud[162]—"Epilogue? But they're still in South Da-fucking-kota. What happens? What kind of crazy antics do the girls get into on the way home? And . . . oh yeah, you're totally including Gil in that, when you ask it.

Well the truth is a whole lot of stuff went down on the way back and since then. Some of it's for other books and some of it's for right now. So here are some postcards from the road trip back, just so you'll feel special.[163]

1. *Rapid City, South Dakota to Cody, Wyoming (of all places)*

[162] After all, I don't really know you all that well. You could be completely bat shit crazy, pretending to read this book on some park bench, chattering away at squirrels with pigeon poop running down your shoulders. You never know.
[163] You like to feel special, don't you?

- We packed Scott, Randy and Darryl (yes, all three alive and healing) into the camper and made the decision to drive only at night. That way Ethel and Gil could actually do something other than congratulate each other on being the most fabulous creatures ever. Gag.

- Our first stop was Devil's Tower, which looks like absolutely fucking nothing in the middle of the night, and certainly not the hotbed of alien light shows, as I'd been led to believe by an overzealous Wendy in full-on tourist/U.F.O. geek mode.

- In Sheridan, we stopped for a bite to eat and to gawk at the world's largest spool of human intestines. Quite an achievement for the elderly curators of the attraction, Roberta and Gregory Walthers, who were so damn cute I would have eaten them had they not been a couple of rotting corpses. Still, I highly recommend the joint. That bobbin was totally huge and Roberta made us some bomb-ass meat margaritas.

- Somewhere atop the Big Horn Mountains, west of that big Indian tourist attraction named after a wheel, Gil nearly tore the car apart trying to get out and pee. I know what you're thinking: vampires don't pee, right? Well get some bad blood in 'em and watch 'em go. He screamed throughout the entire thing and the steaming puddle looked like autopsy run off, swear to God. There's a lesson for ya. He never did figure out where he got the bug, but I suspect it was that creepy hitchhiker back near Sheridan.

2. *Cody, Wyoming to Old Faithful, Yellowstone National Park*

- Were you aware that Wyoming has drive-through liquor stores and cocktail lounges? Well they do. It's the weirdest thing, but so convenient, particularly when you're driving cross-country three vehicles deep. So. We were at this one in some town that could barely support a grocery store— but sure enough the liquor store was open[164]—when a car pulled up behind us. Gil and I were in the Volvo, while the rest were sorted between the RV and the Mustang. Well, we have a big order, obviously, and the guy behind us starts honking. I mean crazy honking like he's got somewhere to be. When Gil got out to confront him he pulled away. He was driving a blue Dodge Dart. Keep that in mind, it's important, later.

- Yellowstone was magical, the scenery is amazing and we did run into a pack of werebison that were hospitable and worked as seasonal help for the lodges. Nice kids.

3. Old Faithful to Jackson Hole, Wyoming

- Gil let me in on the Oatmeal Scotchie incident while we watched a predawn geyser explosion at Old Faithful, said it reminded him of the experience, which—you'd be proud—only made me gag a little. It seems Markham played a trust game with his associates. Scott denied it, but I suspect he might be covering up. Apparently, Markham was an enema freak, but rather than water or something equally hygienic he used oatmeal—something about the way it "squished".[165] Well, if he was dealing out millions, he'd demand that his business associate play a game of "hold the oatmeal" (the "scotchie" came about as a result of the massive amounts of single malt the Beaver King consumed and always seemed to be toggling in a lowball). They'd stand over metal tubs and hold that breakfast food

---

[164] Because alcoholism trumps hunger, any day.
[165] Yes. With the quotes. When you repeat this—and you will—make sure to use them.

inside as long as they could, before finally . . . well, you know. Can you believe Gil told me? It's like he wanted Oatmeal Scotchie as a nickname.

4. *Jackson Hole, Wyoming to Boise, Idaho*

- Thank God for Jackson Hole, it was the first real shopping of the trip, though unfortunately for Wendy, they had a Häagen-Dazs. I kept my promise and my mouth shut. But most of that day Honey and I were alone, if you know what I mean.

- The town was important for two reasons. Honey had her first solo meal there and I bought the cutest dangly silver earrings. We were watching an antler auction—which I'd never even heard of—and this guy plunked down a ton of money for a stack of antlers. While I watched that, Honey ran into this weird guy, who tried to talk her into getting into his BLUE DODGE DART. Well, I'm not one to hold a kid back from her life lessons so I egged her on. The fucker thought he had us, too. Probably was planning to kidnap her or something. Instead, two got into the car, one got out. You know the story.

5. Boise, Idaho back to Seattle

- Boise had a Macy's. Do I need to go on?

So there you are, just a few snapshots. Now we'll move on to a proper epilogue. I was getting tired of remembering the trip anyway.

Scenery. Scenery. Food. Scenery.

Epilogue Two

The Pretty Princess Party Palace

Many supernaturals capitalize on human egocentrism by setting up shop in the Emerald City. A veritable hotbed of paranormal commerce, Seattle's elite have expanded their businesses to cater to a growing crowd of living "fantasists," usually with benefits secondary to profits.
—Howard Hughes in a recent interview on *NightMarket*

The Pretty Princess Party Palace appeared to be a fairy tale, complete with streaming pink pennants and the ability to stimulate my gag reflex. Coming into view from the bottom of Queen Anne Hill, its flesh-tone spires poked from the trees like erections from a thatch of wild pubic hair, appropriate considering the Starbucks across the street was filled to capacity with foggy bespectacled child molesters when we arrived, each drooling into his cold drip coffee, while rows of little girls filed across the Palace drawbridge, giggling. Some skipping.

Normally, I wouldn't be caught dead near such a theme park atrocity, but with the holes in my cheeks gaping like hungry mouths and the cave in Wendy's gut whistling with every step of her spiked heels—not to mention the pungent aroma of garbage scow wafting off her—I didn't have a choice. Scott and his boys were good as new by the time we rolled back in to town. Some of us weren't so lucky.

The Pretty Princess Party Palace served multiple purposes (outlined here in this handy and time efficient list).

1. A fun and fantastical escape from the harsh realities of elementary school (or so said the brochure). It, further, promised a whimsical tea party atmosphere, Alice in Wonderland theme parties, and a professional staff. It neglected to mention their shark teeth, but I digress.
2. An endless source of fresh recruits for its proprietors—those heinous little bitches, the reapers. As well as a healthy crop of deviant souls right across the street. Just wipe the slobber off the pervs and they're good to go.
3. A large enough facility to house a ballroom full of squealing girls, a dorm for the squadron of supernatural cleaners and several floors of a purportedly luxurious therapeutic clinic for the undead.

Never mind the décor was decidedly Pepto-Dismal, the Pretty Princess Party Palace was the cure for what ails you.

We parked on a residential street and fell in line behind a herd of soccer moms clad in high-waisted jeans, flats in a variety of middle-class colors and—Jesus—cardigans, the lot of them reeking of a Liz Claiborne clearance sale. Wendy clutched her trench coat tight around her damaged stomach, and lurched forward on shaky legs. Her skin had gone green and necrotic. The road trip had been lousy for beauty maintenance.

"Just a little further, Grannie." I put my arm around her shoulders.

She shrugged it away. "Shut up."

The nearest mother tossed a glance in our direction, scanned Wendy's shuddering figure. I sneered. "Don't you have some private school drama you could be discussing?"

The woman let loose the kind of gasp normally reserved for catching a vagrant shitting in your yard. She clawed at her friend's forearm, a woman with hair as white as a cotton swab, and whispered frantically, "Did you hear what she said?"

The other bitch scowled. "Bitch."

Oh no. I wasn't about to be judged by a walking Q-tip, regardless if she'd hit the mark on my character.

I handed off my Alexander McQueen green croc Novak bag[166] and dropped straight into ghetto fabulous. "You wanna bitch? I got a *bitch* for you." I started at the woman who squealed like the pig she was and raced into the building. The first woman simply crossed her arms and pouted. "You tell her I'll get her after the ball." She rolled her eyes. "I'm not kidding. I'll be waiting."

Wendy poked me in the side. "Seriously?"

I shook my head "no." Of course not. We'd be busy recuperating in the luxurious new clinic.

Just then, the doors opened and all the pretty princesses stampeded, followed by their mothers, each clinging to last season's patchwork Coach, as if that could make up for the fashion travesty.

Inside, we nearly choked on the scent of bubblegum pumped thick into the room; you'd expect that kind of thing in a Vegas casino, but not in a glorified Chuck E. Cheese. The girls took to it like freshman crackheads, bouncing up and down one minute, swaying contentedly the next. All eyes were on the hostess stand and the blond reaper, Hillary. Her head bobbed with every word, pigtails twirling like tasseled stripper pasties.

"Ladies! Attention please!" she yelled. "Are you read for a cotton candy fantasy?"

The girls screamed, their shrill voices cried in unison, "Yeah!"

Curtains on the far wall swept back in a flashy rustle to reveal the horrific aftermath of a pink tsunami. That most egregious of colors had spread through the room like a medieval plague, infecting table linens, candelabras and floral sprays. Even the waitstaff had been given the cherry treatment, though none

---

[166] Oh yeah, I bumped up. How could I not, really, what with my fascination with Hitchcock heroines? Go look this little number up on the internet; it's to die. Plus, it goes *too* well with McQueen's black tulip skirt. Sexiness!

looked particularly happy. That's where Gretel came in. The brunette reaper marched through the space like a prison warden smacking a star-tipped fairy wand into her palm like a riding crop. As she passed, each of the waiters grew instantly toothsome, and of course, rosy-cheeked.

The crowd rushed the room, leaving us standing over Hillary, whose smile lost its magic and distorted into rows of shark teeth. "Amanda Feral," she judged and looked Wendy up and down. "And your little dog, too."

"Well that makes me a little bit uncomfortable." Wendy's smile creased a bit, still somehow smitten with these little freaks.

The girl smirked, twitched and screamed over her shoulder. "Heidi! Get in here." Then directing her gaze back at us, "Trainees. I can't stand breaking them in. Heidi!"

Another reaper bounded from a hall behind her, with pink flats sandpapering the tile floor, and a peasant girl dress seemingly swiped from Strawberry Shortcake, who'd probably been dissected for party canapés. "Yes, Hillary." She bowed.

"I don't give a shit about the slack Gretel or Gretchen give you. When *I* call I don't expect to repeat myself. Please make a note of it."

The girl shrugged, a wide grin of razor sharp teeth spread across her chubby face, making it impossible to look sheepish, which was undoubtedly what she was going for.

"No. I mean make a note of it." Hillary drew letters in the air with an invisible pen.

The girl nodded, swept her curly red hair behind her ears and pulled out a little pad of paper, scribbled something and then slipped it back inside the folds of the dress, again nodding.

"Now, Amanda and her friend Wendy are frequent clinic customers. They never miss a chance to trip over something or get themselves into trouble as you can clearly smell." She waved her hand in front of her nose. "Uh, can you say, 'ripe'?"

"That's a tad dramatic, don't you think?" I asked.

She dismissed my words with an eye roll and turned toward a massive stone staircase. "Follow us, zombies, and please . . . watch your step. If you fall in here, you won't be getting a discount." To her protégé, she mumbled, "A couple of real oxen, those two, and clumsy as hell."

"I can hear you," I said.

Without turning around she responded, "Oh . . . I know."

At the top of the stairs, a waiting room was filled to capacity with the bored and damaged. Battered zombies shared space with elves carting their severed limbs, probably after some sort of bar melee—elves do love a good brawl. Faeries with broken wings sputtered around gimpy yetis, headless horseman and the odd wheelchair-bound mummy.

Wendy groaned clutching at her stomach all the more. Good girl, I thought, play it up.

"You needn't bother acting, either. You'll be going right in. Nothing but the best for our best customers."

The waiting room erupted in sighs and arguments. One particularly incensed gargoyle shuffled over dragging a cement leg. "But, I've been waiting three days! You can't treat me like this."

Hillary stomped her foot and spun on the creature, her pigtails slapping the sides of her contorted face. "Sit your ass down and shut your mouth. You should be used to waiting, you lazy rooftop layabout, and just for your little outburst, I'm tacking on an annoyance fee. 'Cause guess what?" She poked an angry finger into the gray flesh of his chest. "You've just annoyed me."

The demon's face crinkled, his tail literally tucked between his legs, and he limped back to his seat, grumbling.

"Come on ladies," she tossed a glance our way. "Quit dragging balls. Keep up."

The girls led us down a hallway and into a sparsely furnished room. An uncomfortable looking table stood in the center opposite a black fleshy trunk, strapped and buckled, and undulat-

ing and puffing as though containing a set of lungs.[167] We'd
seen the trunk before, as Hillary would surely point out, if you
ask. But each time, a different curative was employed.

"Open the chest, while I take a look at this piece of meat."

Wendy's mouth hung open. She clicked a warning with her
jaw. Apparently, they weren't so cute anymore.

"You must be joking. Open the trench and let's see what
we've got."

Wendy untied her belt and let the coat slide to the floor, revealing the gaping hole in her abdomen, now oozing with a
brackish green slime. The reaper approached, staring into the
chasm.

"Come here." She whistled to her trainee. "Look at this."
She lifted her hand and stuck it into the hole, passing her entire
arm through Wendy's gut and wiggling it out of her back. "This
is what you call a catastrofuck."

She looked up at Wendy. "Get on the table and relax. You
don't mind spiders, do you?"

"What?" I shivered. I'm not afraid of much—poverty, loneliness, blemishes, Ethel—but spiders were at the top of the list. I
couldn't imagine what one of the god-awful creatures would
have to do with fixing Wendy and I didn't really want to find
out.

"Yeah, what?" Wendy recoiled, reaching for her coat and
drawing it around her like a security blanket.

Hillary grinned. Heidi crossed the room and began searching inside the trunk.

"I'm afraid it's the only way."

The trainee turned toward us; a hairy black tarantula-thing
squirmed in her hand. Wendy screamed.

I passed out.

Three hours later, we were freshened and on our way. Wendy's

---

[167] The reaper's medicine cabinet was a tad unconventional and um, gross.

skin was bronzed and healthier than I'd ever seen it. She even remarked that the spider kind of tickled as it wove her flesh back together. I wasn't sure what they'd used on me, but my face was flawless and my pores tighter than a priest's ass. Regardless of what you think of the reapers—evil devil children, Satan's little abortions, whatever—their work was astounding.

And so was their bill.

On many days, when we can pull ourselves away from the pressures of work, relationships and celebrity, Wendy and I enjoy haunting the patio overlooking the drive-through lane at Starbucks. It usually begins with me purchasing two double espressos and Wendy securing good seats. From there it's all about sniffing the thick pungent steam from paper demitasse cups, gossiping with alacrity and hunting for dinner.

"So how's your mom?" Wendy snickered, leaning back and rolling up the legs of her shorts in a vain attempt at energizing her dead melanin.

"Let's just call her Ethel, okay? That woman bears only a passing resemblance to my mother."

"She's changed then?"

I thought about her transformation, her new life as the *de facto* ruler of Markham's Bottoms empire, how she and Gil spend so much time together, how, back when I was in high school, she glommed onto my friends as if they were her own. "No. Not at all."

"But she's happy." Wendy said.

"Whatever." I shrugged. "The topic of my mother is never going to be light Starbucks banter. I'd rather leave it for the sequel."

"Oh yeah. How is the book coming?"

"It's coming, just kind of difficult to schedule a time to write, between functions and work."

"Dude. What about Scott?" Honey flopped down in an oh-so-stylish black silk organza dress by Chanel, over skin-tight jeans and black flats.

"Dude." I pinched the single gossamer sleeve. "Been raiding my closet much?"

"Do you mind?" Her face dipped into a sheepish grin. So cute.

"Of course, not. But you're going to have to ask."

"Got it."

It doesn't take a stretch of the imagination to figure out that Honey's living with me now. After all, I kind of feel responsible for her—um . . . condition—or am responsible, as the case may be. We haven't discussed it really, but sometimes I catch her staring at me and wonder if it's resentment in those smoky MAC-smudged eyes.

Kimmy hasn't mentioned anything, but he wasn't angry that I'd turned his sister, just sad that it was the only way to keep her around. Two months have gone by and he's just begun to give the girl some privacy. Having him in the house is a little bothersome, particularly now that he's developing some new talents. Changing the TV channel is his favorite and our biggest point of contention. Have I mentioned I'm not a fan of the couch commando?

If it happens again, I've threatened an exorcism.

Wendy's another story. She's writing copy for Feral, Inc. now. Our road trip had an added cost in the form of Wendy's job. Her editor at the *Undead Science Monitor* wasn't having any of her missed deadlines and left her a message saying so on her cell. Too bad she'd forgotten it at home on the night we escaped the city. She didn't find out she'd been fired for weeks. Still, she wasn't the least bit upset about it, half the time she called in those crap pieces anyway.[168]

---

[168] And between you and me, I can't find a single one that is clip-worthy for one of my memoirs. I'm rewriting her ad copy myself. She's just not that interested. Now a club opening or a trunk sale at Barney's, she's all over that like fleas on a dog.

"Are you avoiding her Scott question?" Wendy asked.

"No. No. He's still in the picture. I just haven't made up my mind about him. On the one hand the sex is *très* animal."

Wendy and Honey giggled, so I paused, naturally.

"On the other, he still thinks he's in a porno movie. There's only so much kink I'm willing to endure."

"At least it's just talk," Honey said, looking around for a lurking Mr. Kim. "I had this boyfriend that got off watching me pop balloons with my bare ass. Made him freak out. It was nauseating."

"Well, I've got you both beat. I was with this one guy—" Wendy's voice dropped into a clandestine whisper. "Who wanted me to fart while he went down on me."

"Ew." Honey and I screamed in unison.

"Did you do it?" I asked.

She nodded.

"Dude, that's nasty." Honey shook with laughter and reached for a cup to sniff. "Makes me want to clear my sinuses."

"So are you gonna keep the nice officer in your stable?" Wendy cocked her head.

"I don't know. Too early to tell."

Wendy fished her cell phone out of her purse. "Shall I see what Madame Gloria predicts?"

"You better not." I reached for the phone. She tossed it into her other hand, held it out of my reach. "I'll tell her you're a pottymouth. I swear to God."

"Whatever."

I mean, Scott was going to be around until he got tired of me, or me of him. I wasn't particularly concerned either way. I needed to change the subject, quick. "Isn't it about time to eat?"

A black Range Rover pulled into the drive-through queue, its owner shouting some harsh eastern European language into an iPhone. His face was sharp and angular. His eyes were secreted away behind Ray-Ban Aviators.

"How about something from the Borscht Belt?" Wendy pulled her sunglasses down and peered over the bridge.

"Well, you know what they say. Russian is the new Latin Fusion." I stood up and sauntered to the car, hips swiveling like a salsa dancer.[169]

"Dinnertime." Honey sang the word in a light jazzy breath and followed Wendy.

Our duo of super sexy undead glamour killers was a trio, now, like Destiny's Child, or the Supremes, except with sharper teeth and healthier appetites.

---

[169] Do I need to say, it caught his eye?

Amanda's
Très Importante
Authorial Acknowledgments

They said I'd rot before I got out a second memoir. Said I didn't have it in me. Who's they, you ask? The press. My mother. Those idiots at the *Supernatural Seattle*, who should know I took the review for *Happy Hour* and wiped my ass with it. I'm talking to you Meredith Martin, you might remember a certain stink coming from your in-box. All me. I ate some cake special for you.

Oh yeah.

And you high and mighty literary critics, do you remember those free pizzas that showed up during the elections? Guess what? They had a special topping on 'em.

I proved the bastards wrong, anyway.

Road Trip was a living hell to put to paper, and this time, the only person worth thanking is myself.

So thank you, me.

Good job!

Please turn the page for an exciting sneak peek of
Mark Henry's
next Amanda Feral novel
BATTLE OF THE NETWORK ZOMBIES
coming in March 2010!

Chapter 1

Hillbillies, Whores, and Horrors

> **Saturday**
> 2–2:30 A.M.
> CH. SS12
> *Tapping Birch's Syrup*
>
> The remaining "ladies" share a group date with Birch and another challenge: create evening gowns with the local flora . . . poison ivy! Plus, Ludivine reveals a secret deformity.

It's official name was the H & C Gentleman's Club—that's what it said on the tax statement, at least, and in the phone book—but everyone in Seattle knew it as the Hooch and Cooch, the Northwest's first hillbilly-themed titty bar, and it certainly lived up to its backwoods inspirations. The exterior was dilapidated, a hodgepodge of boards nailed up at weird angles and intervals as siding, while rust from the corrugated-metal roof striped the building a gritty orange. It clung to the hillside above Fremont on pilings so rickety, the slightest bump threatened to dump the shack's smutty guts onto the quiet neighborhood underneath.

I'd applaud the audacity, if the owner weren't Ethel Ellen Frazier, vampire, mega-bitch, and, worst of all, my mother.

I considered leaving the car idling in the space—a sound getaway plan was looking like my best option—then fished out my cell and hammered in Marithé's number.

"Seriously?" I asked the second she picked up, fondling the address she'd written on the back of my business card.

"What?" My assistant's voice always sounds annoyed, so it's difficult to assess her tone. A good rule of thumb is just to assume I've interrupted something very important like saving time in a bottle, writing the great American novel, or ending the plague that is zombie crotch rot—more likely, at that hour, she'd be using the Wite-Out to create a budget French manicure.

"The Hooch and Cooch? Since when is one of my mother's strip clubs an appropriate meeting place?" My eyes took in the stories-tall cowgirl on the roof, lit up old school—in lightbulbs rather than neon. Several were burnt out, but most notable were the cowgirl's front teeth; on closer inspection, those seemed to be blacked out on purpose—it's nice to see an attention to authentic detail. The ten-foot-tall flashing pink beaver between her legs was a subtle choice, if I do say so.

"He insisted," she said, her voice echoing on the speakerphone.

"Fucking pig."

The pig's name was Johnny Birch, and he was famous for three things: crooning jazz standards like that Bublé or Bubble guy or whoever, screwing anything with a hole (including donuts), and doing it all publicly on his own reality show, *Tapping Birch's Syrup* (shown exclusively on channel SS12). He was also a wood nymph, but even though that's all ethereal and earthy, it's really secondary to the pervert stuff. Apparently he had a proposition and from the look of the Hooch and Cooch, I had a pretty good idea it wasn't business related.

"Seriously, this better be a for real deal or I'm gonna be one pissed-off zombie."

"Karkaroff was very specific that this was a *priority* meeting." I could imagine her making air quotes in the cushy office chair, leaning back with her ankles crossed on the desk admiring her trophy shoes.

My business partner was already fuming from our recent clusterfuck with Necrophilique. How was I supposed to know the fecal content of the cosmetics? Do I look like a chemist? Still, we needed the money after word spread and the launch tanked. What was the saying, beggars can't be choosers? Not that I was a beggar by any count, but . . . shit, mama's got bills to pay.

"Fine." I gripped the phone to my ear as she yammered on about her day and I started loading my purse with all the important undead accoutrements. Flesh-tone bandages (you never know when you'll get a scratch, and humans are normally surprised when they don't see blood seeping), cigarettes (why the hell not) and lastly, Altoids, of course, because dragon breath doesn't even begin to describe the smell that escapes up this rotten esophagus.

I did take a moment to wonder if I was dressed appropriately for the venue. The Gucci skirt was definitely fitted and might draw some roving hands, but I could certainly handle those. My big concern was the white silk blouse.

It was Miu Miu, for Christ sake.

The Hooch and Cooch didn't look like the kind of place that any white fabric could escape without a stain, let alone designer silk.

As if on cue, two drunken slobs slammed out of the swinging doors and scattered out onto the red carpetless cement.[1] One landed on his ass with his legs spread, an expanding dark wetness spread from his crotch outward. His buddy clutched at his stomach in a silent fit of laughter, but then fell against a truck and puked into the open bed. The rest dribbled off his chin and down his loosened tie as he slid to the concrete. I guess that answered my question about fashion choices. Pretty much anything will do if your competition is piss and puke stains, though

[1] No. No paparazzi, either. Yeah. I was glad about that.

clearly the blouse was in danger and the stains were much more dubious than I'd imagined.

"Ugh. Christ. Call me in ten minutes. I know I'm going to need an excuse to get out of here."

I stuffed the phone in my Alexander McQueen red patent Novak bag—yes, you need to know that, if for no other reason than to understand that I've moved on from the Balenciaga; it's a metaphor for my personal growth—and headed in, stepping over the passed-out figure on the threshold. The urine smell was unbearable. Someone had enjoyed a nutritious meal of asparagus.[2] I shoved the splintery doors into the strip club's lobby and was greeted by a wall of palsied antlers, Molly Hatchet blaring some '70s bullshit, and my mother's pasty dead face beaming from behind the hostess stand.

"Darling." She crossed the room in three strides, cowboy boots crunching on the peanut shells coating the floor and arms reaching—the effect was more praying mantis than loving mother, I assure you. "You should have called."

I submitted to a hug and, over her shoulder, caught a glimpse of Gil, arms crossed and leaning on the open bed of a Ford F-150 that seemed to have been repurposed as the gift shop—how they got it in there, I have no clue. A pair of those ridiculous metal balls dangled between his legs from the trailer hitch behind him. I couldn't help but giggle. He tipped his Stetson in my direction and winked.

"You're right, Mother. I'll definitely call next time."[3]

She pulled away, concern spreading across her face. The vamping achieved the kind of freshening a top-dollar Beverly Hills facelift aimed for, but no amount of magic could revive Ethel's sincerity.

---

[2] Don't pretend you don't know what I'm talking about. That piss is rank. Good for getting rid of some quick water weight, though. Just a tip.

[3] The authorities, that is; nothing disrupts business like a vice raid.

"It's just, we haven't had a whole lot of time to sort out this . . . tension between us, and I'd like us to be a family, again."

Again. Just like that. Like there'd ever been anything remotely resembling a "family." Unless her definition of family was the people one ridiculed, judged, and rejected, then yeah, I guess we had a "family."

I clenched my fists. If blood flowed through my veins rather than thick yellow goo, I might have turned beet red. But instead of appearing angry, I took on a sickly jaundice, which is never cute.

I decided to stuff it and pushed past her to find Johnny Birch. "Sure, Ethel, let's work on that."

"I don't appreciate your sarcasm." She sang the final word, as she did when pretending something didn't actually bother her. I grinned, triumphant.

I bounded up to Gil. "How do you put up with that bitch?" I stabbed a thumb in Ethel's direction.

"Who, your mother? Oh please, she's wonderful to work for and so funny . . ."

His voice trailed off, replaced by the twangin' guitar of Southern rock. Mother had obviously brainwashed Gil to spout this pro-Ethel propaganda, and I wasn't about to listen to it. "Yeah. Yeah. Awesome. A real peach."

"A better question is, how do I put up with this seventies ass rock."

The music changed. "Slow Ride," by Foghat. "Seriously. What's the deal?" I asked.

"Part of your mom's plan; it's all she'll play here. She says seventies rock forces guys to buy beer. Something in their genes. Oh . . . and look at this." Gil reached into the truck bed, which was lined with various Hooch and Cooch promo items, T-shirts, CDs, pocket pussies—that sort of thing—and retrieved a DVD. A sleazy, greasy-haired dancer grinned from the cover, one of her front teeth was missing, and she wore a wife-beater that didn't

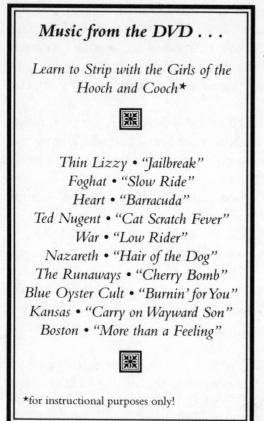

do a good job hiding the fact that her boob job looked like two doorknobs. It read: Learn to Strip with the Girls of the Hooch and Cooch (see inset).

"Jesus. Like one of those Carmen Electra striptease workouts?"

"Yep." He tossed it back in the truck. "Sells like hotcakes."

"I bet."

I looked past Gil into the club for the first time and witnessed the horrors of uncontrolled testosterone production. A drunken mass of homely men and a few semi-doable ones, surprisingly, crowded around two spotlit islands, shouting obscenities and waving dollar bills. It was nearly impossible to distinguish them as individuals; they'd reverted to some sort of quivering gelatinous state. A few appeared near death, eyes rolling in the back of their heads as though they'd never seen a used-up hooker—I mean, nude woman—writhing in a metal washtub, scrubbing herself with a moldy bath brush and kicking suds off dirty feet at her sweaty admirers. Maybe it's because we were indoors.

Between the two performance spaces—though really I'm being overly generous with that description—was a large shack built into the back of the club complete with everything you'd expect to find in the backwoods of the Ozarks, or in a typical Northwest suburb, for that matter—a covered porch, rocking chairs, even a butter churn.[4] Everything, that is, but a little inbred blind kid playing the banjo and showing off the graveyard of teeth in his mouth.

He must have been on a smoke break.

Booths lined the edges of the room, where hillbilly chicks chatted up customers under the watchful glass eyes of various stuffed animal heads. Fog lights on truck grills jutted from the walls lighting up the tables and the assorted (or sordid) activities taking place there.

"This place is a regular Rainforest Café. Only instead of cute plastic animals, you've got dirty whores."

"Absolutely." Gil crossed his arms and beamed, as proud as a new father—sure, he had a stake in the place, but he was overdoing the satisfaction considering the place reeked of bleach and I'm pretty sure it wasn't emanating from a big load of laundry.[5]

"Pays the bills," he said.

"Listen. I'm supposed to be meeting a guy. Johnny Birch, that fame whore from TV. Have you seen him?"

"Um." He scanned the room. "Totally. What a freak. I think he's just finished up with Kelsey." Gil pointed to a hallway flanked by two columns of chicken coups. A lanky, dark-haired man emerged with a jug of moonshine in one hand and a skanky redhead in the other.

"Christ."

The guy was tonguing the girl's ear as I approached.

"Excuse me," I said. "Are you Mr. Birch?"

He spun the girl away like a Frisbee, absolutely no regard for where she might land. She twirled a few times, collapsed in

---

[4] I didn't want to even think what these girls would use *that* for.
[5] It's a curse that my sense of smell is so acute. A curse!

some other perv's lap, and started gyrating. Birch measured me in long, sweeping stares. Head to toe, lingering on the tits and back to the head. "Sure am." He extended his hand. "And you're Amanda. Lovely to meet you."

He pulled at my hand as though planning to pull off a gentlemanly knuckle kiss, but I snatched it back, wishing for a Clorox wipe. "Yeah. Um, you have some sort of business proposition, I've been told. Do you want to talk about that here, or do you have a table somewhere? Maybe a private booth they reserve for regulars."

"You mean V.I.P." He winked.

"No." I shook my head. "Just regular."

Birch nodded and chuckled off the jab under his breath.

The next moment, the blaring '70s rock was silenced, an apparent signal for the strippers to make way for the principal dancer in this redneck ballet. They scrabbled off on bruised knees, wet hair dangling in clumps, and bulldozing collapsing pyramids of dollar bills in front of them.

Birch pointed toward the shack.

The lights dimmed, and a jaundiced glow rose behind the dirty shower curtain covering the front door of the facade. At the edges of the porch, slobbery men set down their jugs and hushed each other as though in reverence to approaching royalty. It became so quiet, I could hear the chickens scratching in their cages and crickets chirping or rubbing their legs together or whatever the fuck they do. Though that last bit was probably being pumped in through the speakers to set the mood. The stage light brightened until columns of dust motes stabbed into the audience from between the rusty metal curtain rings, stretching across the waves of corrugated roofing above and the five o'clock shadows of drooling businessmen below.

And then *she* stalked into silhouette—no . . . shuffled is a better word—to the opening cowbells of Nazareth's "Hair of the Dog"—'cuz really, what else would you expect?

"Harry Sue!" I could have sworn someone yelled.

"Harry Sue!" the crowd shouted back in liturgical response.

"*Harry* Sue?" I asked Birch.

"Short for Harriet, maybe?" He shrugged without taking his eyes off the dirty play unfolding.

When the guitar roared in, Harry Sue snatched back the curtain and stomped out onto the porch in Daisy Duke overalls and the most hideous high heels—since when did Jellies make a heel? Her blond hair teased and tortured into massive pigtails, hay jutting from the strips of gingham holding them in place. Her face was pretty enough, if you could get past her wild eyes, bee-stung lips, and the mass of fake freckles that sadly recalled the broken blood vessels of an alcoholic more than the fresh sun-kissed face of a farmgirl.

She didn't tease the crowd of howling men much, making quick work of the denim overalls with two rehearsed snaps at each shoulder; they slid off her bone-thin frame and pooled around her ankles. The ensuing slapstick of Harry wrestling her feet out of the denim mess would have been charming had my eyes not been stuck to her undergarments. Not satisfied with a dirty wife-beater and some holey panties, the stripper wore cut-off Dr. Dentons complete with the trapdoor. Of course, in true trashy stripper fashion, Harry Sue wore hers backwards.

The room was filled with redneck boner and there I stood in the middle of it, without a vomit bag, a designer cocktail, or a canister of mustard gas. You couldn't move through the room without rotating aroused men like turnstiles and I had no intention of doing that. I did notice that Johnny Birch was standing awful close to me.

Glad to see you, close.

Too close.

"That's my asshole, asshole." I jerked away from his probing fingers.

Johnny grinned in response, totally deserving the punch I threw into his kidneys.

"Ow!" He ran his fingers through his hair, eyes darting nervously at the men around us, as if any of them were looking for anything other than a beaver shot. "Jesus. It's all in good fun."

"Touch me again and we'll see who's having fun."

"Aw." He scowled.

Harry Sue slunk down in one of the rockers, and the men whimpered in unison—apparently prepared for what Harry Sue had in store for us. She rocked slowly, pivoting her ass forward on the edge of the chair until the flap was front and center. She toyed with the buttons, tweaking them like nipples.

I glowered. Shot a glance at Birch. Wished I were drinking.

The stripper got my attention when she unbuttoned one side of the flap, then the other, finally, exposing the biggest 70s bush I'd ever seen.[6] It was massive. Afro-like. Harry Sue needed to be introduced to the wonders of Brazilian waxing, though she'd likely be charged extra. And then it clicked. The men weren't yelling Harry Sue.

They were shouting *Hairy* Sue.

Still. It didn't make sense.

I've read *Cosmo*. I know men prefer shaved to bouffant. Yet they were clearly enthralled by this stripper. I watched more closely.

Hairy (let's just drop the Sue part; it never had any real value, anyway) reached for the butter churn and pulled out the plunger dripping melted butter down the front of her jammies.

She peeked at the mess, frowned, then licked the end of the plunger before returning it to the churn. In one motion, she slipped out of the Dr. Dentons and reached into an aluminum pail next to the rocker and retrieved an ear of corn, which she preceded to shuck using her teeth. She sprinkled her breasts with corn silk. With the ear she traced circles across her belly, her thighs, and then, as though by accident, she dropped the cob on the porch, gasped, and then slipped from the chair into a full

---

[6] Hey. I've always kept mine neat and trim. Don't go making assumptions.

splits, hovering briefly above the ear before nestling it against her buttery crotch.

I shifted from one foot to the other.

There was absolutely nothing sexy about this. These guys were all perverts.

Hairy Sue rose then and bowed to the wild applause and showers of dollar bills. She posed there like she owned that porch, corncob dripping and a fat smile spread across her face.

The lights dimmed.

"I'd sure like to see *your* bush." Birch again. His lips curled into a lewd smile.

I nearly vomited up my dinner (let's not go into what that might have been, just yet). "Is that some kind of wood nymph joke? 'Cause I'm done with your poor impulse control."

"Hey." He stepped back, spread his arms, and wiggled his fingers. "I can control the trees and stuff."

I let my eyes wander down to the tent in his pants. "But not the wood?"

He sagged.

"Maybe we should just talk." He covered his crotch with cupped hands, a flush rising in his cheeks.

I followed him back to a booth underneath a monstrous moose head, where he laid out the scenario. It was the first time I'd seen his face in full light. He wasn't hideous, though his features were sharp and his nose a bit too thin. The brown of his eyes shimmered with veins of gold, and his lips, though pale, were full and unexpectedly alluring. He looked much better on TV, but that was probably the makeup.

Mmm. Makeup.

"The calls started coming about three months ago," he said. "At first the caller wouldn't say anything. Just hang up after I'd answered. The phone company said they were always from phone booths. I didn't even know those still existed, but they do."

I nodded, though I couldn't remember the last time I'd seen

one, either. Still, why do people feel the need to tell me the most random crap? Like I care. I'm dead.

"About a month ago, they started getting threatening. Not overtly so, just freaky. Like letting me know that I was being monitored. 'You're at the Texaco on First.' Like that. And then they'd just hang up and I'd be standing there at the pump, not just worried that my cell was going to spark and blow me up, but now that someone was nearby watching. Then a couple of weeks ago I get the first one."

"First what?"

Johnny reached into a briefcase he must've stored under the table before his lap dance and pulled out a plastic shipping envelope, the kind lined with Bubble Wrap. He placed it on the table between us and leaned forward, searching the room for observers. Half the crowd had been culled into the back rooms, and the other half were busy drinking themselves into stupors.

I made eye contact with Gil across the room. He looked concerned. It must have been my expression of pure boredom. My eyes dropped back to the envelope.

"I'm not a private detective, Birch. I'm in advertising. Can we get on with this?"

"I know. I know. But, I don't need you for that. I need you for your celebrity."

Celebrity?

Oh, yes. He'd snared my attention with that. "Go on."

He opened the end of the envelope and pulled out a thin shingle of wood. Stretched across it and attached with thick pins was a creature like none I'd seen, almost insect-like, with wings that clung to its sides like a termite. Its flesh was as black as obsidian and shiny from toe to its segmented abdomen to its horribly humanoid head. The creature's waxy face was frozen in a torturous silent scream.

"Gross. What the hell is it?" I was unable to look away from the little body, pinned as it was like a lab experiment. Better there than flying around, though, or I'd be snatching a flyswatter.

"I don't really know. But it looks like a fucking threat to me." He slid it back into the envelope and tossed it into his bag. "Anyways! I'm going on tour this spring and clearly, with this shit going on . . ." He kicked at the briefcase. "I'm going to need some protection."

"All right. How is my 'celebrity' going to do that?"

"It's not. I'm putting together a team of bodyguards, and what better way to do it nowadays than with my own fabulous reality contest show? Can you see it? Celebrity judges and weekly death matches. It's exactly what Supernatural TV is aching for. Cameron Hansen would host, of course, and all we'd need is our Paula. You'd be our Simon."

"Simon? I'm too cute and, anyway, you'd be our fucking Paula. What we'd need is a Randy." I reached for my purse and began to scoot out of the booth. The idea was ludicrous.

"Maybe." His voice thundered. "But I'm a nut with financial resources and I'd be willing to pay."

"So you're looking for more than just a guest judge here, then? We're talking about exclusive advertising contract with product placement?"

"That could be arranged."

"Let me think about it." I looked around the Hooch and Cooch and couldn't quite believe that such a gross experience might lead to a potential financial windfall. "All right, let's plan to meet somewhere less . . . disgusting, and then we'll talk about it. Sound good?"

"Up to you."

"Well, let's figure it out in the parking lot. I don't think I can stomach this place much longer."

As we stood to leave, a commotion began in the hallway to the private rooms. A steady stream of men were rushing from the exit, most of them screaming and none of them attempting to shield the bulge in their trousers. Following them was a roar that vibrated through the room and a crash as the chicken coops shattered sending several birds flapping and skittering off toward the door in the shack. Gil and Ethel ran into the room, my mother brandishing a machete, Gil some sort of short club.

"We better get out of here." I turned to Birch, but he'd already darted for the front door. Behind him a massive hairy beast emerged from the tangle of metal cages. Its bulbous head sheared the ceiling as it lurched, creating a groove across the ripples of metal. Its thick, muscled arms ended in rakish claws that shredded the floorboards into mulch with each powerful swipe. It stopped in the center of the room, head twisting wildly from one patron to the next until it found its quarry.

The creature howled with such force, the floor shook under me, slobber clung to foot-long fangs like sloppy pennants flapping in the direction of Johnny Birch, who let out a quivering whimper.

It rushed forward.

Dammit, I thought. There goes the TV show.